Lu Etchells

First published in Great Britain in March 2018 by Silver Girl Books.

www.luetchells.com

Lu x

TO MY PARENTS
For raising me to believe I can do anything.

TO MY HUSBAND
For reminding me I can.

TO MY CHILDREN
If I can, you can.

Also by Lu Etchells

Short Stories
Beware The Penguins
Dead Flowers

PART ONE

Making the decision to have a child is momentous. It is to decide forever to have your heart go walking around outside your body.

- Elizabeth Stone

CHAPTER 1

The sound of voices drifted up the marble stairs, and Adrienne realised they were no longer alone. She'd been awake, but in that halfway place between sleep and consciousness. Coop climbing out of bed had disturbed her, and she'd listened to his footsteps padding over to the bathroom. The gentle splash of water hitting the hard tiles, and the thought of him naked under that tropical shower had almost persuaded her to follow him, but in the end, she wasn't ready to open her eyes.

From inside her Eiderdown cocoon she could replay the events of last night over in her mind, before the cold light of day forced her back to reality. She wasn't quite ready to be her usual self just yet, and was happy to cling to the moment before it slipped away, like a message written on sand when the tide comes in.

They'd agreed weeks ago that he would pick her up after work so they could spend as much time together as possible before he had to head out of the country again. As promised, he'd met her at her flat, and had whisked her away to the latest hotel he was staying in. It changed every time he visited, and she now felt well acquainted with the various luxuries a five-star lifestyle had to offer.

Since he'd announced this visit she had begged him for a quiet night out; just them, a local restaurant for an understated romantic meal, a bottle of house wine and a shared chocolate fudge cake. Nothing fancy. To be honest, she'd have preferred it if they'd just stayed at hers, ordered a take away and put Netflix on, but she knew he'd never go for it. She wasn't even sure Coop would know what Netflix was.

With all his assurances that he wasn't going to bombard her with extravagance she'd been mortified by her favourite t-shirt, jeans and Converse combo when they'd arrived at one of the most prestigious addresses in London. She should have known he had no intention of changing his habits, and instantly chastised herself for not bringing a change of clothes.

As soon as his chauffeur glided up to the imposing hotel entrance she realised it was the type of night that ended with a sleepover, and was all too conscious of the similarity between the image she cut and Julia Roberts' infamous Vivian.

As usual, he'd dismissed her concerns, and in the end, he was right, it didn't matter. They had gone straight to the Penthouse and by the time the heavy door had closed behind them her jeans were round her ankles. He made no apologies for having her there and then, and she needed none. It had been two months since their last encounter and she was as unable to control herself as he was. She smiled to herself as she recalled the squeak her shoes had made on the Marquino flooring as he'd pinned her against the wall.

After they had finally managed to untangle themselves from each other, they'd ventured up the sweeping staircase and discovered a king-sized bed with an impressive en suite. He'd opened the champagne and they'd spent over an hour in the Jacuzzi. She blushed as she recalled the effect all those different bubbles had had on her, and how she'd quickly forgotten about her skin pruning.

Her reverie was interrupted by the sound of a tray being placed on the table beside her head. She rolled on to her back, gave the stretch of a blissfully contented cat and finally opened her eyes. Coop was standing on her side of the bed, a white towel wrapped around his waist, beads of water still clinging to his perfectly chiseled chest.

His physique gave no hint of his 52 years. He had a pot of cream in one hand, a strawberry in the other and a glint in his eye that made it clear she was going to be late for work.

*****

Sarah had been awake for hours, but despite the early start wasn't feeling remotely tired. When she had woken after a brief and fitful sleep she had initially tried to drift back off. After what felt like an eternity of staring at the ceiling and coaxing her mind to think of nothing, she'd admitted defeat and gently edged herself out of bed so as not to wake Pete.

Of course, she didn't need to be quite so careful, he was the sort of man who was unconscious before his head hit the pillow, and would have struggled to wake if the house had been on fire. In all the years they'd been together she could never understand how he slept so soundly, whilst the slightest stress or worry would have her tossing and turning for nights on end.

They were entirely different in that regard. He always said he was more dog, able to live in the moment and be content with his lot. She, on the other hand, was definitely more cat; highly strung, prone to anxiety and over-exaggerated tail twitching.

Giving sleep up as a bad idea she'd crept downstairs and made her way to the small, but serviceable kitchen, and poured a glass of milk. Sitting at the breakfast bar she surveyed her kingdom and smiled, in the short time they'd lived in this new house she had definitely made it a home. Now they were ready to take the next step to complete the picture.

No matter what she did, nothing captured her attention for long and nothing could take her mind off the importance of today. She'd already finished reading her book, a non-descript tale of a woman who'd stayed in bed for a year. It made no sense to her, why would any woman want to give up and stop being a wife and mother?

She could never do that to Pete. The thought of him having to make his own meals or iron his own socks made her feel uneasy. That was her job, and she was proud to do it. Once, when she'd been bedridden with food poisoning she'd talked him through putting a store-bought pizza in the oven. She'd never felt so inadequate in her life, and had vowed never to be ill again, or to touch another oyster.

By 7am she'd scrubbed the kitchen tiles and had disinfected the grey wheelie bin in the garden, taking a moment to haphazardly pull up some weeds whilst she was there. Next on her distraction list was the DVD cabinet in the front room, which she had a sudden urge to alphabetise. She couldn't help wondering if Pete would even notice, or if he would simply carry on oblivious as he did with all of the little touches she added to their domestic bliss.

She'd even gone for a walk around the block before the sun had started to spread in to the black sky. Stopping outside the Maguire's house for a few minutes she couldn't help but notice the nursery light was on, and she knew Janice would be in her rocking chair, nursing baby Jack and singing him a lullaby. This time of night was made for newborns and their mothers. Sarah had laid her hand over her stomach, telling herself it wouldn't be long before she had her own night time companion to take care of.

A shiver brought her back to reality and she checked her watch. She had to hurry home before Pete realised she was missing. She wanted everything to be perfect, and there was no way she was going to be late to her appointment.

*****

The sound of the alarm pierced the air and Jenna reached a perfectly manicured hand out from under the silk covers to silence it. Truth be told she'd been awake for hours, staring at the ceiling and mentally planning her wardrobe for the day. She'd never been able to sleep well when she had the bed to herself, though goodness knows she'd had enough practice over the years.

She swung her long, naturally tanned legs out, placed her feet on the floor, stretched and headed straight for the en suite. Minutes later she was dressed in leggings and a t-shirt and was setting up her yoga mat in the conservatory. Every move was well practiced, deliberate and executed perfectly. She took her time, enjoying the feeling that her body was waking up and getting ready to face the day.

She'd always taken such pride in her appearance and knew she had an amazing body, though it was never her own approval she sought. He'd stopped noticing years ago, but she refused to give up, just in case he decided to take an interest again. She had a duty to be ready if he did, though she had long since stopped holding her breath.

Precisely 45 minutes later she rolled her mat away and poured herself a glass of orange juice. She checked her watch, more out of habit than necessity; she knew she was perfectly on schedule. She had plenty of time, could probably even afford an extra five minutes in the shower.

Standing under that hot water made her feel every worry in her seemingly perfect world was disappearing down the plug hole. She didn't believe in God, there was too much badness in the world to believe in an all-knowing and powerful entity overseeing it all, but she imagined that's what faith felt like. A hot presence enveloping you, making you feel safe and clean. It was comforting.

*****

Pete could hear the birds singing outside the bedroom window, and he could tell it was already quite light out. For a moment he lay motionless, hoping if he didn't think or move he'd be able to go back to sleep immediately. Without opening his eyes, he already knew she wasn't lying next to him, and he couldn't work out whether he was relieved, or not.

The part of him that was stereotypically male wished she had been there, so he could roll over and innocently cup her breast whilst giving her a good morning squeeze. He knew sex was off the cards, but the day always started better with a little bit of spooning. On the other hand, she'd been so uptight for so long he couldn't help feeling he was better off her not being there. His visions of what a morning cuddle would look like these days were definitely viewed through rose-tinted glasses. Still, he was a naturally optimistic soul and would always hope for the best.

He rolled over and checked his phone, realising his alarm must have woken him, before eventually silencing itself when it failed to rouse him in the required time. He knew that meant he was officially late, and he'd already be in her bad books. The sex-deprived part of him decided it therefore didn't matter whether he got up that instant, or made the most of the remaining peace and quiet. With that, he rolled back over, closed his eyes and was fast asleep again within seconds.

CHAPTER 2

Covered in sweat, Adrienne fell back on the bed and laughed. They might go months without seeing each other, but they certainly made up for lost time when they did manage to secure a few hours together. Coop rolled on top of her, kissed her nose, then kissed her passionately on the lips. She admired his virility and longed to match it, but knew time was ticking on, and she had to get to work. It was going to be a busy day and she couldn't let her patients down.

She kissed him back, and started to roll him off her. She maneuvered herself from underneath him, straddled him briefly, her long hair engulfing them both, before she jumped up and ran to the bathroom. She could hear him pleading her to come back to him as she turned the shower on. She knew there was a good chance he would follow her in, but if she was quick, she'd be able to get her hair washed and rinsed before she could no longer ignore him.

As she washed the last of the suds out of her hair, he stepped in behind her. He scrubbed her back, and she found herself willing him to go further. She had her excuses planned, of course she'd protest, remind him of her need to get home and changed before heading to work, but it was redundant. Her back washed, he gave himself a cursory freshen-up before grabbing a new towel, and stepping out of the cubicle.

Her disappointment must have been plain to see. "Two can play that game, besides, I have a meeting I need to get to," he said as he admired himself in the mirror.

"Tony's made an almighty cock up on one of our biggest accounts and I've got to go get shouted at. The clients are monumental pains, and frankly scare the crap out of me, but they're loaded, so needs must."

Adrienne smiled. She couldn't imagine Coop being scared of anyone, much less anyone having the audacity to dress him down. He was an animal; primal and unpredictable. One minute you could be tickling his tummy and the next he was scratching your arm to ribbons. She was always thankful she'd never been on the receiving end of his temper; however, she'd witnessed it repeatedly when he'd had to make work calls during their time together.

By the time she came back in to the bedroom he was dressed and looked immaculate in his suit. She knew nothing about fashion, but assumed it must be Armani or Givenchy. They did make suits didn't they, not just cologne? Not for the first time she was reminded of the fact they had very little in common other than their sexual desires. They lived in entirely different worlds; he was a have and she was most definitely a have-not. Yet, fate had hurled them together and here they were two years later still … actually, what were they doing?

It had been two years of fancy meals and luxury hotel rooms. When she talked about him with friends she always focussed on the romance and the glamour of it all; the thrill of being whisked away, the passion, the intensity, and the late-night phone calls. Filthy phone calls.

She tended to leave out the way he'd kiss her goodbye the morning after, a perfunctory gesture, an almost formal close to business. She tried not to think too much about the feeling she was left with each time, where she should be searching for money left on the nightstand. For some reason she suddenly wasn't so sure their relationship was all she made it out to be.

As she stood in her fluffy white robe watching him pack his briefcase and order his chauffeur to come around for him, she genuinely had no idea where he was going. What was it that he did, even? It involved lots of travelling, lots of being elsewhere, constant phone calls with his assistant and seemingly never-ending meetings with people he apparently despised.

Come to think of it, did he really know what she did? He knew she was a doctor, he'd originally joked that he'd have preferred her to be a naughty nurse. It hadn't taken her long to enact that particular fantasy, in a room very similar to this in fact on the other side of the river.

Lost in her thoughts, she was caught off guard when he approached her, undid her dressing gown and cupped her breast. "I'm going to miss these," he said as he planted a kiss on each erect nipple in turn. "I'll call you when I land in LA. Alice will let you know what my schedule is."

And with that, he was gone. Who knew when he would next have time for her? Alice would know. She'd call, she'd arrange a time and Adrienne would drop everything to accommodate his availability and desires, like a faithful dog waiting for its master to come home.

She picked up the towel he'd discarded on the bed and used it to take the wetness out of her hair. She knew she'd have to wait to get back to her flat to do anything remotely meaningful with the now tangled mop on her head, so instead focussed on finding her underwear.

Not for the first time she cursed herself for not packing spare knickers in her bag. She knew how a night with Coop was going to end, and invariably it meant spending precious time the morning after on her hands and knees, trying to locate her latest Agent Provocateur ensemble.

As she scouted the room she caught a glimpse of the time. Fuck. She pulled on her jeans and t-shirt, grabbed her shoes and legged it out the room, hoping no one would notice as she made her dash of shame, and the taxi rank would be full enough to ensure a swift return home.

*****

Sarah was trying very hard to be patient. Today was going to be a good day. It was *the* day. Nothing was going to spoil it and she'd already made a promise to herself that she was not going to lose her temper. However, Pete was making that promise increasingly difficult to keep. So far, he had refused to get up when the alarm went off, and instead had worked his way through five separate snoozes. When she could finally take no more and had insisted on him getting out of bed he'd tried to persuade her to get back in with him.

That had very nearly caused an argument. Not only was she already dressed, but he knew the rules. He knew she couldn't, even if she'd wanted to, and today she most certainly did not. Her refusals of his advances always left him looking like a little boy scorned, and she felt guilty for swotting his hand away. She knew she should be grateful he still found her attractive and only had eyes for her, but honestly, it was so tiring. Besides, she had more important things on her mind.

While he showered, she prepared his breakfast, a bacon and egg sandwich. She thought that would soften the blow of the sex ban, but again, it nearly led to an argument. As per the rule of Sod the runny egg had dripped all over his clean shirt, necessitating a change of clothes and another five-minute delay. Now she sat at the breakfast bar wearing her new coat, and tapping her nails impatiently on the counter top.

Seconds felt like minutes. It was torture. She desperately wanted to be in the car, on the way. There already. She wouldn't feel safe, confident that this really was it, until she was safely there, sitting in the welcoming comfort of the waiting room, flicking through glossy magazines and attempting small talk with the man she wouldn't let touch her.

Finally, he appeared in the kitchen doorway, smiling as though he didn't have a care in the world.

"You ready then?" he asked, as he pulled on his jacket. There were times she could kill him, but that playful smile always got him out of jail. She jumped up, poked him in the ribs and walked past him to the front door. Her hand had just touched the handle when he said, "Meet you outside, I just need a wee".

She groaned as he rushed back upstairs, but continued on her way outside. Just being near the car made her feel they were making progress and could still be there on time. She reminded herself that today was the day, stress wasn't good for her. Today was the day. It was like a mantra, and she was determined to keep her cool. Today was special, she wanted it to be perfect and Pete was not allowed to ruin it by being his usual happy-go-lucky self.

After what felt like an age he was sitting in the seat next to her and starting the engine. They were off. This was it. It was happening. At last. She had imagined they would talk on the drive across town, plan their future, make predictions about what today would bring for them but instead, he reached for the dial on the radio and the silence was filled with Bruno Mars Uptown-Funking.

She turned her head and stared out the window, resigned to being alone with her thoughts. Bruno wasn't such a bad name. Perhaps they would have a boy and she could one eventually tell him of the day he was conceived and how he got his name.

Deep down though, she hoped for a girl. With four older brothers she'd always wanted a sister, a companion to share clothes, make-up and secrets with. A daughter would be even better. They would be best friends forever. Inseparable.

Pete would unintentionally take a boy away from her, teaching him to love football and spend all their time together, splashing about in mud and generally making her life dirty. She never could understand the fascination. Surely if they all wanted the ball so much they should put 22 on the pitch and be done with it?

Lilly. That's what she'd call her. Although, on second thoughts, it was becoming a very popular name and she didn't want to be seen to be following the crowd. Her daughter would be special, and the name had to reflect that. She couldn't have something that just any child might have. That said, she didn't want anything too unique. They didn't live on the type of estate that could accept a Tiger Princess or Apple Blossom.

Janice kept telling her not to worry about such things for now, that none of it really mattered, but what did she know? Jack was their fourth child, the second boy. Janice had no idea what it was like to really want a child, to think of nothing else. She was disgustingly fertile, pregnancy just happened to her. With four perfect children in little more than seven years, she couldn't possibly understand what it meant to Sarah, and why every tiny detail occupied her every waking minute.

Pete didn't get it either. He was just along for the ride, doing as he was told. He'd wanted to adopt, but Sarah had managed to talk him out of it. Looking back, he was really quite passionate about it. His eyes used to light up when he talked of rescuing a child from uncertainty, and giving them unconditional love and a home.

He didn't understand that she needed to carry his child. As far as she was concerned, as his wife, that was her job; really, it was as simple as that. Maybe they could adopt when their daughter was three. Or perhaps they could get a puppy instead. Children loved puppies and they'd always talked of getting one. That was it, she'd steer the conversation to adorable Labradoodles if the adoption thing ever came up again.

The traffic was unusually clear and they made good time, arriving at the clinic 10 minutes early, despite their delayed departure. Pete fumbled around in the glove box looking for spare change while Sarah re-applied her lipstick.

“Sweetheart, you look fine. Besides, they’re not going to be focusing on your face today.” He thought he was being funny, but Sarah had to fight the urge to scowl at him. Today was going to be a good day, she repeated to herself.

They made the short walk from the car to the large reception doors in silence, booked in and then took up their seats in the waiting area. As soon as he sat down Pete pulled out his mobile. Sarah tutted, “Really? Now? It can’t wait?”

Pete looked put out, was about to reply that he was expecting an important email, but thought better of it. There would be no suitable excuse for not being 100% in the moment, no matter how potentially tedious that moment was. He mumbled an apology and put the phone back in his pocket.

CHAPTER 3

When Jenna got out of the shower she sat looking at her reflection in the dressing room mirror. She was impressed with how youthful she still looked, but gone was the sparkle in her eyes Will had once found so attractive.

As she surveyed her face critically, she marvelled at the irony; the thing he had once loved so much about her was gone, because of him. All those long years of marriage had taken their toll on her, yet, here she was, always hoping for the best. Praying that one day it might just start being different.

She was disturbed from her thoughts by the sound of her phone ringing. It was him. For a second, she considered letting it ring, and wondered if he would bother to leave a voicemail. Either way, she already knew what he was going to say. He was running late. Some disaster at the office, a traffic jam, or some idiot hadn't done their job properly. There was always something. He'd meet her there. It would be fine. She'd heard it before.

Once upon a time these calls had upset her, but now they were as much a part of their marriage as their wedding bands. She wasn't really needed for these conversations, they were just a formality. She offered the occasional 'don't worry' or 'oh no, how frustrating' and ended with a reminder about their dinner plans for that evening. It never occurred to her that her lack of feeling should mean something, it had been this way for so long.

Jenna was the type of woman who firmly believed you could waste time worrying about things, or you could just get on with them. Her approach to life, and the occasional difficulties it threw her way, was to just keep on keeping on. When you didn't have control over something there was no point in losing sleep over it.

A lot of water had passed under the bridge since she realised she couldn't control Will, or really have any say in what he did or didn't do. It had been a painful thing to accept, but now she had, her life was easier. Shallower and largely devoid of meaning, but easier all the same.

She hung up and turned the hair drier on, already relegating Will's excuses to the back of her mind and returning her focus to the plans for her hair style. Today wasn't about him, it was about her; her needs and her dreams. She'd waited long enough and everything was going to be perfect, with or without him.

*****

The driver picked Coop, or Mr. Cooper as he insisted staff call him, up from outside the hotel and headed straight for the office. Tom knew better than to make small talk, and instead kept his focus on navigating the early morning rush. Within seconds Coop had the contents of his briefcase spread over the back seat, and was already on the phone to his assistant.

Tom could hear Alice's Australian accent over the speakerphone, running through Mr. C's schedule for the day.

"You have a breakfast meeting with the Disraeli family at 8am in the Acorn room. Everything is already prepared and waiting for you. I then have you booked for an external meeting at 9.30am. Is this still going ahead? We've allocated two hours."

Coop stared out the window, "Shit. I doubt I'm going to be able to make that on time, you know what the Disraeli's are like. Just in case, will you ensure Tom is still available to collect me? I'll give him the address when we set off."

Tom shook his head, it never failed to amaze him how he was not allowed to manage his own diary and organise his day. So much time could be saved if Mr. Cooper would just talk to him directly, instead of insisting on this divisive hierarchy. However, it was a good excuse to speak to Alice. She'd phone as soon as Mr. Cooper was in the office, and maybe this time Tom would find a way to ask her to dinner.

"If that's all Mr. C, I shall finish checking your emails and await your arrival."

Coop terminated the call without saying anything more, and returned to the papers on the seat next to him. He frowned. Things were exceptionally busy at the office, and he already had more on his plate than time on the clock, a trip back across town would just make matters worse. He wished he could get out of it, but he knew his life wouldn't be worth living if he cancelled again.

Not for the first time he found himself feeling frustrated that his life couldn't be simpler. The day had started so well, and now he had to go back to reality and deal with all the crap everyone else expected him to take responsibility for. It was one of the things he liked most about Adrienne, how utterly uncomplicated and undemanding she was.

He knew it bothered her that they couldn't see each other more often, but at the same time, she never made a big deal out of it. She willingly accepted that his work kept him out of the country for large periods of time, even if it actually didn't. He refused to feel guilty about that little white lie, instead believing he made up for it by regularly calling her, which seemed to satisfy her need to be in touch.

That said, he always believed their relationship was far more physical than anything meaningful, and assumed she felt the same. They didn't have long moody walks on the beach and didn't discuss their feelings. That's why he was convinced she was actually the perfect woman.

Accepting he couldn't put it off any longer, he picked up his phone and hit speed dial. Maybe she wouldn't be available, and he could just leave a message. That would save a lot of unnecessary discussion and excuses.

The phone rang twice and then she answered, a hint of irritation in her voice. He took a deep breath and tried to sound jovial, "Hola chica bonita, I hope you slept well?"

Silence. He immediately knew this was going to be harder than he'd hoped.

"I know we have an appointment scheduled for this morning, but I'm going to be a bit late. I have a crisis meeting first thing and there's a good chance it may run over." He paused in case she had something to say, but when he was met with silence from her end of the line he ploughed on.

"I'll do my best to be there, but you know what it's like. Alice has double-booked me again and there's just nothing I can do. It's out of my hands. I really will try to be there but if I can't, I promise to make it up to you."

She barely said anything before hanging up but he shrugged it off, knowing there was nothing he could do about it, or her mood now. Instead, he turned his attentions to packing up his papers. Tom was just turning in to the office underground car park. He checked his watch and realised he had enough time to grab a quick coffee before heading to the first meeting.

He needed it after his lack of sleep last night, it was certainly going to be a long day.

*****

Adrienne dashed out of the reception area and jumped in to the first taxi in the line. She gave her address to the driver as she fought to pull her shoes on. Honestly, she was far too old to be behaving like this. She was going to have to put her foot down next time she had a chance to really talk to Coop. There was no logical reason why he couldn't stay at hers when he was in town. OK, so it was no Hilton or May Fair, but it was comfortable and clean and would save her a fortune in lost underwear.

She gazed out the window at what promised to be another glorious day, and wondered how she had become this woman. She had always put her career first, something she would never regret, but now at nearly 36 she felt it was time she finally settled down. She adored Coop, was still as madly in love with him as she had been when they first met, and desperately wanted them to be *something*.

She wasn't too concerned with putting an official label on it, she didn't need a ring on her finger but she did want to know they were going somewhere. Did they have a future? Did that future involve children?

To be honest, she wasn't sure she really wanted any herself. If Coop did want to be a father, he was going to have to get a move on. She smiled to herself, what on earth was she doing? They'd never even been on holiday together, and here she was thinking about fertilising an egg and creating a whole new human being with him! It was ridiculous.

The longest they'd spent together was 48 hours, and for the vast majority of that time they were either asleep, ordering room service or doing things her Catholic mother would disapprove of.

She vowed that next time they saw each other she would force the issue, and try to pin him down to giving some form of commitment. This time she laughed at herself. It was all very well talking the big talk when she was sat on her own having a one-sided conversation, but it was quite another when Coop was involved.

He wasn't a big conversationalist, especially when it came to feelings, so she worried trying to push him in to a meaningful discussion would have him running for the hills, and she wasn't ready for that. If this was nothing but a good time, she'd rather it went on for a bit longer yet. She was having far too much fun to quit just now.

The taxi pulled up at her apartment block, "Can you wait please?", she asked as she handed over a £20 note. "I'll just be 5 minutes, and then I need to head over to Albert Street. Is that OK?"

The driver looked at the money in her outstretched hand, and nodded before opening his window and lighting a cigarette. Adrienne jumped out of the car and ran up the stairs to her flat. Even when the lift was working, the long way was infinitely quicker.

She stripped off and stood naked in front of her wardrobe, trying to decide which outfit was least likely to need ironing. She flipped through the hangers and came across a pale pink blouse and her black pencil skirt. She threw them on the bed and grabbed at some underwear before getting dressed. She raked a brush through her hair and tied it back in a ponytail; quick, neat and professional, even if it was still a bit damp around the edges.

She gave a quick glance in the mirror propped against the wall and gave herself a nod of approval. Putting on her office shoes she snatched up her work handbag and headed back down to the taxi.

CHAPTER 4

Jenna had arrived with plenty of time to spare, and decided to take a walk around the block to calm her nerves whilst she waited for Will to arrive. She wasn't convinced he would actually make it at all, but she always felt guilty when she gave up on him, even when she was eventually proven right.

She stopped briefly outside the Baby Boutique and took in the display. Cute yellow baby grows and an oversized rabbit with big floppy ears filled the window. Her mind drifted back to Will. She knew he didn't let her down on purpose, his haphazard timekeeping in relation to their mutual appointments wasn't malicious, she just didn't think he cared. Their things, which he generally regarded as her things, didn't register on his importance radar.

Over their 25 years of marriage she'd found a way to come to terms with it and nothing was going to change now, not even if today went according to plan. She checked her watch and moved on, making her way round the last side of the square before finding herself back at the reception doors.

This potential baby was not about them. It wasn't going to be a band aid to bind them together and make him see her with renewed love. She wasn't a teenage girl, she'd been around long enough to know that sometimes when things were broken they stayed that way. You simply made do with what was left. She was fine with that. It wasn't perfect, but they managed.

This baby was about her needs, and him fulfilling his promise. She had earnt this baby, she'd done her time and made a million sacrifices already. She'd forgiven the ambivalence that had pervaded their marriage, his late nights at the office, and that 21-year-old blonde temp from last summer. She'd never complained, she'd never tried to fight or take anything. All she wanted was her baby. He owed her that, before it was finally too late.

She stood outside the glass doors and surveyed the street. She couldn't see his silver Mercedes, and she reluctantly accepted there was no way he was going make it on time now. She checked her watch once more, sighed and went inside, preparing to go through it all one last time on her own.

Her stilettos clicked on the tiled floor as she made her way to the reception desk, booked in and took a seat. An anxious looking couple were already seated, and for the first time she wondered if she was better off going this alone. From the corner of her eye she could see the woman was a nervous wreck, and the man looked as though he'd rather be anywhere else.

It probably was easier sitting here, silently, in her own little world, not having to worry about anyone else's emotional reactions and requirements. Will would never want to be sat in this room, with these people, and she was glad she'd never forced the issue.

He was welcome, of course, but it had never been demanded.

No sooner had she precariously balanced on the edge of one of the designer chairs dotted around the waiting room than a young girl in a white nurse's smock approached her and asked her to follow her to the consulting room. She took one last look at the reception doors, half hoping to see him striding in, late but nevertheless there. It was just habit to hope. Sometimes when everything else was gone, hope was all you had left.

*****

It was five minutes past eight and he was sitting in his office, catching up on the Disraeli client file when Alice came in. He looked up and was again taken aback by her beauty. She had the sort of red hair women paid good money to replicate, and the body of a 1950's pin-up. He always found it hard to concentrate in her presence and preferred to keep the desk between them at all times.

He wasn't unduly sold on the idea of being faithful, monogamy sounded far too much like monotony for his liking. While he had no doubts about his ability to keep one woman happy for the rest of his life, he was far more doubtful about one woman being able to satisfy all his wants and needs.

That said, he did believe strongly in the idea that one did not shit on one's own doorstep. Alice was the best assistant he'd ever had and he had no intention of jeopardising that for a quick fumble, no matter how enjoyable he often imagined it might be.

"They're not coming," she said abruptly as she handed him his coat. "Some sort of family emergency involving Raffa, they didn't elaborate. I've spoken to Tom and he's waiting downstairs to take you to see Ms. Sanchez."

She saw the colour drain from his face, and for a moment felt sorry him. Despite his reputation for not taking any prisoners she knew Ms. Sanchez was the one person he couldn't charm in to submission. It was strange, as Alice had always thought her to be a perfectly friendly lady whenever she had met her or spoken with her on the phone.

Taking a deep breath, Coop pushed himself out of his chair and reached for the coat Alice was holding out for him. He knew he had to make the effort. He should go and do his duty, but by God he couldn't be bothered.

It had all been so much easier when she'd just been a shouter. Back in the days when his failings had been met with screams and the sound of china whizzing past his head, before it inevitably smashed against the wall. There was something comforting about that level of anger, it showed a passion that could often be reasoned with, if not tamed.

He knew where he stood with that, he'd learnt when to duck and dodge, and over the years had realised her anger bomb would often diffuse itself. However, he hadn't yet worked out how to cope with the silent treatment and the aloofness she had started to wear like a shawl.

As he passed Alice's desk on his way to the lift she felt as though she was sending him to the lion's den. "Good luck", she said before returning to the pile of papers on her desk and the flurry of emails that had already started coming in despite the early hour.

By the time Coop had made his way to the basement, Tom was ready and waiting for him. "Hello again Mr. C, where are we off to?"

Tom opened the car door as Coop replied, "The Hope please Tom, I am about to face the wrath of Ms. Sanchez".

Tom closed the door behind him and Coop sank back in to the seat, closing his eyes whilst cursing the Disraeli's and their bloody family emergency.

*****

Jenna was shown to the room she'd been in countless times before. The room where she had first started this journey, where she had discussed her options, where those options had reduced over time and she'd been on the verge of shedding countless tears. All on her own. Will had never made it to any of the previous appointments, today really shouldn't have been any different.

Dr. Barker was seated behind his desk when she walked in, but stood to shake her hand as she approached. He was always so warm and knew how to put her at immediate ease. Not for the first time Jenna wondered if his convivial bedside manner had gotten him in to trouble in the past. Being constantly surrounded by emotionally distraught, vulnerable women in need of comfort could definitely lead him in to compromising situations.

She quickly brushed off the thought that if things didn't go well this time she would happily be compromised herself. It was a thought she'd never allowed herself before, and it jumped unbidden to her mind now.

Despite the neglect of her marriage, she had never been anything but faithful, and she never saw that changing. Will was hers, for better or worse, and she certainly stood by those vows they'd made so many years ago. Sitting down she crossed her long legs and smiled at the man she hoped would change her life.

"So, Jenna, how are you feeling today? Ready to be a Mum?" he asked as he leafed through her unusually large file on his desk.

Jenna smiled. She'd heard all the spiel about having a positive approach and remaining upbeat, but after six failed IVF attempts she was past the point of holding her breath. Today was her last shot. Only one embryo remained and had thankfully survived the thawing process. She knew the chance of this tiny cluster of cells making it safely into her arms in nine months was slim.

It wasn't that she wasn't optimistic, she simply favoured realism. As a young girl starting out a career in fashion she'd learnt the hard way that no matter how positive you were, you had no influence over the outcome. Positive or not, if your face wasn't right, you didn't get the gig.

No amount of smiling and repeating of mantras was going to get her pregnant today. The odds were slim, and whilst she allowed herself to hope, she'd always preferred to know what she was dealing with; it saved disappointment in the future.

"OK then." Dr. Barker closed the file and looked directly at her. "We're just going to check on everything in the lab, you get yourself set up and comfortable, and then we'll get cracking." With that he left the room through the staff door at the back, and the nurse guided her to the exam bed.

Here we go again she thought as she picked up the hospital gown, and began to get undressed.

*****

Sarah was flicking through a copy of House and Garden in an attempt to keep herself occupied. She knew they were early when they'd arrived, but she couldn't help thinking they should have been seen by now. "What if there's a problem?" she whispered nervously to Pete. He looked at her, uncertain what to say.

“There won’t be a problem”. He hoped he’d struck the right balance between confidence and non-commitment. The look on her face suggested he’d failed, and he decided not to press any further.

Sarah had always been high maintenance, anyone who knew and loved her couldn’t disagree, but the last few months she’d become harder to handle. He’d put a lot of it down to hormones, and a fair amount of stress, but he was concerned that even when all of this was over and done with, she would remain the same.

Suddenly a nurse appeared and said, “I’m sorry, Dr. Harper is running a little late, but you’re welcome to come through.”

CHAPTER 5

When Adrienne arrived at the office she was pleased to discover she'd made up time, and was therefore only about 20 minutes late. The taxi dropped her off round the front, so she decided to head in through the main doors, rather than the staff entrance at the side.

Kate was on reception and gave her a wave. "Morning Dr. Harper, Mr. and Mrs. Jenkins have already gone through. Denise is just going over the procedure with them again. She said you wouldn't be long, and that you'd just got caught up on a consult."

Adrienne blew her a kiss and mouthed a quick 'thank you' as she rushed passed, determined not to be any later than she already was. She'd need to take a moment to drop off her stuff, make herself a cuppa and compose herself before she actually went in to them. Her bombing in to the room in a hurry didn't necessarily give the right impression, and she was only too well aware how precious Mrs. Jenkins was. She often reminded her of a highly-strung racehorse, easy to spook and always on the verge of bolting or kicking out.

As she walked through the waiting area she caught the familiar scent of Jean Paul Gaultier and automatically turned her head to see if she could locate where it was coming from. She knew it was a popular fragrance, but she always associated it with Coop and she couldn't help but look. To her amazement there he was, sitting with his back to the window, completing the crossword puzzle in The Times, looking as though he entirely belonged there.

She couldn't believe it, and for a moment stood dumbfounded. What on earth was he doing here? When they'd parted a little more than an hour ago he had been on his way to the airport for a flight to LA. Had his meeting been cancelled? Was there an emergency? Her mind whirled with possibilities, none of which made any sense.

Her heart raced as she tried to figure out what was going on. She stood staring at him for a second longer, initially unable to speak before finally uttering, "Hey, you", to get his attention. He looked up at the source of the interruption and the colour instantly drained from his face. In her state of confusion, she didn't notice.

Instinctively he stood up, and Adrienne came over to hug him. "I didn't expect to see you so soon, is there a problem?" she asked, but all he could do was stare at her, open-mouthed.

"Is everything OK, Coop?" she tried again. He nodded and smiled as he started to regain his composure.

"Of course, why wouldn't it be?" he eventually replied, hoping a slight deflection would buy him more time.

Adrienne squeezed his hand, "What on earth are you doing here?" she asked, feeling disconcerted by her utter lack of understanding of the situation. She hadn't realised he even knew where she worked, so his presence didn't make the slightest bit of sense. None of this was helping her feel any less flustered before going in to see the Jenkins.

Coop smiled again, rapidly ticking off his options in his head, and weighing up their chances of success. There was no plausible explanation that would get him out of this mess, and he couldn't help feeling it was only a matter of time before the bubble burst. However, his natural instinct was always to deflect and do everything possible to save his own skin.

Before he could find the right words, Adrienne shook her head and laughed at him, "Give me a minute, I'll check in with my patient, dump my stuff and we can grab a coffee in the kitchen. I don't have long though." In an instant she was gone, disappearing down the corridor and in to one of the side rooms.

Coop looked around, unsure what to do. Should he sit, wait and see how this played out? Should he pick up his coat and leave? Tom was parked a little down the street waiting for him, he could easily get out and be away before Adrienne came back. Then what? Yes, that would get him out of his immediate predicament, but he'd still have questions to answer later.

He could see it now, she'd phone once she had finished work and demand to know why he'd rushed off without saying goodbye. He'd had years of coming up with excuses and plausible stories to explain his absence or need to be elsewhere at any given moment, so he wasn't unduly concerned by that.

An explanation as to why he'd been at her office in the first place was perhaps a little harder to come by. A last-minute attempt at romance before he disappeared again for a few weeks? That might just about swing it for her.

Rooted to the spot, he stood perfectly still, considering his options and trying to gauge how much time he had to make a plan. He marvelled at his own dumb luck; of all the fertility clinics in all the city, she had to work at this one. He afforded himself a wry smile.

Suddenly the door of a consulting room opened and Dr. Barker walked out, extending his hand to Coop despite being a good 10 feet away. He had no idea who this stranger approaching him was, but quickly determined it must be the consultant the receptionist had phoned to advise of his arrival.

"I trust you are well, Mr. Cooper? Your wife is prepped and ready to get going if you'd like to come in and sit with her? I know she'll be thrilled that you were able to make it."

Coop watched Dr. Barker as he retreated back to his office. This was his escape, this was his chance to get away from the situation. Time would afford him a credible justification for bailing on Adrienne and he was confident he'd be able to make things play out the way he wanted them to.

*****

Adrienne dumped her coat and bag in the staff area and hurried over to her consulting room, conscious her patients were probably tearing their hair out by now. Well, Sarah would be; Pete would no doubt be pacing the floor like a caged tiger, anxiously looking for an escape route.

The Jenkins' were an interesting couple; he always seemed completely disinterested in the process and as for his wife, she had comfortably slipped in to neurotic obsession by their second appointment. It was clear whose idea IVF had been, she just wasn't sure how many arguments it had taken for Mrs. Jenkins to be declared the victor, or what the ultimate cost to their relationship might be.

She had an image of Mrs. Jenkins fidgeting in her chair, checking her watch and fiddling with her Pandora bracelet in that infuriating way she had. She no doubt thought it made her look cute and vulnerable, but it just confirmed what an anxious mess she was. Adrienne had seen it all before, but for some reason it grated with her on this woman more than it had with others.

Adrienne was feeling disconcerted after her encounter with Coop in the waiting room. Her mind was racing a mile a minute, but there were no coherent thoughts coming out that she could work with. He was as out of place in her world as a hippo would be at a dance class, it just made no sense.

She had to clear her mind, she couldn't breeze in to the Jenkins full of nervous energy, that would never create the air of quiet, professional confidence she always aimed for. She took a deep breath, composed herself, opened the door and went in.

*****

Jenna looked up as Will came in to the room. Of all the things she thought might happen today, this certainly wasn't one of them. "What on earth are you doing here?" she asked, realising how accusatory she sounded without meaning to. He laughed, "Now that's a fine welcome right there!"

She straightened the sheet the nurse had placed over her lap and readjusted her wedding and engagement rings. "You know exactly what I mean, William." She paused, "But it is wonderful to see you, I just wasn't expecting you to make it."

Will walked over to her, took her hand and kissed it. "I've been crap. You don't deserve to go through this alone. Again." He was amazed at the level of sincerity in his voice, then was taken back by the fact he genuinely meant it. The encounter with Adrienne just now, and the realisation that he had come perilously close to his world falling to pieces, had stirred a semblance of guilt within him.

Jenna had stood by his side for 27 years. She had supported every one of his decisions, plans, goals and ambitions. Even the most hair brained and risky of deals he'd developed or backed, she'd been by his side, wiping his brow and saying it would be just fine.

Even when it went wrong, she was right. It all worked out OK in the end and he was becoming increasingly convinced it was because of her. She was the steady hand that steered his ship, and for at least the last 10 years he had taken her for granted.

In fact, it was worse than that. He had totally forgotten she was there. He had belittled her importance and the value she added to his entire world, to the point of almost ignoring her. He had assumed she was nothing more than a trophy wife who was getting older with every passing year, and was therefore less deserving of his affections.

As he looked at her now lying in this clinical environment, the harsh light somehow softening as it hit her face, he was reminded just how beautiful she really was. Her skin was softer than any 45-year-olds had the right to be; the little crow's feet hugging the corners of her eyes made her look exciting and fun to be around, and her hair was always immaculately coiffed.

The only thing that let her down was the sadness lurking behind her once bright and sparkling brown eyes. Will studied her intently and reluctantly concluded age had nothing to do with that. Whatever light had gone out in her was his doing. Years of neglect had done that and in that moment, he knew he would never be able to forgive himself, and would never be able to make it up to her.

He settled himself on a small black stool placed near the top of the bed she was lying on and kissed her hand again. "It's going to be fine. This is the one, I just know it. We're going to have our baby, you're not going to have to go through it all alone anymore."

Jenna turned to look at him, not fully understanding what he was saying. The first pinprick of tears began to form behind her eyes, but she blinked them away and stared in to the light. Jenna Maria Sanchez didn't cry. She couldn't even remember the last time she had. Was it when her father had died all those years ago?

Even then she might have been practical rather than emotional. Emotions were too exhausting and time consuming, she'd rather be *doing* than weeping, no matter what the situation. This unexpected display of warmth and compassion from the man she had once worshipped caught her completely off guard though.

It was one thing to have him here, but she had assumed he would sit dispassionately in the corner, responding to emails or scheduling meetings with Alice over the phone. She had never assumed that, were he to be present he would actually be in the moment, attentive and interested.

Dr. Barker coughed, "I'm sorry, I just have to take a phone call, I'll be back as soon as I can and we'll get started." Jenna looked up, nodded and told him there was no rush. She meant it. Her and Will hadn't exchanged this many pleasant words with each other for months, it made a nice change and she had no idea how long it might last. She wanted to make the most of it while she could, regardless of the bizarre environment they found themselves in.

CHAPTER 6

Adrienne shook hands with both Pete and Sarah and seated herself behind her desk. "I'm sorry for the delay, I got caught up on a consult. I trust Denise looked after you?" she asked as she pulled open the file on her desk, not really caring about the answer. Pete nodded while Sarah replied "I thought we might have started by now. Are we still going to have time to do it properly?" Pete shifted uneasily in his seat.

Looking up, Adrienne took another deep breath. "Sarah, please try not to worry. It's only a few minutes and I assure you, I never rush. We will take as long as we need to, and we'll do everything right. You just need to concentrate on staying calm and being positive, leave the rest of it to us."

She closed the file and nodded to Denise. "I just have to go check how things are looking in the lab, Denise will get you comfortable, and then we can finish making this dream come true." With that she stood up and exited back in to the main corridor.

Closing the door behind her she shook her head. Some women were easier to work with than others, and Sarah Jenkins was definitely not one of them. She desperately hoped she was one of the few to have a successful birth after their first attempt at transfer. Adrienne wasn't sure she had the emotional resilience to go through repeated cycles with this couple. Their journey so far had been trying enough.

As she walked back down the corridor towards the waiting area, she started trying again to work out Coop's reasons for being there. In the two years they had been seeing each other they had never had anything to do with the other's professional life. They didn't talk about their careers, co-workers or the trials and tribulations of office politics. Come to think of it, they barely talked about their personal lives either.

She knew he came from a wealthy family and he'd spent a few years living in New York, but that was about all she could piece together about his past. He had never mentioned an ex-wife, so she assumed he'd never been married, and he certainly didn't have any children.

It suddenly struck her as strange that through their entire existence as a 'couple' they had somehow remained entirely separate entities, little more than strangers who spent the occasional night together. Really, she knew very little about him even now, only that he had a stressful and complicated job which required him to spend a lot of his time in America, which was the sole reason they saw each other so infrequently.

Was it the sole reason though, really? She'd always assumed it was, taken for granted that it was simply distance and conflicting time zones that kept them apart more than it put them together, but what if it was more than that? Coop wasn't an open or affectionate man, and whilst that didn't bother her, she now found herself wondering if he was ultimately incapable of committing.

When she reached the waiting room she was dismayed to find it empty. Where on earth could he have gone now? Surely, she hadn't imagined it? She wasn't that sleep deprived! She turned around and headed back to the reception desk.

"Kate, did you see where the gentleman who was waiting in here went?" she asked, hoping it hadn't all been a figment of her imagination.

Without looking up from her computer screen the young receptionist replied, "Mr. Cooper? Yeah, he went in to Dr. Barker's room."

Mr. Cooper? Coop? Her Coop was with Dr. Barker? Why on earth would he be seeing Dr. Barker? Perhaps they were friends. Surely Coop would have mentioned that when she found him in the waiting room? There was no logical reason to hide it. He knew she would be right back, why wouldn't he have waited for her? She was even more confused now.

"What the Hell would he be seeing Greg for?" she found herself asking out loud, more from shock than an attempt to find the answer. This time Kate looked up and made eye contact with her, "Well, his wife Ms. Sanchez was in there. They're having their final session today. Such a sad story, she's been coming here for years. Never seen him before though."

Kate paused, then added for good measure "I really hope it works out for them this time." With that she returned to her typing, leaving Adrienne groping for a response.

Wife? He had a wife. He was here, in her clinic, with his wife, trying for a baby. She grimaced, at least that answered her internal query about whether or not he wanted to have children. It wasn't the answer she was anticipating, but then things never went quite according to plan where Coop was concerned. This was undoubtedly a curve ball though, and something that would take more getting used to than a change of venue for dinner.

She leant against the reception desk for support, her legs suddenly weak and her head spinning. Kate looked up again, this time with concern etched on her face, "You OK Ade? Can I get you a glass of water?" Adrienne shook her head and stumbled towards the lab at the back of the building. It would be quiet in there, she could gather her thoughts and figure out a way to get back in to deal with the Jenkins before completely losing the plot.

On automatic pilot she sanitised her hands before swiping her pass and entering the cool capsule of the storage lab. The sound of the door sealing shut behind her made her feel safe and protected, isolated from whatever dangers were lurking in Dr. Barker's office. She sat down and tried to compose herself, running through her thoughts and prioritising them.

Coop was married. She had no idea how to process that right now and would have to figure out how to deal with it later. Realistically, she couldn't gain control of that situation any time soon, so she might as well focus on things she could deal with; the Jenkins.

Pain in the ass or not, Sarah needed her. Today was her day, and they had been working towards it together for months. It had to be today and Adrienne knew she had to be on top of things to make sure it happened.

She stood up, shook it off and took another deep breath. Work. That's the only thing she could think about right now. Coop and whatever the Hell complication he had just dumped on her would simply have to wait, at least until Pete and Sarah were safely implanted and on their way home.

Turning she looked at the bench behind her and saw the dish Denise had already prepared for her. As she reached for it she heard the doors open and Greg came striding in to join her. Quickly, she blinked back her tears and flicked her hair out of her eyes.

"Everything OK?" he asked as he stopped in front of her. Unsure how much control she had over her voice, Adrienne simply nodded and picked up the dish she had been reaching for. Checking it under the microscope she breathed a gentle sigh of relief. Everything looked perfect, this was going to be a healthy little baby; she could just feel it.

Greg collected his own supplies and gave her a wink, "Let's go make some babies" he said as he turned and left the room. Fixing a smile on her face she gathered everything she needed, left the lab and returned to her office, refusing to look at the door to Dr. Barker's room as she passed by.

*****

By the time Dr. Barker returned to the room Jenna and Will were giggling like school children. They'd been reminiscing about a disastrous holiday in Antigua in which Will drank too much rum and had fallen off a boat, breaking his ankle in the process. "I'll get Alice to book us on the next flight, we could do with a holiday", Will suggested as Jenna wiped tears of laughter from her eyes.

Dr. Barker had never seen them together before, but this is not what he expected of the elusive Mr. Cooper. Reading between the lines there was no love between the couple, he'd always assumed they remained together out of convention rather than a desire to be with each other specifically. It was clear they were independently wealthy, she had enjoyed a successful career as a model whilst he was a hedge fund manager, or something to do with investment.

They clearly had a good lifestyle filled with fine food, expensive wine and fast cars. He'd often imagined they slept in different parts of their mansion, communicating via personal assistants or housekeepers. The couple he found in front of him now took him by surprise. They appeared to be good friends, genuinely fond of each other and comfortable in their own company. It threw him for a loop and he rarely got things so very wrong.

He remembered Jenna had told him that she and Will had met when she was just 18, and here they were many, many years later still lighting up the other's world. It was a beautiful thing to watch and he found himself saying a silent prayer that this, their last remaining embryo, would complete their idyllic family.

He knew from his many conversations with Jenna that they had just waited too long. Will was not entirely paternal, and had no overriding desire to father a child, but he was prepared to do what it took to keep up appearances. The sad thing is, by the time they were settled and in a position where they should have children, they never managed to get around to it.

The jet set lifestyle, the parties and the frequent conflicting schedules meant they spent much of Jenna's fertile years in different time zones. From things Jenna had hinted at over the years, Greg suspected Will might have found comfort in the arms of other women while Jenna's eggs whittled away.

It was such a shame, looking at them now. He could see that under other circumstances it could have been so different. However, he was glad he could be on hand to offer some hope and potentially make all the difference. He wasn't holding his breath though.

This was their seventh attempt and the embryo floating in his petri dish was the remaining survivor from their initial egg harvest all that time ago. There wouldn't be any more now unless a miracle occurred.

Dr. Barker cleared his throat and asked Jenna to move closer to the end of the bed. It was time to begin. She did as he asked, more familiar with the process than she had ever wanted to be. As she cast her mind back to the first attempt, she remembered feeling so confident that everything would be OK.

She knew now that at over 40, her chances of conceiving and carrying to term were reduced, but she also firmly believed that it would just be too unfair if she wasn't given the chance to be a mother. She had waited far too long for this, perhaps literally, and remained hopeful that nature would be on her side. She just hadn't counted on nature needing quite so much scientific help along the way.

Now she was facing her last possible attempt she wasn't sure how she felt. In the past she had always been comforted simply knowing she had at least one more shot before they called it a day. It was a kind of safety net, ready to catch her if that second line failed to appear on her pregnancy test. Today the safety net was being removed, and she was terrified of falling again.

Will changed position slightly so he could hold her hand and stroke her hair, "How long is this likely to take?" he asked. Jenna scowled, "If you have somewhere else to be you didn't have to come."

He was crushed by her response although he knew he deserved such an attack; however, in this instance he was more concerned with how long she would have to endure this process, rather than his own itinerary. In fact, he was only concerned with her, he'd already decided to cancel the rest of his appointments for the day and take her shopping.

He wondered if he should put her straight, but was concerned his real explanation would make her feel guilty, which in turn would embarrass her in front of the dapper Dr Barker. Instead he continued to stroke her hair and turned the blame on himself, "It's shameful to admit, but it just struck me I know nothing about how our baby is being conceived".

While Jenna closed her eyes, and tried to locate that positive energy everyone was always talking about, Dr. Barker explained in brief the process to date, and what was occurring this very minute. Jenna pretended not to listen, but of course could not help herself. She marvelled at how interested Will genuinely appeared to be, and wondered what had sparked this sudden change in his attitude.

When she had first raised the subject of "actively trying" for a baby he had been unenthusiastic. Admittedly, he'd taken the time to check his work diary to see his availability for "doing the deed" as he called it, but it had quickly become apparent he was not going to be around at the right times to help her out. As usual he had found a solution, and unsurprisingly it had involved throwing money at the problem.

One morning as he was preparing to leave for the office he broached the subject with her. His precise words were: “Let me know how much IVF is going to cost and I’ll cover it. Call it an anniversary present.” With that, he had left for a business meeting goodness knows where and they hadn’t been in the same place together for another three weeks.

She had long since given up being upset or even insulted by his offhand approach to her emotional needs. He wasn’t a nasty or vindictive man, he was just inwardly focussed and pragmatic. She wanted a baby, he understood she’d be waiting far longer were he to oblige the traditional way, and he had presented her with an alternative option.

He had never suggested she use a donor, the baby was to be biologically his, and he assured her he would find the time to make the requisite deposit as and when it was necessary. That was as romantic as Will got these days, and she was grateful to accept the offer.

As she lay there with Will holding her hand and Dr. Barker seated between her legs she tried to recall the last time they had made love. Unable to conjure up any memories of the event at all, she queried how long it had been since they were last intimate, on any meaningful level. This moment was probably the closest they had been, both physically and emotionally for years. She felt like crying at the thought. When had it happened, and more importantly, why?

Yes, Will worked hard and he was often away, but shouldn't absence make the heart grow fonder? Had he been the one that stopped trying, or had she? She never really considered it before, just accepted it for what it was and hoped that one day it would magically change. The reality was it wasn't going to, they would have to do something about it, but what? And who was to make the first move?

In all honesty Will had, just by being here. She racked her brain to think of what she could do to encourage him not to give up. Would a baby help now? He seemed so keen, as though he had suddenly woken up to the idea of a new life entering their world, a life they had created together, albeit slightly unconventionally. She could work with that. Images of her lying on the sofa with his hands on her belly, waiting for their baby to kick, appeared unbidden in her mind.

She was brought back to reality and the cold light of the consulting room by Dr. Barker pushing his chair back and announcing he'd finished. She opened her eyes and the first thing she saw was Will looking down at her, "We just made a baby!" he said, grinning from ear to ear. She really hoped so. More than ever before as she realised the pressure stakes had just doubled.

Will joined Dr. Barker at the table in the other corner of the room while the nurse pulled the curtain around the examining bed to afford Jenna some privacy. She imagined Will would launch in to a discussion about the latest James Bond film, or whether Dr. Barker was a keen golfer, but instead she could hear him asking advice on what to do over the next few days.

As the fertility expert outlined the importance of a healthy diet, Will nodded along earnestly like a student attending a fascinating lecture. “Do you think it’s OK to travel? A week on a warm beach would do us both good.” Dr. Barker was delighted by this suggestion and agreed it could be the perfect way to get some R & R before they hopefully found out their lives would change forever.

It only took her a minute to get dressed, and before she knew it Will had dismissed Tom, and was seating himself in the driver seat of her Audi, preparing to take them both home together for the first time in months.

CHAPTER 7

Sarah had finished getting dressed again after her procedure, and returned to her seat opposite Dr. Harper at the desk. Dr. Harper looked up from her notes and smiled, "That's it all done now Sarah. All you have to do is wait and keep your fingers crossed."

Sarah wasn't sure what to expect, she had hoped she would immediately feel different, that somehow, she would know whether she was pregnant or not. "When can I take a test to find out?" she asked, conscious of the impatience in her voice.

Dr. Harper explained it would take a good few days for the necessary hormones to establish themselves, and advised waiting at least nine before testing. Pete looked up from his phone and scoffed, "I appreciate you offering the advice Doc, but I'd be amazed if she didn't go straight home and pee on a stick now!"

They exchanged a smile and Sarah felt she was being laughed at. She desperately wanted to reply, to wipe that look off their faces, but the truth was she had already bought a batch of early tests on the internet and was counting down the minutes before she could be home, safe in the privacy of their en suite bathroom.

After a few more questions they were free to leave, and it was no time at all before they were back in the car, heading home. Pete was thrilled they'd made such good timing so he could get back, get changed and then head out to a job.

Sarah was disappointed, but chose to hide it. She had hoped they would spend the day together; perhaps go shopping for a baby pram, get some ideas for the nursery and have a nice lunch at Giorgio's. She'd skip the wine, of course, but it would still be lovely.

She was hurt that it had never occurred to Pete that today was an important day, and should be treated as such. He'd delayed going to work by an hour and as far as he was concerned that was enough of a commitment to Operation Get Knocked Up, as he kept referring to her treatment. Realising she now had the day to herself, Sarah quickly re-planned her activities.

She'd go home, take that test and then have a hot bath. She might pop round to see Janice too and ask if she fancied a trip in to town. The older children would be at school, so it would just be them and baby Jack. They could look at baby clothes and stop for a scone and pot of tea at that new tea room, Tsp, in town.

For some reason she desperately didn't want to be alone. Deep down she knew the next two weeks were going to be the longest of her life whilst she waited to find out one way or another what her future held, and she wanted to be as busy as possible during that time. Nothing was really going to keep her occupied, but she had to at least try.

The traffic was as clear on the way back as it had been on their drive out, and they were home before they knew it. Sarah walked to the kitchen automatically to make a cup of tea and leafed through a magazine Pete had discarded on the counter top. Unsurprisingly, she failed to be captivated by the latest copper pipe news or advances in solar panel technology.

At times she wished he had a more interesting job, and certainly one that involved him wearing a suit. She despised having to try and wash silicone sealant and goodness knows what else out of his overalls. She should have been a banker's wife, not a heating engineers. Even an estate agent would have been an improvement as far as she was concerned.

*****

Adrienne leant back in her chair and closed her eyes. It was only 11am and she already felt like she'd run a marathon. It had taken her far longer to complete all the Jenkins' paperwork than she'd anticipated, and she knew that was due in large part to her utter lack of concentration.

On top of a foggy head caused by lack of sleep, she couldn't keep Coop and his possibly soon to be pregnant wife off her mind. She wanted desperately to compartmentalise, and had told herself repeatedly over the last 90 minutes that she could wallow all she wanted when she got home, but it seemed her subconscious had other ideas.

She'd lost count of the number of trashy magazines or chick-lit books she'd read involving a philandering husband, duped wife and a provocative mistress. These were the sorts of everyday scandals that made for entertaining reading, but she had always wondered how they were possible.

How could a man do that to the woman he had professed to love so many years ago, and how could the wife not be aware? How did one make a life with someone and have genuinely no idea they were dipping their pen in the company ink? Or anybody's ink for that matter.

Her biggest problem with the scenario she was now facing was that she didn't feel she was the stereotype of the "other" woman. In fact, she felt mortified at the very thought such a term could be applied to her. The reality was, wittingly or not, that's precisely what she was in this relationship.

Coop had turned her in to this thing she despised, and somehow, she had been totally unaware of the part she played in his life, or the impact she could have on this woman she'd not even known about. For the first time her mind turned to the elusive wife, and what discovering Coop's infidelity would do to her, especially now.

Annoyed, she wondered how she could have been so blind. Surely there were signs all around, and for whatever reason she had just missed them? She cast her mind back to when her and Coop had first met.

It had been at a fundraising function for the local hospital and they'd been introduced by his business partner, who happened to be an old friend of Adrienne's brother. They'd hit it off straight away, helped in large part by a mutual love of The Beatles and the complimentary champagne.

The next day she came in to the office nursing a severe hangover to discover a gorgeous bouquet of red roses on her desk with a note saying 'I want to hold your hand'. It had all seemed so incredibly romantic and she'd been blown away by his charm.

The next night they had gone out for dinner, the night after that a trip to the theatre. She had been utterly seduced, yet he'd never laid a hand on her or attempted to do more than give her a peck on the cheek as his car dropped her home.

At the time she'd assumed he was being gentlemanly, taking his time so as not to pressure her or scare her off. She'd told him, on their first date, about her last relationship with an abusive boyfriend so she was sure he was giving her space, being respectful of her need to learn to trust again.

Now she found herself wondering if he was simply weighing up whether she was worth cheating on his wife with. How calculating had he actually been about it all? She shuddered at the thought. It was hard looking back on those early memories given everything she knew now.

Remembering the flowers, she realised he could probably provide her with a legitimate reason why he was at her office that morning. His flight was late, he wanted to see her; it could have been romantic, if it wasn't all utter bullshit.

The reality was though that he probably had no idea she worked here at all, and that's why he was acting so strangely when she saw him. Alice had no doubt spent time researching where she worked and had ordered the flowers on his behalf. Had he even bothered to dictate the message, or had that been delegated too?

She sighed, wondering how many other things he had sent her that he had no real hand in. The Cartier watch for their first anniversary, the diamond necklace from Tiffany's for her birthday last year. Alice no doubt organised it all, perhaps choosing things for Adrienne that she would have liked for herself.

Looking down at her desk she caught sight of the expenses claim form she still needed to complete for the previous month; mileage, stationery and the occasional phone call. Where exactly would one list 'gifts to mistress'? Was she simply tax deductible and a bit of fun? She cringed at the thought of Will and his accountant writing her off, and laughing at her expense.

*****

Jenna and Will had driven home in silence, but not that awkward taciturn quiet they had been sharing for so long. It was pleasant just to be, enjoying their own thoughts, their fingers barely touching as they made their way through the mid-morning traffic.

Jenna was still trying to work out how to respond to Will's presence at her appointment. She couldn't help but feel there would be something deeply whimsical about her finally conceiving their child whilst he was with her. Perhaps that's all the process needed, a little bit of tangible hope that it really would all be OK in the end.

She desperately tried not to get carried away, but deep down she hoped this wasn't just a one-off moment of solidarity, that instead something really had changed. She wanted to ask him what was going on, what he was thinking, but she was terrified of bursting the bubble and scaring him off to wherever his mind had been before.

When they arrived at the house Will called the office and asked Alice to cancel all his appointments for the next two weeks, telling her he planned to take some time off. He offered no explanation, and Jenna imagined none was asked for. Alice had more balls than all the men in that office put together, but it had been her experience that nobody ever questioned Will, it was far easier to merely do what was requested.

"Would you like a cup of tea?", Jenna asked as she placed her handbag on the countertop. It was the most natural question, but again she couldn't remember the last time the opportunity had arisen. Their lives were so entirely distinct from each other that even the act of sharing breakfast or a warm beverage together was noteworthy.

"I should make you one," Will replied, which made her laugh. Not a gentle, ladylike giggle but a roar of noise that started in the pit of her stomach. He turned, surprised by the sound and unsure of its motivation.

"Oh Will, it's a lovely thought but I should imagine you have no idea where the tea bags are kept, and the kettle itself may be beyond your technical capabilities."

He would love to have been able to oppose her, but he knew she was right. There had been no need for him to make his own drink for years. Either Jenna, the housekeeper, Alice or the waitress at his favourite coffee shop would perform that duty.

In fact, drinking tea or coffee out of anything other than a branded paper cup was a rarity these days. He marvelled at how odd life could be, that things could change so gradually that ultimately it was difficult to notice the subtle things that had disappeared from your life.

Opening his briefcase, he took out a notepad and pen then walked in to the kitchen, sitting down at the breakfast bar. "What are you doing?" Jenna asked, surprised by his presence in the one room he had very little to do with. "Taking notes, so that tomorrow morning, I can make you a cup of tea."

They laughed, and quietly hoped something magical had happened that morning.

*****

Pete sat in his van, stuck in traffic and conscious he was already late to his next appointment of the day. He silently cursed Sarah and how her desperation to do things her way had impacted on his ability to get anything done today. He knew he was being harsh, and it wasn't her fault, but he was frustrated and felt impotent with anger.

He loved his wife, but he had become increasingly exhausted by her over the last few months. When they first met she had been fun, and exactly what he needed at the time. Admittedly, despite a few stolen kisses, he'd never planned to be her boyfriend.

The truth was at the time he had been trying to get over a broken heart, and the young girl that looked up at him adoringly and hung on his every word was little more than a distraction. For the longest time he'd actually hoped that the real object of his affections would come back to him, but instead Maggie had turned in to the good time girl that was had by all.

Sarah was besotted from the start, and Pete's ego had been grateful of the attention. It was clear she wanted a real-life romance, a story to tell and wow everyone with, so it had made sense at the time for him to propose. He hadn't really thought about what would come after the moment he placed the ring on her finger.

Of course, within weeks she had booked the wedding and had started sorting all the intricate details. Less than a year later they had moved in to their first flat as husband and wife. He didn't regret it, but now he looked back he wished he'd been a bit more present and had put the brakes on a little.

The only thing he had managed to slow down was the start of a family. Sarah had been desperate the second they'd said 'I do', to join the club. She'd wanted nothing more than to come back from honeymoon with some good news. Instead, he'd refused. He'd used every excuse in the book; money, security, the need for a bigger house, they were too young, it was too soon in their marriage. For a while a combination of them all had kept her off his back.

However, as time ticked away so did her biological clock and eventually he'd had to relent. After so many years of excuses he no longer felt he had the right to simply say he wasn't sure he wanted children. Well, it was more complicated than that. He did want children, he wanted a large family, he just wasn't sure he wanted it with Sarah.

Said out loud it sounded terrible, but he had never been convinced they were well matched enough to stand the test of time. He had no doubt he could blunder his way through the rest of his life married to her, but he wasn't sure he wanted to subject a child to that sort of existence.

It wasn't something he'd ever admit to anyone else, but he'd been delighted when they'd been unable to conceive naturally. He should have known Sarah would press for alternative methods, to see what else could be done to ensure she got her perfect little baby.

He shook his head when he thought of the arguments they'd had. It was easy to chastise himself for not standing up to her and refusing to go ahead with it all, but in the moment, with the constant rows, it had been far easier to just relent. It was always easier to just let Sarah have whatever it was she wanted.

CHAPTER 8

Leaning against the counter, waiting for her tea to brew, Sarah cast her mind back to when her and Pete had met. They'd been childhood sweethearts and had first spoken at a youth dance at their local church. Neither of them were particularly religious, but there was nothing else to do in their neighbourhood at that time, and it was a great place to meet members of the opposite sex. She'd been 14 and had immediately been impressed by this tall, handsome, dark haired 16-year-old with the hazel eyes.

They'd stood awkwardly next to each other by the drinks table for a while and she watched as he tore a plastic cup to strips. Eventually, she had taken his hand and dragged him to the dancefloor. She was glad she had because they'd spent the rest of the night talking and laughing together.

When the dance had finished he'd walked her home, holding her hand and leaning in for a goodnight kiss on her doorstep. Or had she leant in? She couldn't remember now, but decided it was more romantic the other way around.

They'd never looked back. By the time she was 17 she was sporting a suitable sized diamond on her finger and they were married the year after. Her family absolutely adored Pete, otherwise they may have had something to say about their only daughter marrying at such a young age. She knew she was doing the right thing though, Pete would always stand by her and give her anything she wanted, and the only thing she wanted at the time was a baby. Nothing had changed in the last 17 years.

Pete had refused to try for a family immediately, believing instead they should focus on their marriage and being a happy couple. She'd agreed at the time because it made sense, but now, at 35 she wondered if maybe they'd left it too late. Initially Dr. Harper had said she could find no reason as to their failure to conceive naturally, but after their first course of treatment further tests revealed her egg supply was dwindling.

That word, dwindling; it made her feel so old. The truth was her ovaries had probably given up after being made to wait so long for Pete to be ready. They could have started trying when she was 20 and she'd have a teenager by now. In all the time they'd been waiting, it had never occurred to her to ask why Pete was so hesitant about parenthood. Now, it didn't matter; she had got her way and with luck, a baby would be theirs soon.

*****

Still unable to concentrate, Adrienne found herself wondering how on earth she'd become a mistress, especially without even knowing it. Had she been so blown away by his charm, and the money, that she didn't stop to think carefully about his constant absences and his reluctance to be contacted at certain times of the night? If he had been like any of the other men she'd attempted to date in the past, would she have seen it sooner?

She felt sick, how long would this have gone on for? The piecemeal truth she had uncovered today was pure luck, he hadn't come clean; he hadn't even spoken to her. In that moment she was sure it hurt so much more because it hadn't come from him, she was reeling from that as much as the truth itself.

It suddenly dawned on her that he wasn't even aware she knew anything other than he had abandoned her at the clinic. Immediately she felt the urge to check her phone, he might have called or left her a message to provide some form of explanation for his sudden disappearance.

Nothing.

She felt cold and empty, unable to digest what had happened, and incapable of guessing what the next 24 hours would bring. If he didn't get in touch soon would she have to bring it up, come clean about her brief conversation with Kate? Would he deny everything or try to placate her with the clichéd excuses "But she doesn't understand me" and "I never meant for this to happen"? The thought made her feel ill.

What if he had weighed up the probabilities and concluded she might well have figured out the truth, somehow? He might decide to just vanish from her life, cut his losses and hope she'd be a good little girl and not contact him again. If he chose to do that, could she oblige?

The thought of not having closure, of never really knowing anything about the last two years was more than she could bear, though a full revealing of the truth didn't necessarily appeal to her either.

While it was clear they weren't what she had initially thought they were, she felt she was entitled to some form of explanation from him. He owed her something, even if it was an attempt at honesty before he walked out of her life.

*****

After she'd finished making her tea, Sarah rushed upstairs. It only took her a second to locate her secret stash of pregnancy tests, and she immediately went to the bathroom to try the first one. She deliberately waited the suggested three minutes before turning the test over, hoping to see two beautiful lines.

However, as Dr. Harper had predicted, there was only one. She skulked back in to the bedroom and sat down on the bed, test still in hand. Despite knowing there was no way she would get a positive test, even if everything had gone perfectly this morning, she felt a deep sense of disappointment looking down at the space where a second line should appear.

She had a vague understanding of the biological processes along with the time that was needed to show her the result she wanted, and to a certain extent accepted them. However, she had taken a pregnancy test nearly every day for the last three years, and it had become more than a habit for her now. She couldn't stop herself.

She even found herself wondering if she would be able to stop when she did finally get two lines. Would she still continue to test every day of her pregnancy, just to make sure? Or would she feel better once she had seen her baby on an ultrasound screen?

Occasionally she wondered if she was going mad, but was too scared to talk to Janice or Pete about it in case they laughed, or worse, agreed. There was no way they would understand what she was going through, and she wasn't eloquent enough with words to really make them get it.

Sighing, she wrapped the little strip of card in a tissue and hid it in her knicker drawer alongside the others from this week. It was always the same; she would wait until Pete put the bins out on Monday and then she'd sneak out to put them inside once he'd gone to work. She'd be mortified if he found out her secret. Having suspicions about her level of obsession was one thing, having him able to confirm them was an entirely different matter.

In an attempt to calm herself and regain control of her emotions she reached in to her bedside drawer and pulled out all her IVF leaflets. She read through them again, reminding herself of the journey she had already been on, and how much they'd achieved. The statistics always scared her, only one in every three would get pregnant on a first attempt. Well, that was fine, she could be one of them.

Dr. Harper had spent so much time saying there was no physical reason why they hadn't been able to conceive. Pete had perfect sperm apparently and she was ovulating regularly, even if she did have a dwindling supply. In many ways Sarah had found that more frustrating than if they had identified a problem.

Problems were meant to be fixed, but this had been impossible to understand. The knowledge that 'it was what it was' didn't help her move on at all and she had found it hard to accept the need for treatment if there was, to all intents and purposes, nothing wrong with either of them.

Since they had started trying for this baby she'd read many things online, in various forums and baby groups, about women who essentially psyched themselves out of getting pregnant each month. Women who wanted it so badly that all they thought about was conceiving, and their bodies just turned against them.

She didn't understand why nature would do that, but it seemed it was the case and she sometimes wondered if that was what Dr. Harper was getting at when she kept reminding her to relax. She wanted to, desperately. She did yoga and even took Pilates classes, but nothing seemed to help. She had charts for her temperature and each month she'd worked out the best possible times for them to have sex, and had made Pete keep to them.

She'd even made love one night when she had a pounding headache, but two weeks later, nothing. Actually, worse than nothing, evil Aunt Flo had arrived and it was back to square one. To a certain extent going for treatment had made things easier, she no longer had to worry about sex or what her body was doing, that was Dr. Harper's job.

They still had a strict schedule but it focussed around hormone injections, blood tests and ultrasounds now which were all out of Sarah's control. She felt that, on many levels, there was nothing she could do and she relished the thought that if it didn't work she could now blame someone else.

The leaflets weren't helping so she put them away, lay down on the bed and closed her eyes. There was nothing she could do now. Her embryo, the first cells of her potential baby were where they were meant to be. All she had to do now was trust in nature, fate and anything else that had any sway in this situation, that all would be well.

Closing her eyes as she started to daydream about her daughter, within minutes she was asleep, the early start catching up with her at last.

*****

There was a knock at the door and Kate came in. "Everything OK, you feeling better?" she asked as she sat herself down on the chair opposite her. Adrienne welcomed the distraction from her painful thoughts whilst at the same time wishing she could remain alone.

"A bit, thanks," she mustered. She knew Kate was fishing for an explanation for her behaviour so followed up with, "I forgot to have breakfast this morning, so I'm probably just hungry."

It wasn't entirely a lie, the food from the breakfast tray had not been used for the purpose it had been intended for. She shuddered. Recollections of this morning, of last night, of it all, made her feel violated.

Yes, she loved Coop, would do anything for him and with him, but he wasn't who she thought he was. He had lied, no matter what way you looked at it, she didn't actually know the man she had been so intimate with for so long.

"OK, well as long as you're not about to pass out on us" Kate said cheerily, standing up preparing to leave, "I just need to get the Jenkins paperwork to update their file. You all done with it?"

Adrienne nodded and handed the small manila folder over to her. For a second, she wondered whether her next appointment with Sarah Jenkins would be for an ultrasound, or to discuss recommencing treatment. "Fingers crossed it's good news for them", she said as Kate opened the door and left.

Adrienne checked her diary, suddenly unable to recall the appointments she had left for the day. Thankfully she only had one more face to face meeting;

a consultation with a new couple. She usually loved these appointments, it was all new for these people, and they were often scared by the unfamiliar world they were entering. She enjoyed being able to answer their questions and tell them there was always hope. More often than not by the time they were sent on their way they felt much better and positive for what the future may bring them.

It was often hardest when the man was the one with the fertility problem. They invariably saw infertility as a slight on their manhood, as though somehow it was something that could, and indeed should, be controlled. She saw it time and time again, and found it amusing how simple and predictable they all were.

Women on the other hand usually had a guilt-based response; a feeling of letting their other half down, but as soon as you told them they could still carry a child, even if it wasn't theirs biologically, they came around.

In her experience, many of her male patients would have been more than content to draw a line under having a family and using the IVF money to have a good holiday instead, or build a games extension on the side of the house. Most failed to understand the emotional and biological need of their wives or partners to carry a child, birth a child and then raise it.

For them, if a child was all they wanted, why not adopt? Men were so much more practical when it came to this than their significant others. Of course, she was grateful for the emotional needs of women, without them she'd be out of a job.

There was another knock at the door and Kate came in again before Adrienne had time to reply. She had a serious look on her face which Adrienne hadn't seen before.

"Is everything OK?" she asked, and Kate shook her head, "I think we've got a serious problem".

CHAPTER 9

Adrienne returned to her office and slumped at her desk. The meeting with Kate, Dr. Barker and the clinic manager Evelyn had been called unexpectedly and had been exceptionally fraught. As she sat staring at nothing, completely unable to focus, Adrienne found herself marvelling at how quickly things could change.

In all the time she'd been at the clinic she'd never had any encounter with the management that wasn't exceptionally positive. She felt that today, within seconds of the meeting starting all that had been forgotten and counted for nothing. Of course, under the circumstances it didn't necessarily feel entirely unfair, but still it stung more than she was prepared to admit in this moment.

During the meeting it had been made clear she was to take the rest of the day off, her afternoon meeting would be handled by Greg. After collecting her coat and handbag Adrienne made her way out of the building via the staff entrance at the back. She contemplated ordering a taxi, but she wasn't sure where she wanted to go. The obvious choice was home, but for the time being that didn't feel as inviting as it should have. She checked her watch, it was only 11.30am; she could walk around for half an hour and then find somewhere to have lunch.

The thought of lunch didn't really appeal though. Eating was an automatic response, a reminder she hadn't had breakfast and should, from a purely physiological perspective at least, consume calories to sustain her, but she knew she couldn't stomach anything. The only reason she was really contemplating food was to create a socially acceptable scenario in which she could have a glass of wine. Perhaps a bottle. No one would notice a bottle if she accompanied it with a large bowl of pasta.

It certainly felt like the sort of situation in which alcohol, and copious amounts of it were required. Today had most definitely not gone according to plan and it wasn't even half way done yet. Goodness knows how many other twists and turns could await her over the next 12 hours. She kept walking and passed the local convenience store.

While the bottle of wine continued to appeal, the thought of surrounding herself with other diners, many of whom were no doubt having a significantly better and more jovial day than her turned her stomach. She decided to opt for a ready meal and a bottle of Shiraz instead. That made the thought of going home slightly more palatable, and she made her way to the nearest taxi rank.

*****

Sarah opened her eyes and glanced at her mobile phone lying on the bedside table. She couldn't believe she'd fallen asleep, let alone for three hours. She lay still for a few more minutes, unable to summon the energy required to find something to do to occupy her mind.

After the highs of the morning and the anticipation that had flowed through her for the last few months she felt decidedly down. It was too early to call it depression, it had only been two minutes, but she was definitely feeling funky and out of sorts. She wondered if it was a sort of anti-climax, that she'd genuinely thought she would feel different and the fact she didn't baffled her slightly. She had been looking forward to today for so long that, now it had been and gone, she had nothing left to look forward to.

Yes, she knew she had the confirmation of pregnancy to look forward to but there was a nagging voice at the back of her head, probably Pete's, that made her doubt this. There was always a chance that day may not come, or if it did, it might not be as a result of this cycle. She couldn't hang on to that hope firmly for fear it might send her over the edge.

Each month was a new month, a new chance to get pregnant, but underneath all the prayers and positivity she never really expected it, always knew there would be some barrier. Now there wasn't, now there was a bunch of cells which should be her baby inside her, all she had to do was hope they hung on in there.

It seemed more likely than ever that the end result would be positive, but she knew it just meant that failing would hurt even more than before. She was conscious that technically she was now pregnant, regardless of what the test had said. If she wasn't pregnant in two weeks that meant she'd miscarried. It was an entirely different prospect to contend with.

It was going to be a long wait before she would know for certain, and she wasn't sure she was mentally strong enough to cope with it. Pete thought she was completely neurotic, and on some levels, he wasn't entirely wrong, but she couldn't help it and she felt so entirely alone. She worried that she often pushed people away with the things she said, or perhaps more the way she said them, but she couldn't change the way she was.

She pushed herself out of bed, determined not to waste any more time lying there feeling sorry for herself. It was about time she stopped focussing on what might be around the corner, especially as she had no control over it, and instead paid more attention to what was here right now.

Pete had been going on and on about going away, and she kept refusing. She didn't really know why, now she came to actually think about it. There was some fear that she might get ill if they went abroad, and that would put a pregnancy at risk. On the flip side, if she didn't get pregnant then she'd just be miserable and she'd rather not waste the money.

Now she realised how childish she'd been and that Pete had a point. A holiday, no matter where, would do them both good. They hadn't been away for ages and they could both do with a change of scenery and something to look forward to. She practically skipped downstairs, made another cup of tea and logged on to her laptop.

He had wanted to go camping, but it had never really appealed to her. She'd never been the most adventurous of individuals and regarded staying in anything less than a 4-star resort as slumming it. She'd rather not go anywhere than end up somewhere below par. That said, she found herself looking for camp site information. It still didn't exactly rock her boat but she was suddenly conscious of the fact that Pete had done everything he could to give her this baby.

Whether it worked immediately or in the future was neither here nor there, he had done it. He had done extra jobs at weekends to help fund Operation Get Knocked Up, and he'd driven her to every single appointment. He had given her all the hormone injections and had put up with all her entirely irrational mood swings and tantrums, not all of which could be blamed on the treatment. The least she could do was give him something he wanted.

A few minutes of reading about pitching tents and communal wash areas had her reconsidering though. She shuddered at the thought of having to walk anywhere in the middle of the night to attend to her toilet needs. It just wasn't going to happen and would most definitely not lead to a nice, relaxing or romantic getaway.

She’d tried, and while Pete may never be aware of it, she knew the truth and it made her feel better. Suddenly she stumbled on glamping, and quickly realised it may just be the compromise they needed. A bit of outdoors for him, and a flushing toilet with running water for her. Before she could talk herself out of it she had booked 10 days away, leaving tomorrow.

It felt good to be so spontaneous, all she had to do now was let Pete know and hope he didn’t have any big jobs on that he couldn’t reschedule. He’d probably be annoyed at first that she’d made such a relatively large purchase without consultation or consideration of the implications, but she didn’t care. He’d wanted a holiday and now he was going to get one.

*****

Adrienne reached for the bottle of wine to top up her glass and realised it was already empty. She checked again, just to be sure, tipping the bottle upside down over her expectant glass. “Bugger”, she said out loud as disappointment surged through her. She knew it wasn’t a big deal but she felt this perfectly summed up the shitty day she’d had.

Catching sight of the time on her phone she noticed it was far later than she’d imagined, and realised she had a choice. She could either pop on her shoes and head over to the Co-Op across the road for a third bottle of wine, or she could make a night of it. A proper night of it, that didn’t involve her drowning her sorrows whilst sitting in her apartment, lamenting the fact she didn't even have a cat for company.

It didn't take her long to make up her mind, and within minutes she was in her bedroom frantically looking for something more suitable to wear. The fermented grapes had definitely worked their magic, and now she had the semblance of a plan, she was no longer feeling sad and pathetic; she felt empty, and in need of doing something to make her feel something else. Anything else.

She grabbed at a few dresses, held them up in front of her to review in the mirror, and then promptly discarded them on the floor. Finally, she settled on an off the shoulder black number she'd been saving for a night out with Coop. Stripping off down to her underwear she decided that needed changing as well. Unclipping her sensible, mid-week work bra she turned to her drawers to look for a replacement, then a tiny seed of a thought began to grow in her mind.

If she wanted attention, which right this minute she undoubtedly did, then nothing would achieve that better than a tight black dress and no bra at all. That meant the comfy knickers had to come off too and she replaced these with a pair of black lace Brazilian panties, which were always a crowd pleaser. Or at least had been when the crowd had been Coop.

CHAPTER 10

Sitting in the reclining armchair, Will tried to recall the last time he'd spent the night with Jenna like this, simply doing nothing. It must have been years, in fact, he wasn't convinced it had ever happened in this house, and they must have lived here for nearly 16 years now.

Glancing over, he smiled when he realised she was fast asleep on the sofa next to him. Worried she might be cold, but reluctant to wake her, he pulled the faux fur throw over her. She stirred slightly, but not enough to cause her any real disturbance, and within seconds she was lightly snoring again.

After filling his glass from the half-finished bottle on the coffee table, he returned to his seat and closed his eyes. He found himself wondering how it had all gotten so complicated. Looking back, he didn't really understand how it had happened.

One minute he was wining and dining this beautiful younger woman, and the next he was embarking on a long-term affair; one he even kept from the woman in question. It had all started innocently enough, but then he was sure all these things always did. Nobody planned to completely cock-up, things just played out that way.

He had never intended to cheat on Jenna, but equally he accepted it was no doubt an inevitability. Part of him felt Jenna understood that too. Sex was simply that, something to keep you occupied and entertained, but even he accepted he had overstepped a line by seeing Adrienne regularly.

Jenna had known about other women, the ones that had come and gone so quickly no one could be bothered to recall their names. There hadn't been many, he reminded himself, but there had been enough. At first his wife had been furious, her Latino temper exploding with the slightest provocation. It seemed every week he was arranging for the plates to be replaced, or the First Aid kit to be replenished.

Suddenly though she'd stopped fighting. Now he stopped to think about it he realised that was what had been so different for the last year or so. Instead of raising her voice and challenging him, she'd simply accepted his excuses, no matter how pathetic or clichéd they were, and let him leave without question.

Part of him was hurt that she no longer cared, but he also accepted it was his fault she had been pushed that far. Now guilt surged through him. When they had first met, countless men were vying for Jenna Maria Sanchez's affections, and despite the odds, she had chosen him. Turning to look at her once more he wondered how often she had come to regret that decision over the years, and if he had enough time to make her happy now.

*****

Three hours later Adrienne found herself half hidden in the corner of the Cave Bar, talking with a lawyer called Mike, or Mick … or was it Rick? She hadn't cared enough to listen properly, and she sure as Hell wasn't going to ask him to repeat it. She had no intention of remembering him in the morning.

He'd already bought her three G&Ts and she knew if she had many more she'd probably spend the rest of the night throwing up. When he made the motions to go back to the bar for another round she looped a slender finger in his belt and pulled him closer to her. It was time to wrap this part of the night up and move on.

If he was surprised by her forwardness he didn't show it, and instead took it all in his stride, meeting her gaze and instantly lowering his head to kiss her, gently, once on the lips. She immediately kissed him back, eager to let him know it was OK, and she didn't need him to back off. He took the hint and kissed her more passionately, running his hands down her back and coming to rest on her hips.

Adrienne leant in, pressing herself up against him, pleased to feel he was already quite aroused. At that moment someone pushed past them on the way to the toilets, and they broke apart. She laughed, and he asked what she was thinking.

"Your place or mine?" was her immediate response.

*****

It was early morning and Will had struggled to sleep. Throughout the night he'd been plagued by a multitude of problems, all clamouring for his attention and he was no closer to resolving them.

He had always prided himself on being able to see a situation for what it was, weighing up the pros and cons, and taking suitable action. He was logical, deliberate and cool-headed; however, for the first time in his life he found himself in the midst of a dilemma, and nowhere to turn for inspiration.

Part of his problem was that he didn't entirely understand where his current feelings of conflict had come from. Ultimately, he was struggling with his overwhelming guilt, and how to manage it; however, he failed to comprehend what had caused the guilt in the first place.

Logically speaking, nothing had changed. He had always been married, and he had never been honest with Adrienne. Therefore, he had always been cheating on the two women in his life. Jenna had always been trying to get pregnant. Yes, so far it had failed, and there was every chance it would again this last time, but something had changed. He couldn't deny that.

The part of him that wanted to believe he was a good man hoped his change of heart was purely part of an epiphany, a realisation that he was doing the wrong thing, and now was the perfect opportunity to set things right. The part of him that was a realist knew it was more likely a direct result of a sense that he'd been caught.

Whilst there was every chance Adrienne would be none the wiser about his real reason for being at the clinic, he was logical enough to assume she had been able to find out. He hadn't called her afterwards to explain his sudden disappearance, and the fact he had not yet heard from her spoke volumes. She knew, and now it would appear they were in a bizarre game of chicken, and he wasn't entirely sure of the rules.

Booking a holiday had been a knee-jerk reaction, and he wasn't entirely sure of his motivations. Yes, being on an island in the middle of the ocean of course afforded him an opportunity to get as far away from Adrienne as possible, but he could have done that anyway. Why he felt the need to take Jenna with him on this trip still wasn't clear to him.

Something felt different between them yesterday. The fear of her finding out what he'd been up to, and the potential for everything to come crashing down around him, had awakened a sense of loyalty and devotion in him he wasn't aware he was capable of anymore. Jenna deserved his time and attention, and it was his duty to actually make the effort to give it to her.

Although he had done everything he could to play no part in the whole IVF process to date, he knew this was the last chance Jenna had to have the family she'd always longed for. He also knew, in the back of his mind, that he had already deprived her of that family for so long, and it was up to him to make the next two weeks as bearable for her as possible.

If the worst happened, and it transpired she wasn't pregnant, at least perhaps they would have been able to rekindle some of the old magic, and it would give her something to cling to. On the other hand, if she did get pregnant, it would be a good start to their new family life – a sense that they did actually care about each other and had a marriage worth salvaging.

*****

The sun streaming through her uncurtained window woke Adrienne up, and sent a stabbing sensation to her temple. She rolled over, desperate to get away from the bright light, and found herself coming face to face with the man lying next to her. Gradually, she edged back away, careful not to wake her sleeping companion and have to face the awkward morning after the night before conversation.

Lying on her back she attempted to open her eyes again, and waited as the ceiling came in to focus. Relishing the silence, broken only occasionally by the deep breathing of the stranger at her side, she tried to work out how best to handle this. She had no intention of last night's fling turning in to a thing, but having never had a one-night stand before she wasn't sure how the etiquette worked.

Would she be expected to make him a cup of coffee, or would he do the gentlemanly thing and leave as soon as he was capable of standing? For the first time in her life, she found herself worrying that the new man in her life would desperately want to see her again, and it was definitely the last thing she wanted to happen.

The only thing she was certain of was that she didn't want to be there when he woke up. In fact, she couldn't imagine anything worse. Quickly, she rolled out of bed and, realising she was completely naked, grabbed her dressing gown and wrapped it around her before making a hasty exit to the kitchen.

Out of habit Adrienne started to prepare a fresh pot of coffee. As she leant against the sink it dawned on her that she should probably prepare something to offer in the way of food. On second thoughts, didn't that suggest she wanted him to stay? The last thing she needed was awkward small talk over a croissant.

Suddenly she realised that if she wanted to get rid of this man who was now outstaying his welcome, she had to simply tell him. It didn't matter if she came across as rude, or if she left a negative impression on him, she had no intention of ever seeing him again, let alone having a conversation with him.

Decision made, she strode in to her bedroom, dumped a hot cup of coffee on the bedside table and nudged Rick, Mick or Mike awake. "I've got a meeting to be at in 15 minutes, which means you need to be elsewhere by the time I get out of the shower."

CHAPTER 11

Pete and Sarah sat in stony silence, surrounded by other travellers on the M25. Although it was only 10am the sun was out in all her glory, creating a stifling heat in the car despite the frigid atmosphere. Of course, the air conditioning wasn't working, why would it be? Why on earth would anything go right today, when everything had been a disaster all week?

Sarah opened her window and fanned herself with an empty crisp packet. Pete turned the radio up and leant over the steering wheel, willing the car in front to move forward even just an inch. She desperately wanted to cry, but knew it wouldn't make her feel any better, and would only illicit derisory comments from him.

Turning her head, she looked at the flowers mixed with litter, on the side of the motorway. Bored of the pretence, she closed her eyes to create a sense of security and isolation. If she couldn't see Pete's tense shoulders she could pretend, for a moment that all was OK. Their brief trip away had been Hell, and now she regretted ever trying to do something nice for him.

To be fair, it hadn't started well. Pete had flown off the handle when she'd announced their spontaneous trip. He'd yelled something about having jobs backed up and already running behind, and for a moment it seemed he was on the verge of refusing to go. Thankfully he'd relented and managed to pull some extra guys in to complete the job. It had worked out very nicely. Or so she'd thought.

He hadn't forgiven her though, and they'd argued most of that evening as she rushed around packing a suitcase for them both. He'd called her frivolous and childish, which she thought was grossly unfair, and he still hadn't apologised for. She knew he'd had money saved in a separate account, so it wasn't as though she'd broken the bank booking a break away – a break, she reminded him, she would never have chosen had it not been for his love of camping.

He'd scoffed at that and had tried to explain that spending a week in a posh shack with a four-poster bed and an external hot tub was not camping, but she didn't understand. There wasn't room service or a concierge on the reception desk and that made it camping in her eyes. Even now, days later, she was riled by his lack of appreciation for the sacrifice she'd made for him.

The next morning when they actually set off things had calmed down slightly. Pete had resigned himself to the fact they were going away, the money had been spent and although he hadn't been consulted, he was determined to have a good time despite his initial reservations. He'd packed snacks for the journey and selected suitable CDs to listen to along the way to keep them entertained. However, not 10 miles in and Sarah had complained about their lack of communication. She'd wanted to talk.

Even now she felt upset by his reaction, "Talk? Talk? The only thing we ever bloody talk about is Operation Get Fucking Knocked Up!"

She'd wanted to reply, to shut him up, but the truth was she'd been about to list her symptoms and ask him when they should start telling everyone their good news, assuming they had good news of course. Hot tears streamed down her face and she'd slumped back in her seat. The rest of the journey had been made in silence.

She couldn't understand his anger towards the IVF process. It's true he had needed a bit of persuasion, but he'd eventually been on board. As far as she was concerned once he agreed he should have been 100% on her side and on the journey with her.

Admittedly he had come to every appointment, and had listened to all her fears, hopes and worries but he seemed to resent it. He would have been happy to have the treatment and then not talk about it again, he didn't understand why it was the only thing on her mind.

The rest of the trip hadn't fared much better than the journey itself. Conversation was strained and she felt she barely knew this man she had spent her entire life loving. He was happy to go off exploring the local woods, but she hadn't brought suitable shoes for hiking and navigating mud puddles. Once upon a time he would have stayed with her, or suggested they go shopping or have a trip to the cinema in the local town, but this time he packed a snack bag and disappeared for hours on end.

Eventually she pulled him up on it and asked him to explain. The holiday had been meant for them, an opportunity for them to unwind and spend time together, reconnecting after the emotional stresses of their first cycle. Pete had scoffed and another argument had started.

Now, with her eyes closed she could clearly recall him standing in the 'snug' of their yurt, alternating between waving his hands wildly and sipping on yet another beer. He kept saying he didn't understand how sitting around talking constantly about babies would be a break, he'd rather be alone and enjoying the countryside. As far as he was concerned that was why she booked a bloody glamping trip in the first place.

Sarah quickly ran out of energy to argue with him and instead just let him get on with it. She spent her days wandering around the site and reading the books that had been discarded by former residents in the communal hall. A large part of her wanted to suggest going home early, cutting their losses and doing something else, but Pete, for all his faults, was enjoying himself. She prayed his time alone in the woods, doing whatever he was doing, was cleansing his soul.

She hoped he'd be able to return to her in a better mood and willing to accept how unreasonable he had been. That hope was dashed when one morning he discovered ten of her used pregnancy tests, all with their miserable solitary line. She'd been hiding them in her toiletry bag, determined he wouldn't find them, but when he accidentally knocked the bag off the shelf the contents had scattered across the floor, exposing her secret. He had stormed in to the bedroom and thrown them at her, demanding an explanation.

"We've only been here for five days, how the Hell have you managed to do ten of these already?" he shouted, unable to retain any semblance of calm. Sarah hadn't known how to react. Part of her was mortified that she'd been found out, and another part of her felt she didn't owe him an explanation. She'd gone through a gruelling round of IVF, she might be pregnant, she just wanted to know if she was or not. She failed to see what could possibly be wrong with that, or why he was getting so annoyed.

As explanation she simply replied "They're cheap ones off the internet, 30 for £5, they haven't cost much!" but that was not the answer he wanted. From nowhere he'd started shouting, arms waving frantically, "I don't care how much they cost, that's not the point. The point is you can't let it go for five minutes! It's dominating every part of our life!"

With that he'd stormed out, and she hadn't seen him again for the rest of the day. He'd gone for a walk and ended up in a local pub, drinking till it was time to shut up for the night. He'd been steaming drunk by the time he staggered back to their pod and had just collapsed on the kitchen floor, refusing to come to bed with her.

That was last night.

This morning she had woken early, but was too scared to go out and face the music. She knew he was going to be like a bear with a sore head, and she didn't want to aggravate him any further. Finally, she plucked up the courage to make a cup of tea and was amazed to find that he was nowhere to be seen.

Two hours passed before he came back, still saying nothing. He grabbed a quick shower, changed his clothes and then started packing up his belongings, "I'm going home" he eventually offered.

Caught off guard she'd been unable to respond, and he followed up with a casual, "You can either stay here or come back with me, but the car's leaving in 15 minutes". She couldn't believe it, and for a few minutes just sat dumbfounded, watching him load things in to the back of the car. Eventually she moved and picked up the last of her clothes and make-up before joining him.

She was crying again when she asked why he was heading home. He looked at her blankly at first, then responded, "I'd rather write this off as a waste of time and money than pretend it's going to be OK. At least this way I can get back and earn some money, so we've got one less thing to worry about."

That was the last thing they had said to each other, and that was nearly two hours ago.

CHAPTER 12

Jenna took her seat in the Clubhouse lounge whilst Will went to collect their complimentary champagne. She leant back in the luxurious arm chair and let her body completely relax. She tried to remember a time when she'd been more content than this, but couldn't. Their wedding day had been pretty perfect and she had been sublimely happy, but it had of course been tinged with anxiety.

Her parents, despite their wealth, were loud and rather obnoxious, most definitely not to her future in-laws' taste. She'd been on edge all day waiting to hear that her mother had offended such a relative, or that her mother-in-law had been declared an uptight toffee-nosed bitch (which, of course, she was). In the end it had all gone perfectly accordingly to plan, Will had seen to that, but still, it was impossible to breathe properly until they were both safely shut inside their honeymoon suite for the night.

The last 10 days had been exactly what she needed, and she frowned at herself for initially being against the idea. Will's decision to whisk her back to Antigua had initially terrified her because she couldn't understand what he was angling for. Now she felt guilty.

Looking back, he was simply trying to rekindle some affection, remind each other why they had said those vows all that time ago, and that underneath it all they still meant every word they'd said on that glorious sunny day.

It had certainly done everything he'd hoped it would. The time alone, free from the distractions of work, away from their friends and the glittering social engagements they found themselves obligated to attend, they had been able to talk. Not that painful, mind numbing small talk they had become so expert at, but properly talk.

They had discussed their past hopes and dreams, what had been achieved and what they regretted losing sight of. Will had lamented the fact he'd missed so many opportunities to support her with her career because he was so focussed on his own.

They'd spent so much time performing the roles other people had ascribed to them, playing the parts people expected of them, that they had inherently forgotten who they really were. Once upon a time they'd just been Will and Jen, young newlyweds with their lives ahead of them. Where had those optimistic dreamers gone?

It would appear they'd been languishing under the surface, and all it took to get them back was 10 days of lying on a deserted beach, sipping cocktails and eating dinner by candlelight. While there was no doubt the entire experience had been fun, and far better than she could ever have imagined, Jenna had to concede she didn't feel entirely at peace.

As wonderful as the past few days had been, she did find herself wondering whether the glitz and glitter of their island paradise had simply given the illusion that all was well again with her marriage. Could a few days of peace and tranquillity really provide a band aid for all that had gone before?

She fervently hoped so, it had been so nice to have her husband back that she was desperate not to lose him again the first time he stepped foot inside the office. Before that day in the clinic she genuinely didn't feel as though she had anything to lose, now she felt entirely differently, and it made her panic slightly.

Suddenly Will appeared by her side and handed her a glass of champagne, "Sorry I took so long, just wanted to check in with Alice and tell her I wouldn't be in until Wednesday", he said as he took the seat opposite her.

"Why the change of plans?" she asked, putting her drink on the table between them. Will stretched out his legs and replied, "I'm just not quite ready to get back to reality I suppose. They have survived this long without me, a few more days won't kill them".

He picked up her glass and handed it back to her, "I propose a toast, to us and whatever the future may bring". Jenna raised her glass but refused to take a sip. Once upon a time Will would have failed to notice, but of late his eyes had been on her all the time, and he couldn't help but comment on her returning the glass to the table untouched.

“I thought you said you could have the occasional sip, until you knew for certain?” he asked with a quizzical look in his eye. Jenna smiled, she had hoped to make a big show of telling him, but the reality was sometimes the news itself was the big bit, the rest was all fluff.

“I know. For certain. No more champagne for 38 weeks” she replied, unable to suppress the smile spreading across her face.

Will exploded from his chair, whooped (a sound she was certain he’d never made before) and pulled her out of her seat so he could give her a bear hug. He then apologised profusely in case he had hurt her, or the precious cargo she was now carrying.

The other residents of the Clubhouse turned to see what had caused the commotion and he gleefully announced “We’re going to have a baby!”, which resulted in an emphatic round of applause and a few more glasses of champagne being placed on their table.

Jenna laughed. On the few occasions she’d allowed herself to imagine this moment, the finding out and then sharing the news with her husband, she had never thought it would look like this. She half fancied she would find out, at home, alone in their en suite and she would simply text him. Or perhaps she wouldn’t tell him until she was 12 weeks and then merely ask for his opinions on which room should be used as the nursery.

Her fantasies hadn't been born out of resentment, just realism that he wouldn't have been in the slightest bit interested. She'd never even been convinced he'd take time off to come and visit her in hospital once the baby arrived, so could never have imagined this as a possibility.

Now, everything was different and she relished the moment. Will was hopping from foot to foot, so full of excitement he literally couldn't contain himself. He was still grinning from ear to ear and shaking the hands of total strangers. She laughed again, he really was going to be one of those Dad's handing out cigars in the maternity waiting room. It was a sight to behold, and one she never presumed she'd have the pleasure of.

After shaking the hands of multiple strangers finally the crowd dispersed, and Will returned to his seat. "When did you find out?" he asked after downing an entire glass of champagne. Jenna explained how she'd brought two tests with her on the trip and had waited until yesterday to do the first one. She thought she'd seen a faint line, but it was much stronger this morning with the second test, definitely no mistaking it.

Will begged to see the test immediately, but Jenna refused, explaining she was not prepared to get a urine-soaked stick out of her bag and wave it around in first class. He exploded with laughter, "You make a valid point", he agreed, and helped himself to another glass.

They sat silently together for a few minutes, letting the news they were to be parents sink in and enjoying the uniqueness of the moment. Eventually Will leant forward and started pumping her for information on how she felt, what happened next and when they could start telling their friends.

*****

Five days had passed and things were still strained between her and Pete, but Sarah remained optimistic as it was gradually improving. He'd thrown himself back in to work, and she had played the dutiful housewife, making sure his dinner was ready when he got home and not begrudging him the occasional pint with his mates.

Usually she'd pull a face or sigh if he announced he'd be 'a bit late', but this week she'd resolved not to rock the boat and give him any more cause to be frustrated or annoyed with her. Suppressing her natural tendencies was difficult, but it seemed to be working, and ultimately that's all she cared about.

This morning he'd left the house early, wanting to spend some time in the gym before he started work on the new bathroom renovation over on Chatterley Drive. He'd at least given her a kiss on the forehead before he'd left, a sure sign that he was starting to calm down. For her part, Sarah hadn't mentioned the potential pregnancy since they'd come home, something that was killing her inside.

That didn't mean to say she'd stopped thinking about it, in fact she spent a large part of her day on the baby and trying to conceive forums, asking questions and analysing symptoms with a myriad of other desperate women hoping to become mothers. They'd become her lifeline, a virtual support group and she genuinely felt, without them to turn to and be honest with, she'd go mad. Either that or she'd be getting divorced, as it was clear Pete could not cope with any more of her agonisings on the matter.

She rolled over, checked the clock on her phone and realised it was probably time to get up. She sat up, rubbed the sleep from her eyes and stretched. As she made her way to the bathroom it suddenly dawned on her that today was day 14. Today was the day. Despite her natural inclination she hadn't done another pregnancy test since they'd left the glamping site. She daren't in case Pete found them and lost his temper again.

Today was the day she could legitimately do one though, and even he couldn't argue with that. Now in dire need of the toilet, she pulled open her bed side drawer and rummaged around until she found what she was looking for, then made the mad dash to face her destiny and relieve her bladder.

As always, she waited the obligatory three minutes, not daring to look at the result ahead of time. She had a perfect routine to while away the time; she'd wash her hands, tidy up the towels, and then clean her teeth and brush her hair. By the time that was done she'd allow herself a look.

While every time she tested she was hopeful, this morning she was also nervous. She knew in all likelihood a negative at this stage indicated she was not going to get pregnant. It meant another trip to the clinic, another round, another long and agonising wait. She wasn't sure Pete would be ready to go through it all again so soon, if at all.

Holding her breath, she plucked up the courage to turn the test over and find out where she stood. To date she had only ever been met with one line, so it came as a shock when this time two unmistakable deep blue ones looked up at her.

CHAPTER 13

"That's wonderful news, congratulations! I'll book you in for an appointment with Dr. Harper for Friday, if that's OK? How's 10am work for you? Great stuff, and congratulations again."

Kate hung up the phone, updated the diary and then walked over to Dr. Harper's office. After knocking lightly on the door, she went in and found Adrienne typing away furiously at her computer.

"Sorry to interrupt you," Kate said as she approached the desk, "but Mrs. Jenkins just called." Adrienne lifted her head, a look of concern immediately etched on her face, "I'm not going to want to hear this am I?" she asked.

Kate shook her head, "No, it's not the answer we'd hoped for, that's for certain". Adrienne pushed her chair back, closed her eyes and gave a deep sigh. "Fuck. Fuckity, fuck, fuck!" she exclaimed, before opening them again.

It was such a bizarre feeling, wishing your patient, who you'd worked so hard to get pregnant in the first place, would be phoning with negative news. Not that long ago she would have been amazed to think such a conflict could ever arise in her world. A positive result was always good news; but yet, here she was, hoping against hope that for once, the odds being stacked against them would be a lifeline.

"Any word on Greg's patient?" she asked in a vain attempt to avoid thinking about Sarah and Pete.

"No," Kate replied, "but he said if she hadn't called by the end of today he'd try her first thing in the morning. Mrs. Jenkins is scheduled to come in for her blood test on Friday, so we have until then I suppose." Adrienne nodded and Kate left the room.

Left alone again Adrienne picked up her coffee cup and threw it against the wall. It was most unlike her to lash out in such a way but the last two weeks had been exceptionally difficult, and she didn't feel she had any outlet for her frustrations or anger.

Admittedly, throwing things didn't solve anything or change the situation, but for a brief moment she felt as though she had been able to vent. That was until she looked at the smashed pieces of crockery and the coffee stains on the wall. Now she'd have to clear it up.

She picked up her waste bin and walked over to the newly formed crime scene on her laminate floor. As she bent down to pick up the small sharp shards that had once been her University cup she chuckled to herself, at least this was one mess she could clear up relatively easily.

Standing up, she straightened her skirt and put the bin back before making her way to the staff kitchen to pick up a dish cloth. She needed something to soak up the spilt coffee and start to dab away at the stain. As she left her office, Greg Barker came out of his.

Their eyes met and he shook his head, "Sorry Ade, we need to talk". Her shoulders slumped and she immediately felt like crying, but now was not the time. She followed him back to his office and took a seat. For a minute they just stared at each other, neither of them really knowing what to say.

"OK," Greg said, realising it was his job to break the silence. "Ms. Sanchez has called, and has confirmed she is pregnant. I understand Mrs. Jenkins is, too?" Adrienne nodded, a gamut of emotions hitting her at once. She genuinely didn't know what to think.

Coop was going to be a father. She still hadn't spoken to him since his disappearing act from the waiting room nearly two weeks ago, hadn't had the chance to tell him she knew about his wife, and yet here she was finding out that he was going to be a father. She felt crushed.

Over the last week or so she had tried in vain to process all the information that had been thrown her way at once. She wasn't sure if it was the sheer magnitude of each thing, or a combination of everything coming together at once, but nothing was sinking in and she still hadn't figured out how to handle it all.

Her initial reaction, to drink and screw around, had been short lived. It was an immediate, knee jerk and had given her something else to think about, but it certainly didn't solve anything. In fact, she now felt ashamed of how she'd behaved, which added to the myriad of things she was unable to think about clearly.

The reality was, nothing was going to make any of this better. It wasn't going to go anywhere any time soon, though it was being dragged out in part by Coop's radio silence. This morning, one more part of the puzzle was confirmed – it was no longer a what-if situation, Coop's wife, Ms. Sanchez, was pregnant.

She mentally slapped herself. Now was no time to have a personal response to events, she had to put her doctor head on and keep it in place, at least for the next few weeks. She sat forward, "OK, so we're not getting away with this then. What are we going to do?"

Greg shook his head, suddenly showing how drained he was feeling himself. Of all the ways this could have panned out, of course both women had to end up pregnant. He followed Adrienne's lead and stopped wallowing.

"The way I see it," he said, "we only have one option. We know the truth, but we've not reported anything yet; we can discover it later, buy ourselves a bit of time. We can bring the women in, do their blood tests and send them on their way until their ultrasounds. Let's get them both to heartbeats at six weeks, you never know, they could both miscarry and then we no longer have an issue."

While Adrienne completely understood his stance, she was appalled that they were actually discussing this. The hopeful tone in his voice that both women could go on to lose their babies was unmistakeable, and made her feel sick to her stomach. Keeping their mouths shut and not admitting their terrible mistake did nothing to help the soon-to-be parents, but everything to potentially protect their own asses.

She didn't feel comfortable with the approach, but knew she probably wasn't going to get much of a say. Besides, such a revelation so early in a pregnancy, under any circumstances, could lead to complications anyway. Adrienne didn't think she could cope with being the potential cause of that tragedy, on top of everything else she suddenly found herself at the centre of.

"What are our other options?" she asked, hopeful they may be slightly more palatable than the first. Greg shrugged, "To be honest, I'm not entirely sure. We could always come clean now and see how that plays out. I'm reluctant though at this delicate stage of the process. I'd rather we ascertained viability and went from there."

He was right, she knew he was, but it still seemed so barbaric.

"The fact is," he said, "we need to be honest, I don't want to contemplate hiding it, but we want to cause minimum distress. Equally, we have to give both women the time and support to be able to make a decision regarding the future of their pregnancies."

Adrienne nodded.

Being realistic there was no option that wasn't going to cause distress. There was no way to sugar coat events or put a spin on them that would make anyone feel good about the situation. The damage had been done, and at no point would the unveiling of what had happened not be the most painful thing these families would ever have to face.

"Mrs. Jenkins is coming in on Friday for her blood tests," Adrienne offered. Greg nodded again, "And the Cooper-Sanchez's", he replied. "My preference would be to keep them on the same time line for visits and screening so we always know where both of them stand with their pregnancies. It will no doubt be easier to manage that way."

He sighed, appearing to take a moment to contemplate his next steps. "I'm going to have to inform the regulator, and of course get in touch with our lawyers to find out the best way to go ahead with advising the couples. I also need to work out precisely how much we need to say at this stage."

Adrienne looked up, confused. What did he mean how much to say? Surely saying sorry, we made a mistake, you were implanted with another patient's embryo and you're now having their baby kind of covered it all? What the Hell else was there?

Sensing her confusion, he explained they would need to decide how much they admitted in terms of what happened, what had led to the mistake, and what they would offer in terms of compensation.

Adrienne left his office feeling even worse than before. She couldn't imagine what these two women would think, or how they would feel finding out the babies they had been so desperate to conceive were not even theirs. If she thought the last two weeks had been bad, the next two weren't going to be any better.

PART TWO

Biology is the least of what makes someone a mother.

- Oprah Winfrey

CHAPTER 14

Adrienne sat at their favourite table patiently waiting for him to arrive. It had taken her all morning to get ready, trying on and discarding a multitude of outfits before settling on a simple black dress. She didn't want to be sexy, but she didn't want to look frumpy either. The problem was there weren't any articles in Cosmopolitan that dealt with what to wear when you confronted your boyfriend about his secret pregnant wife. She'd looked.

Although she hadn't been waiting long she'd already nervously shredded her paper napkin in to hundreds of pieces. Looking down, her lap was hidden by a pile of red paper confetti, and it looked like a tiny massacre had taken place. She hoped it wasn't a sign of what was to come with Coop.

Inexplicably, *Murder on the Dance Floor* started playing in her internal juke box and she was momentarily distracted, tapping her foot in time to the tune only she could hear. The woman at the next table looked over at her and Adrienne reluctantly returned to reality, aware once again of the mess on her lap.

She wondered what on earth to do with it all. She couldn't leave it on the table, a symbol of her anxiety, and she wasn't sure she could make it to the toilet without dropping them all over the floor. While she mused over the best course of action she saw Coop approaching the door. In a blind panic she picked up her handbag and shoved the tiny scraps in it; she'd deal with them later.

As Coop approached their table she automatically stood up, a huge smile on her face. Just laying eyes on him felt so good, and she hated being reminded how much she was drawn to him. While distance and lack of contact had allowed her to relegate him to the back of her mind it had been possible to hate him, despise him, minimise his importance in her life; but now, with him in front of her, she just wanted to throw herself into his arms and forget everything that had happened.

They hugged, but she could feel him withdrawing from her even while they embraced. Come what may, this was going to be a difficult lunch and nothing was ever going to be the same again. She admired his tan and remembered he had been in LA since they last met, or had he? There was no way of knowing what was, and wasn't true anymore.

For the first time it crossed her mind that everything could have been a lie. His frequent trips abroad for 'work' might simply have been a result of his inability to get away from his wife. While part of her would have liked nothing more than to ask him outright how much bullshit he had fed her over the last two years, the other part of her was still too fragile to hear it.

In the end she settled for asking how his trip had been, hoping she'd managed to keep a semblance of normality about the question. He looked up from the menu briefly, replied "It was good", and then returned to studying the wine list. Adrienne sighed, nothing about this was going to be normal or natural it seemed, even on the surface.

Food and wine ordered they had nothing left to legitimately distract them from talking. The comfortable silence had long since ended and both looked at the other expectantly to get things started. Adrienne decided she might as well be the one to make the first move.

While she hadn't exactly planned what she'd say in advance, she had imagined it would be something intelligent and heartfelt, a well-constructed and moving monologue of pain, love and betrayal. When she eventually managed to open her mouth, the only thing she could force out was, "What the fuck is going on?"

It wasn't precisely what she'd been aiming for, and although she'd tried to minimise the accusation in her voice, she clearly failed miserably. Surprised by her tone, and the frankness of her question he floundered, wondering what she'd managed to glean for herself.

He knew it wasn't beyond the realms of probability that she'd found out about Jenna, had put two and two together and that, in reality, she knew as much as he did. He hadn't come to this meeting planning to lie, but the realisation that there may be no point in trying to cover anything up meant he was mentally ticking off escape routes.

Once upon a time he would never have dreamt of ending things with her. For so long, Adrienne had been everything he had ever wanted in a companion, and he'd never felt any reason to jeopardise that. However, now, with all that was happening with him and Jenna, and them being on the same page for the first time in years, he found himself wondering if he could be the happily married, father of one so many of his friends had seemed to evolve in to.

The silence was deafening and the longer it continued the more frustrated Adrienne felt. He had asked to see her, he had to expect she would demand to know what had happened. Besides anything else, he had been at her place of work, and then minutes later disappeared without explanation. They hadn't spoken since, and now he sat here as though nothing had happened. She was entitled to an explanation for his behaviour, and was annoyed by his apparent reluctance to elaborate.

He was about to open his mouth and speak when the waiter appeared with their wine. Coop made a great show of tasting it, drawing out the precious seconds before they would be left alone again and he'd have nowhere left to hide. Wine approved and poured he raised a toast, "To us and the long and winding road; wherever it might lead us".

She raised her glass and took a long, hard drink. It was a good choice, but then Coop always did have impeccable taste when it came to the finer things in life.

Suitably empowered by the hit of alcohol, she asked again with significantly less venom, "What's going on? Where did you disappear to at the clinic?".

Coop shifted in his seat, realigned his already perfectly symmetrical cutlery and took a deep breath, accepting that Adrienne had questions and he would have to answer them, somehow. He looked up from his empty plate and met her gaze, calmly and with an air of resignation.

"I don't know what you know," he started, "nor what you may have guessed. I see no point in beating about the bush so please forgive my bluntness, but I am married. I was at your clinic because my wife had an appointment with your colleague, Dr. Barker. A final appointment, that clearly worked, because she is now pregnant."

He stopped, took another sip of wine and looked at her expectantly. He had an air of a man who had just attended confession and was now waiting for the verdict on how best to absolve his sins. Adrienne was in no mood to afford him the mercy of five Hail Mary's and an Our Father, he didn't deserve to get off so easily just because he had finally decided to be honest with her. She was well aware this honesty was borne of the fact his lies couldn't take him anywhere now.

"I know," she replied, suddenly feeling deflated. His frankness had done nothing to ease her pain, though for a moment she had thought it might. He nodded, half expecting that to be her response and glad it was the case. "I'm glad, I would have hated it to have been a surprise to you."

Adrienne felt winded. Did he genuinely believe that just because she wasn't shocked at this very moment in time, the time of his finally coming clean, that it had not been a near mortal blow when she had initially found out?

She sneered, "What you mean is you're glad you didn't have to witness the surprise, because let me assure you it was bloody well there when I worked it out for myself!" Adrienne quickly took another long gulp of wine in a bid to regain her composure and avoid causing a scene.

Coop didn't react, so she continued. "When you disappeared on me I asked our receptionist where you'd gone. She told me the gentleman I'd been speaking with had gone to support his wife during their last attempt at IVF. I found out from our bloody receptionist, Coop! Please don't pretend you're doing me a favour by being honest with me now!"

"I deserve that," he replied, refusing to look up. "For what it's worth, I am sorry you had to find out like that. It was never my intention." Her confidence buoyed by the wine and incensed by his nonchalant approach to the situation, she could no longer hold back.

"I have no doubt you would rather I hadn't found at all. After two years I can't imagine a situation in which you planned to tell me about your wife, or the potential for a baby. I mean, when on earth would it ever have come up? During dinner? After sex? You tell me Coop, when were you going to tell me?" With each question her voice rose another octave.

He winced, but she wasn't sure if it was what she said or the volume at which she'd said it. The couple sitting closest to them had turned to see what was going on, and she knew how much he abhorred a scene. It was one of the main reasons she'd desperately wanted to meet in public, somewhere that would create a bigger impact on his psyche. Again, he was saved from replying immediately, this time by the arrival of their starters.

When the waitress had moved away he continued, "I owe you an explanation, I know that, but to be honest Ade, I'm not sure I have one. Not one that is going to suitably answer your questions or salve your pain.

"I'm married, I have been for 25 years. I loved my wife intensely once but things change, people grow apart, they stop making an effort. It's no excuse, not a satisfactory one anyway, but it's the way it is. She stopped making an effort, I stopped caring; or it may have been the other way around. It's been so long, I can no longer remember."

Adrienne listened intently, but daren't take her eyes off her mussels. She had expected to hear the traditional tale of a wife that no longer understood her husband, how she didn't meet his needs as a man.

Hearing this clearly heartfelt explanation of the flaws of their marriage made her feel uncomfortable.

She knew she was in danger of feeling sorry for him, for almost understanding what had happened and why he'd not said anything sooner. She didn't want to understand. She didn't want to say it was OK to have lied to her for so long. She didn't want at any point to feel capable of condoning what he'd done to either of the women in his life. For a fleeting moment she found herself hoping there were only two women. More would be impossible to cope with.

"When I met you at that gala I felt something for the first time in who knows how long", he continued. Given a platform to express himself openly for the first time Coop was relishing the opportunity, and found his thoughts falling in to a degree of order.

"It wasn't just sex," he continued, "though I can't pretend that's not been an amazing bonus, but I felt alive. I felt wanted, validated and cared for. Jenna hasn't felt like that for years, and looking back I must be honest and say I can't blame her. On a long enough timeline there's every chance I would have one day made you feel about me the way she has felt for so long. Ultimately, I am the one to blame."

He stopped and looked at her, seeking reassurance that it was OK to go on. She had to stop him. She knew she had to take control of the situation, otherwise his words would charm her in to forgiveness, and she would be furious with herself. "Were you ever going to tell me?" she asked, suddenly desperate to know how far his deception would have continued.

He shrugged. "I would love to say it had crossed my mind, but I'd be lying, and it's clear I've done enough of that. I would have told you, eventually, though I confess some external event would have forced my hand in to doing so. That unforeseen event has now occurred, but had it not, I am not sure when we would have found ourselves having this conversation."

Ironically, Adrienne admired his honesty. In so many of the books she'd read the guilty man had always tried to convince his unwitting wife that the truth had been on the tip of his tongue the whole time, and it was just plain bad luck that had allowed her to find out accidentally.

The fact he had no plan to tell her, that he would have been more than happy to continue the deception indefinitely was of no comfort, but she knew where she stood with his current candour. There was little more she could ask for at this time.

"Do you love her?" As soon as she asked the question she regretted it. It was an automatic one, it made sense in her head, but deep down she knew it wouldn't make the slightest bit of difference. What answer did she want to hear?

Did she want to know that he didn't love his wife? Would that make things better? Would it make her feel more important to him as The Mistress? Or did she want to hear that he did love her dearly and that he was going to stay with her, ending things with Adrienne?

How would still being in love with his wife help? It would show he was capable of doing terrible things to someone he professed to care for, and she knew she couldn't handle that. Coop seemed to struggle with the answer as much as she struggled with the validity of the question.

"Yes," he replied eventually, "I do love her. Over the last few weeks I've realised she is still the woman I first fell in love with and chose to spend my life with. She has stood by my side faithfully for 27 years, and has never demanded anything. She is everything that is good in my life, and I have done nothing but abuse that goodness."

Adrienne felt the tears well in her eyes and knew she was wrong to ask. She didn't want to hear this. "If we had been having this conversation two weeks ago, I would no doubt have told you that you were asking the wrong question. Love is such a fickle and transient emotion, asking if you love someone is entirely different to being in love with them.

"Had this all been forced out in to the open before, then the answer to the correct question would have been a no. I cannot remember the last time I genuinely felt in love with Jenna." He paused, straightened his napkin and then continued.

"You, however, yes; I am in love with you. That has not changed, but the reality is with all that has happened I have seen her in a new light. I have made time, I have stopped, and I am now in a position where whilst the love is not entirely there, I can see a way that it can be.

"It is I who needs to make the effort, and the fact a child will be brought in to our ambivalent marriage by the end of the year means I am obligated to do all I can to make that as good as it can be."

In that moment, Adrienne realised she was never going to win this fight, so it was a waste of time trying to work out what she wanted from the situation. Without thinking, she stood and stepped away from the table.

"Coop, I love you. I could forgive you. I could wait. They alone are three reasons why I have to walk away now."

And with that, she left and he was convinced he would never see her again.

CHAPTER 15

Sarah and Pete waited in Dr. Harper's office for her to come back in with the ultrasound machine. Never good at waiting, this minor delay was causing Sarah to become fractious. The numerous pregnancy tests, and even the confirmation by the clinic through the blood test two weeks ago had done nothing to dampen her fears that somehow all of this had been a cruel mistake.

She found it so hard to believe after so many years of trying that, on their first attempt at IVF, they were going to be blessed with a child. Something had to go wrong. There was no way it was meant to be this easy. She'd read so many terrible tales of women who had managed to conceive, but had been unable to maintain their pregnancy. What if she went on to have a miscarriage? The previous obsession with getting pregnant was now replaced with a far more sinister one.

Pete had been brilliant ever since she'd told him the good news. She'd gone out the morning she'd taken the test and bought him a new watch. When she got home she'd placed the positive pregnancy test in the watch box, keeping the watch to one side. Her plan was to have it inscribed at a later date with the baby's name and date of birth, then give it to him for his first official Father's Day.

When he'd opened the box he clearly couldn't believe what he was seeing. At first, she was concerned he might be disappointed there wasn't a watch after all, but when he realised what the two lines meant he was overjoyed.

The entire way through their journey to date he'd seemed ambivalent about the end result. She knew he wanted children, that had never been in dispute, he just didn't seem to understand her overwhelming need. He called it a craving, and maybe that's entirely what it was. That evening though, she could see deep down it meant as much to him as it had to her, the end result anyway. He didn't need to say anything, it was obvious for anyone to see.

It had been hard, but she'd deliberately tried not to let talk of her pregnancy dominate their conversations. Now though it was no longer a what-if, and a theoretical thing to dream about, but a real live tangible life form that was going to happen. Hopefully. If all went well for the next 32 weeks or so anyway.

She had continued to turn to her online friends instead of Pete, sharing with them her fears about the likelihood of miscarriage, determined not to drag him down with her neurotic musings. Their input was invaluable, just knowing if Dr. Harper found a heartbeat today would be a good sign for the future health of their little one had put her mind at ease. Somewhat at least.

The problem was, she now had to wait until that ultrasound was done and the heartbeat was confirmed. It wasn't an easy wait, but then Sarah never found anything she wanted easy to wait for. It wasn't something she was particularly used to. Her parents, her entire family for that matter, had always doted on her, treating her like a princess who could do no wrong.

Pete used to tease her about being spoilt, but he wasn't wrong. The only girl in a long line of boys on her father's side she'd been a long-awaited addition to the family and was treated as such. A miracle. Whatever she wanted she got, no questions asked and all possible delays avoided.

After what seemed like an eternity, but in reality, was little more than five minutes, Dr. Harper returned to the room pulling a large ultrasound machine behind her. "Sorry for the delay," she said breezily, "but here we are. I just need to set up, so do you want to pop on the bed for me, Sarah?"

She slid on to the bed and pulled her top up, revealing her perfectly smooth stomach. Many women worried what pregnancy would do to their figures, but Sarah didn't care. She'd had a perfect body for so long, and knew after years of trying she would give it all up for baby weight, stretch marks and saggy boobs. Nothing else would matter as soon as she had a baby in her arms.

Dr. Harper interrupted her thoughts by saying, "OK, here we go, just a bit of cold as I put the gel on", then a pause. It was the sort of pause that lasted an eternity. As she lay back and tried to relax Sarah imagined this must be what it felt like to wait to find out if you had the last question right on Who Wants To Be A Millionaire.

She could almost hear the suspenseful music in the background, the ba-dum dum dum designed to imitate your pounding heart. Actually, she could hear it, it *was* her heart pounding faster than it possibly ever had before.

Dr. Harper was starting intently at the screen, tilting her head as she moved the probe across her lower abdomen. Sarah held her breath and gripped on to Pete's hand, terrified this was not going to end well. She automatically gritted her teeth, preparing herself for disappointment when Dr. Harper pointed to a tiny flicker on the screen.

"That," she said "is your baby's heartbeat. Exactly where we want it, exactly the size we would expect and beating perfectly." Tears immediately streamed down Sarah's cheeks as she exhaled, the pressure that had been building within her finally releasing and allowing pure joy to flow through her instead.

A few more checks completed, Dr. Harper handed Sarah some paper towels to wipe the ultrasound gel off her stomach while she cleaned up the machine and tidied away. Adrienne felt terrible. This was, without doubt, the happiest moment of Sarah's life. She knew just how much she'd wanted this, and in her mind all her dreams were finally coming true.

It was of course wonderful news that the baby was doing well, and all early indications suggested there would be no problems, but Adrienne knew it was never going to be as simple as that for this couple. Sarah was healthy and there was a strong heartbeat, so she felt confident this pregnancy would go ahead without a hitch. The only problem was the truth that still had to be revealed.

Whilst she had delivered her fair share of difficult news in the past, this was different. She felt terrible knowing what was about to descend on this couple who had done nothing to deserve it. Adrienne checked herself and realised there was nothing anyone could do to actually deserve this happening to them. It wasn't the sort of thing she would have wished on her worst enemy, not that she actually had one.

"If you'd like to take a seat, I'm going to get my colleague to come and have a word with you about what happens next." With that she left the room and for a second leant against the closed door in the safety of the corridor. Yesterday she had sat down with Greg and the clinic's lawyers to discuss how best to proceed with admitting what had happened.

Rightly or wrongly, Adrienne had confessed she didn't feel up to the job of breaking the news herself. She knew this couple, was invested in their outcome, and was realistic enough to know she would be unable to remain strong whilst breaking their hearts. It would be completely unproductive to have her in tears before they were.

The whole situation was made worse by the fact she knew it was entirely her fault. She had been distracted, she'd taken her eye off the ball due to the shock she was in over her discovery of Coop and his wife, and as a result had made this terrible mistake.

Of course, she hadn't been entirely honest with the lawyers, or Greg for that matter. She'd accepted it was probably her who had made the mistake, though she wasn't sure how on earth it could have happened. Investigations were ongoing, and would look in to all their compliance procedures and quality checks.

Ultimately, the lawyers were confident that a simple fine, some compensation and a slap on the wrist would probably be the worst that would happen to the clinic. They'd agreed Adrienne didn't have to admit to any possible involvement as they didn't feel it would help anyone at this stage in the process, and they were probably right.

Sarah was going to need a consultant she felt she could trust, and like it or not, Adrienne was that person. Changing her primary caregiver at this time would possibly do more harm than good as far as a viable pregnancy was concerned.

Deep down she found herself hoping once they knew a mistake had been made in the clinic, regardless of how it had come about, they would want to transfer to the care of someone else. However, after all the time they'd spent together she felt she knew Sarah well enough to know this wasn't likely to happen.

For the first time since working at the clinic Adrienne didn't want to see how this played out, didn't want to be a part of the process, but she also knew that ultimately this wasn't about her. She'd played her part, but now she had to step back and simply be professional about it. Deal with it the way anyone else would if they hadn't been involved, and support her patient through a monumentally difficult decision, and a potentially emotionally draining pregnancy.

She turned to her right and knocked on Greg's door, only entering when she heard his voice beckon her inside. When she poked her head around the door he was already standing, getting ready to put his white coat on. "Are they ready?" he asked as he came towards her. Adrienne nodded. "I assume you've said nothing to them yet?"

She shook her head, "I couldn't. I knew if I opened my mouth I either wouldn't be able to speak, or I wouldn't be able to stop. I'm not sure what would be worse."

Greg looked at her expressionless, "Saying nothing is best. The lawyers told us that. You'll only make matters worse if you allow emotion in to all of this. Right, let's get this over and done with."

With that he pushed passed her and led the way back to her office. There was no more hiding, it was time to rip the plaster off and deal with whatever horrible mess lay underneath.

*****

All morning Jenna had been counting down to this meeting, and after having it confirmed there was a healthy heartbeat ticking away inside her, she should have been on cloud nine. However, in this moment she found herself completely unable to understand what was being said to her. It wasn't because she didn't have the mental capacity, but purely because it made no sense.

She looked from the doctor, to Will, and back again. No one else was saying anything and it didn't look like they were going to start any time soon. Unable to find a foothold on the situation she simply remained silent, looking about her wildly, half expecting someone to burst through the door and yell, "Gotcha!".

It beggared belief how medical knowledge had advanced to the point where it was possible to get a woman pregnant without her having to have sexual intercourse, but so-called experts couldn't stop the most basic of administrative errors from occurring. A lapse, a mistake, a simple mix up. These were all words she'd heard in the last 10 minutes, but none of them adequately described what had actually happened.

Someone had, for whatever reason, failed to do their job properly. A job that was ultimately insanely important, and not the sort of thing you'd leave to chance, or the office junior. It would have to have been someone with training surely? Someone with a high degree of intelligence and understanding of what was at stake had allowed this to happen.

In truth, she didn't much care what had actually happened, it didn't make any real difference, the outcome would be the same regardless of the ultimate cause. The only reason anyone needed to know, at some point, was in a bid to ensure it didn't happen again.

Her mind raced. Of course, it should never happen again, but that didn't help her right now. Right now, in this moment, she sat here pregnant with her first child. It was a miracle in and of itself, but now that initial elation was tainted by the fact her first child was not biologically hers.

The thought mulled around in her head for a while. Not her child; but she was pregnant, and the doctor had only moments before said everything seemed perfectly fine with her baby. The baby. There was no reason to suspect there were going to be any problems. It was a miracle she was pregnant at all, it seemed almost churlish to be upset by the fact that her genetics had no part to play in the process.

Will had started raising his voice, demanding answers and accusing every member of staff down to the cleaners of being incompetent. This was his way, he didn't really mean any of it. When he was upset or felt threatened he lashed out, like some wounded animal that didn't know any better. It had been a long time since she'd tried to stop him when he was like this. The immediate explosion of anger always cleared, and then he would be able to formulate a cold and logical approach.

He'd rant for a few minutes, threaten legal action, at which point she'd usually roll her eyes and then he'd calm down. Come to think of it though, legal action probably wasn't the worst idea in this situation. Something practical would have to be done, but that could wait. It's not like the issue was going anywhere any time soon.

Jenna looked up, put her hand on Will's knee and was amazed it was enough to silence him. She cleared her throat, "Doctor, I'm sure you can appreciate this is a lot to take in, and I hardly know where to begin with processing it, but I do have a question." Dr. Barker nodded, encouraging her to continue.

"If you implanted the wrong embryo into me, what has happened to our embryo? The one we should have been using that day."

Part of her dreaded hearing the answer, there were two responses that didn't particularly appeal, and one she wasn't sure she knew what she'd do with. The look on Dr. Barker's face told her that her embryo was not sitting safely in the freezer, or wherever it was they stored them until they were ready to be used.

"I'm sorry to say that your embryo was implanted in the couple whose baby you are now carrying." Dr. Barker replied quickly, again taking the direct route to honesty rather than sugar coating it.

Jenna inhaled. OK, she thought, that was better than it going to waste, surely. Her momentary relief instantly disappeared as she found herself wondering how that pregnancy was progressing. Implanted didn't mean the other woman was still pregnant. Jenna's biological child might actually have died. Her last possible chance to have her own baby could have disappeared already, and she might never know.

Dr. Barker could sense she was processing the implications of what he'd said, and knew she would be trying to read between the lines. He cleared his throat, "I can let you know the outcome of her latest tests, if you would like?"

It had been tempting to say nothing, or to simply blurt out how Sarah's pregnancy was doing, but it occurred to him at the last moment she might perhaps prefer not to know. However, Jenna nodded slightly, and it was enough to encourage him to continue.

"A recent scan confirmed there is a strong heartbeat, and as things stand, we are hopeful for a trouble free and healthy pregnancy that will be brought to term." He mentally congratulated himself for his delivery of the facts, whilst still maintaining what he believed was a personal charm. As an afterthought he added, "Her due date is the same as yours."

Jenna nodded and exhaled slowly. Her child was inside someone else. At least it was growing and having the chance it deserved to be something. "Do the other couple know?" she asked, without thinking.

Dr. Barker then went on to explain his team had taken the decision to tell both involved parties about the mix-up. Due to the error on the part of the clinic the embryos had mistakenly been swapped, both women were pregnant and as things stood, both pregnancies were viable. However, it was equally up to both couples to decide how they wanted to proceed with those pregnancies.

Will shot the doctor a look and resumed his angry rant, "What on earth do you mean? Are you telling us this other woman has the right to terminate our baby if she wants to?".

Dr. Barker nodded, "It's her body and she does retain that right. She is under no obligation to go ahead with the pregnancy, regardless of your preferences on the matter. Like you, she only found out today and I have no knowledge as to what her decision may be, or when she may make it."

Furious, Will stood up, put on his jacket, said "Jenna, we're going to see our lawyer", and promptly stormed out. Jenna took a while to rise from her chair, still visibly shaken by what had happened. It already felt like a lifetime ago when she was happy, lying there on the bed watching her baby's heartbeat flashing on and off on the screen in front of her. In the briefest of moments, it had all changed and now she didn't know where she stood with it all.

"Do you think the other woman will terminate?" Jenna asked the doctor. He shrugged, "I honestly don't know, I'm sorry", he replied.

Jenna smiled, "It's OK, to be honest I'm not sure whether it would make me feel worse, or if somehow it would make the situation better." With that she slipped on her coat and followed her husband out the door.

CHAPTER 16

They drove home in silence, but not the same silence that had occupied their journey back from their holiday. This was the sort of stunned silence that follows a bereavement, where words are impossible to find and your mind won't stay still long enough to allow you to form a coherent thought.

Sarah was literally numb, barely able to move, let alone interact on any level. Pete was confused. Confused by what Dr. Barker had said, but also about how best to help his clearly distraught wife.

How did you even begin to process the fact that your baby, the baby you had spent ages and a huge amount of money trying to conceive, was not actually yours? There was no training for that. He wondered if there was a support group and found himself fervently praying there wasn't. A support group would suggest this happened a lot, and he couldn't get his head round that being a possibility.

The doctors had been very clinical in their announcement of what had happened, but he supposed they had to be. They were the professionals, as laughable as that word was under the circumstances. They had to tell it like it was, but still, it seemed surreal.

"We're sorry but there's been a mix-up".

That was the way you told a passenger their luggage had been put on the wrong plane and was now half way to India, whilst you had just landed in Cyprus.

It's not what you said when you admitted you'd implanted someone else's baby in to your wife's uterus!

Without thinking, he indicated and pulled over to park the car. Sarah didn't even flinch, she hadn't noticed. He turned off the engine and undid his seatbelt before rubbing his eyes, trying to shake off the fog that had settled over him.

"I can't go home", he said. Sarah looked at him, confusion etched on her face. "If we go home we'll just sit there, probably in silence, staring at the same four walls for God knows how long. I can't do that. It's not healthy."

He paused, hoping she might respond, but quickly realised she still wasn't ready to. "Let's go in and get a cup of coffee. It will be quiet. We can talk, if you want?"

Sarah still couldn't say anything, but she opened the car door and slid out of her seat before following Pete. When they got inside, he ordered them both a coffee, and they sat down in a booth at the back of the room, secluded should anyone else come in.

They continued to sit in silence until the waitress came with their order and Sarah suddenly remembered she couldn't have coffee. "I need decaf," she said. The waitress raised an eyebrow and checked she wanted to change her order before disappearing, muttering under her breath.

"Really?" Pete asked when they were alone again, "you're concerned about your caffeine intake after what's just happened?" She hadn't had time to think, to work out how she felt or what she thought about the clinics revelation, all she did know was that she was pregnant and she shouldn't have caffeine. It was just a knee jerk reaction, and one she didn't think would cause any harm.

"Yes," she replied, "caffeine is bad for the baby. Nothing changes that."

Pete shook his head, "I don't believe you. It's not our baby Sarah. It doesn't matter what's good for it or not, it's not bloody ours!" The waitress returned, placed the drink down and sensing all was not well with the couple, quickly retreated back to the counter and left them to it. "I know that," Sarah replied, tears in her eyes "but it is still a baby, it deserves to be looked after."

They stared at each other for a few seconds before returning their gaze to their respective drinks. He shifted uneasily in his seat, already dreading where this conversation would lead them. As far as he was concerned there didn't need to be any debate about how they proceeded.

This baby was not theirs. It therefore was not theirs to keep, they couldn't possibly go ahead with creating this life. It just wasn't practical or ethical. They still had plenty of embryos left to work with, they could easily try again as soon as the doctors cleared Sarah to.

He'd support her through the process again, he'd be better this time and less surly about it all. It would be fine. It had been easy enough to conceive this rogue baby, there was no logical reason to suppose it would be any different next time around, with their rightful baby. They'd just have to find a different clinic to use.

Clearly though, Sarah had other plans. She was going to be a typically emotional woman about it all and be fundamentally incapable of separating the reality of this random baby with her desire for a child. If she thought for one second, he would support her in keeping another couple's child, she had another thing coming. There was no way he was going to raise a stranger.

While part of him felt it would be kinder to wait to have this discussion, he knew time was not necessarily on their side. The longer she waited to make a decision, the harder it would be for her.

"You're not keeping it!" His words rang out in the silence like a gun shot, physically making her jump. Sarah looked up, appalled by his comment. "How dare you," she replied angrily. "This is my body, not yours. You have no right to dictate what I do, or don't do with it."

He knew he deserved that, but she was missing the point.

"You have no right to tell me to raise another man's child. I won't do it, it's as simple as that. Ultimately you have a choice, me or this baby." She couldn't believe what she was hearing. It had been less than 30 minutes since they had left the clinic and already he was demanding she have an abortion and giving ultimatums.

What had happened to him? This was not the kind, gentle and understanding man she had fallen in love with. It made no sense to her.

"You wanted to adopt," she found herself half saying, half sobbing.

"I don't see what the fuck that has to do with the price of eggs", he retorted, frustration in his voice.

"I just fail to see the difference," she replied trying to keep calm. "You wanted to adopt a random child, one we knew nothing about, but yet this is not acceptable to you? This is so unacceptable that you want me to destroy that little heartbeat we both saw on the screen. That heartbeat which not an hour ago brought both of us so much joy. I just don't think I can do it."

She stopped, wiped the tears away from her face with her napkin, and took a sip of her drink. As she replaced her cup on the table she felt calmer. She took a deep breath and continued talking.

"I have no idea how I feel, and I don't know what I want to do. I don't really understand what our options are at the moment, and I want to take time to understand everything. All I do know is this baby's a miracle for both of us, and I don't know if I can be the one that deliberately changes that."

Pete sighed, deep down he knew if he made her terminate this pregnancy she would never forgive him, and all would be lost anyway. There was no coming back from that, regardless of the biology of this baby. It would still be something that she had done. She was far too maternal to reject a growing being simply on his say so.

This wasn't a mere cluster of cells and genes to her, this was already a living human with a soul and personality. She'd attached her hopes and dreams to it and he knew the grieving process would be too much for her to take were nature to take its course; but to take matters in to her own hands, that would be so much worse.

If she was ever going to make the decision not to go ahead with this pregnancy she had to reach that all by herself, he couldn't force her in to it. The problem was, he didn't know how to lead her to that conclusion without looking like he was trying to manipulate her at all.

"OK," he said eventually. "You're right, it's too early to make any decisions, and I have no place to tell you what to do. I'm sorry, I'm just floundering for a handle on this and don't know how to react. There are so many questions we don't have answers to just yet, I mean, whose baby are we having anyway?"

*****

They walked to the car in silence, got in without speaking and then Will started to drive. "We need to see our lawyer," he said, matter of factly. "We need to know what our rights are. This woman is having our baby, it is our genetic material inside her, surely that's some kind of copyright or something, and it should be legally protected."

Jenna laughed. It was so like Will to be thinking in legal terms, equating this hugely emotional turmoil to nothing more than a legal debate. "I don't think it's going to be that simple," she replied. "It may be our baby, genetically speaking, but it is her body. We can't make her keep our baby any more than she can make us keep hers. We're both in the same boat at the end of the day, let's just take a few days to let it all sink in and figure out how we feel."

"I don't need time to figure out how I bloody feel, I'm furious." He took a breath, and slammed his hands against the steering wheel. "Some stupid bloody idiot has made a massive cock-up, they don't even know how yet, and here we are left to pick up the pieces."

A thought rose in his head, unbidden, that stopped him in his tracks. Surely Adrienne couldn't be the problem? He played that eventful morning over in his head and wondered if the combination of her being tired from their sexploits, then finding out about him being married, had dampened her ability to concentrate. He found it hard to believe, but then none of this really seemed terribly likely.

After readjusting his thoughts, he carried on, "I want to know what we can do to protect our baby. I don't want someone we don't know bringing up our child. What if they're poor? We can offer our baby more than they can! What if they're socialists?" He was almost shouting again now, and all she wanted to do was laugh some more. He was being so ridiculous.

Once again, she put her hand on his knee, "Look, there is no doubting this is a shitty situation. Neither of us know what to do, legally or otherwise, but it's not just a legal problem. We need to take time to let it sink in, to think, to digest what's happening, then hopefully we can make a plan. In a few days we may feel differently than we do now, or at least we won't feel as full of anger or confusion. I'd rather do something when we are able to think clearly and make rational decisions than just react and potentially make matters worse."

They stopped at a traffic light and Will turned to look at her. She was right. She was always right, always the one with the sensible head on her shoulders. He smiled and held her hand, giving it a gentle squeeze. "OK, I won't send the lawyers in just yet. But we do have to come up with a plan, and I am not prepared to just lie down and let someone else control our fate."

Silence enveloped them for the rest of the drive home, it was better that way. Jenna wondered what the other woman must be feeling right now, what her initial reaction to the situation was. Did she want to get rid of the imposter in her uterus, or, like her, did she feel this was a life she'd never dared hope to carry and she wanted to honour it?

She couldn't help but wonder what her story was, how old she was, why she was having IVF. If this was her first attempt, or one in a long line like it had been for Jenna. All these things would no doubt come in to play with her ultimate decision on which to way to go.

Will, on the other hand, remained angry, he just didn't let it show anymore. He was thinking about Adrienne. It was her clinic that had made the gross mistake and he found it hard to believe she genuinely knew nothing about it. He returned to the thought that all of this might inadvertently be his fault. What if it had been her patient that had been caught up in it all? He couldn't carry on the thought, it made him feel faint headed, and he was not a weak man prone to emotional reactions.

By the time they got home they'd moved on to small talk, mostly the weather and where would be good to go for dinner that night. It was easy to lapse into this level of conversation, vaguely comforting. They had been doing it for years, it had become their default position when something was too hard to discuss in full or even acknowledge.

Jenna went straight upstairs for a shower and to get changed, wanting to remove all remnants of their disastrous appointment. Will on the other hand wanted to find out what was going on with Adrienne. He locked himself away in his private office and called her. She answered immediately.

"We need to talk, when can I see you?" he demanded. Adrienne's heart sank. She'd been expecting this call the minute Dr. Barker had confirmed the Sanchez-Cooper's had been brought up to date.

Will was a bright man, shrewd, it was never going to take him long to put two and two together and come close to four. Despite the fact that when she'd walked out on him the other week she had fervently hoped she would never have to see him again, she agreed to meet him.

They arranged to meet at a park, close to her office as soon as her last appointment of the day had finished at 3pm. That would give him time to get to town, see Adrienne, find out what he needed to know and then be back again to collect Jenna and take her to dinner.

CHAPTER 17

"I can't really talk about it," Adrienne said, "please don't make me".

They were sitting on a bench in the park, surrounded by nanny's taking their young charges for walks, hunting for ducks to feed. It seemed like such a normal thing, a couple enjoying the afternoon sun and taking some time to just be together, but it was nothing like it appeared.

"Surely you can understand why I might want to find out how much you know?" Coop asked. "Your clinic isn't exactly being forthcoming with specific information." He was amazed how quickly the tables had turned on their relationship, and the quest for truth.

"So far all I know is that my wife went in for treatment, and came out pregnant with someone else's baby. There is no conceivable way you wouldn't know something about it!"

He was shouting again. He hadn't wanted to, he'd wanted to be calm and not frighten her off, but he hated the thought of being lied to, or kept in the dark. He just wanted to get to the bottom of it all and understand what had happened.

Adrienne had tears in her eyes and struggled to speak. "It's hard, I'm not meant to be talking to you about this. If it wasn't for the fact we know each other outside of a professional setting, we wouldn't be having this conversation."

It sounded so pompous, but it was true. If this had happened to anyone else's wife, she wouldn't be sat here on a park bench getting ready to defend herself. The husband wouldn't be able to pin her down and demand answers from her, answers she desperately didn't want to give. Answers she wasn't technically allowed to provide. An entire conversation she didn't want to have.

As far as anyone at the clinic was concerned, what had happened had been nothing more than a terrible mistake. The reality was, that's exactly the way it had panned out. Having taken statements from everyone concerned, it was clear that Adrienne had been the first to pick up her dish, but Greg had followed suit. Neither of them had checked they had the right embryo for the right patient, so in reality were both as culpable as the other.

On some levels, Adrienne felt completely reassured by that. She knew she had played her part, but in no way could she be held solely responsible, and that eased her guilt tremendously. The problem was, she didn't know how honest to be with Coop. Would he really care who was to blame? What difference would it make to him and his wife now?

The only difference it could make moving forward was how he felt about her. Did she want to admit she had any real part in it? Would he assume she'd done it on purpose, and think she was nothing more than a vindictive scorned woman? There was no way she could cope with him assuming she was capable of that.

Eventually, she decided to go with the company line, “The senior partners are conducting a full investigation, but at the moment it seems like it was a simple lapse in our security and quality procedures.”

Coop shook his head, “So you’re essentially telling me it’s just one of those things?”.

She nodded. “It shouldn’t have been able to happen, but it did. Dr. Barker took his sample for his patient, and I took what was left. We both should have checked, and for whatever reasons, we didn’t.”

“But it is your fault?”, he asked, although to Adrienne, it sounded more like an accusation.

Caught off guard Adrienne stared at the floor, unsure what else she could say without getting herself or the clinic in more trouble. “I didn’t mean to”, she sobbed eventually. “I didn’t even know a mistake had been made until later that day”. She stopped, realising too late that she’d said too much already.

Will glared at her, a look of thunder passing across his face. “You knew? You knew straight away? You knew when we had lunch, when you made me feel guilty for not being entirely honest with you?”

“I couldn’t tell you, the lawyers had told me not to talk. We needed to know if the pregnancy was viable before we held our hands up. That’s why we waited to tell you. Please Coop, I’m in an impossible position here." She reached out for him, but he shrugged her hand away.

Scoffing, he said, "You're in an impossible position? My wife is pregnant with someone else's baby and *you're* in an impossible position?" He stood up and stormed off, leaving her to sit alone with her thoughts and regrets.

*****

As he walked around the park trying to calm himself down Will knew Adrienne was right. There was no way any of this had been done on purpose, he hadn't thought that for one second. It really was just one of those things, as ridiculous as that actually sounded given the severity of the situation. If he was going to blame Adrienne for making a mistake and taking her eye off the ball, then he was going to have to accept some of the responsibility himself.

He had put her in a position, albeit unknowingly at the time, whereby her judgment could be compromised because of a personal issue. He'd love to pretend it was possible to separate the two, that one did not belong in the other world, but the reality is human beings didn't behave like that. Even he was capable of accepting that.

He imagined how she must have felt when he disappeared on her that day in the clinic. She'd described finding out from the receptionist what had happened and who he was. It must have been like being hit in the face with a baseball bat.

When they'd spoken about it weeks later, she had still been visibly shaken, he knew it was not something she was ever likely to get over. For her to then try to carry on with her work, under pressure to perform for this other couple, unable to confide in anyone it was little wonder she hadn't concentrated fully.

No, he didn't blame Adrienne. He blamed the system that allowed such an error of judgment to take place. He blamed this Dr. Barker, who had been just as lax in his approach as Adrienne had been, and probably with no real reason.

There should have been better processes in place to ensure nothing like this could ever have happened. He prayed, for Adrienne's sake, that she would be protected from everything, at least as far as her career went. Emotionally there was no turning back, she would always have to live with what happened, no matter how things played out.

That was the next thing he had to worry about, what he and Jenna were going to do. In the brief conversations they'd already had about it, he knew that was never going to be an easy question to answer.

*****

Sarah sat on the sofa, staring in to space. Once they'd finished their drinks in relative silence, Pete had driven her home, and immediately gone back out again. It was a Wednesday, his traditional day for visiting his Mum. No matter how busy he was, he always made time to pop in to see his beloved Elsie, armed with a bunch of flowers to brighten up her week.

On some levels Sarah had always resented the way he adored his Mum. The first woman he'd ever loved, and the one no one else could compete with. It didn't help that it always felt like a competition. Elsie had never warmed to her, and although Pete would invariably take his wife's side in arguments, she still never felt he really defended her as much as he could do. It often seemed more like lip service, and that behind her back he was secretly agreeing with Elsie instead.

Today though it hurt even more that he'd abandoned her, in her moment of need, to deliver a bunch of sodding tulips. Tradition and routine aside, this was a moment of crisis, and surely his place was by her side? Never before had she felt so let down, and utterly alone.

The conversation with Dr. Barker kept swimming around her mind as she desperately tried to make sense of it all. It didn't matter that she couldn't understand how such a mistake could happen, and she'd moved on from silently screaming 'it's so unfair', all she wanted now was to understand how she felt about it all, and how they could move forward.

Part of her longed for a leaflet, outlining the process, and the emotional stages she'd pass through. Of course, no leaflet could possibly exist, and she was entirely alone in this. Pete would never understand how she felt, not really.

He might not believe it, but she didn't for one second think this wasn't happening to him, but the truth was it was her body that was growing this life. Any decision they made was going to have a greater impact on her, than it would on him. At least in the short term.

It was in that moment she realised there was only one other person that could possibly know how she felt. There was only one person who was going through the exact same thing she was. That's when she knew she'd have to find a way to get in touch with the mother of the baby she was carrying.

*****

Jenna nursed a cup of tea and looked around her perfectly manicured garden, full of flowers and designer accessories. Whilst she was proud of the way it looked, she couldn't take any of the credit, other than hiring the most expensive landscaper in Surrey. That's as far as her involvement had gone.

As far as she was concerned, a garden was nothing without children's playthings scattered around it. She longed for the day there would be a slide scuffing up her grass, and a football trampling her carefully tended flower beds. That was all she wanted, the reality of a family, not the magazine perfect image she'd been cultivating for so long.

The news this morning had momentarily made her think it was all being taken away from her, but the more she thought it over, the more she realised that didn't need to be the case. As far as she was concerned, a baby was a baby. It had been Will that was adamant that any child they raised would have to biologically be theirs.

Personally, she had no interest in establishing a genetic legacy. If truth be told, she didn't even have an overwhelming urge to carry a child, or give birth. She wanted to be a mother, and she knew it involved a lot more than simple dumb luck and biology. She didn't need the badge of pregnancy or the war stories of labour to feel bonded with a child. All she needed was love, and she already knew she had plenty of that.

Before Will had left for the office they'd agreed they'd talk later, but she already knew what her decision was going to be. There was no way she was going to end this pregnancy, and she was more than prepared to raise the resulting baby as her own child. Of course, she hoped Will would be by her side as she did so, but if it came down to a choice between the two, there was only going to be one winner.

CHAPTER 18

Pete walked round the side of the house and found his Mum sitting in the garden, reading the local paper. "Hello dear," she said without looking up and waved him to the seat opposite her. He kissed her affectionately on the head, placed the bunch of flowers he'd bought for her on the iron table, and took a seat. He leant back and stretched out his legs enjoying his first real moment of relaxation all day.

She finished reading the article on the council's decision to move to three weekly bin collections and sniffed to signal her displeasure. "Bloody Council, if they spent less money on that Mayor's fancy car they could afford to empty my bin more often! Bloody disgrace, I don't know who elected them, I really don't. Doris down the road, you know her, the one with the bad hip? Anyway, she said she saw the Mayor shopping in Waitrose last week. Who can afford Waitrose these days? Not on a pension you can't, and he's got to be 68 if he's a day."

Pete smiled and looked around the garden, taking in the immaculately kept flower beds. His Mum was a proud woman and would have spent her last penny ensuring her garden was the talk of the estate. She hated mess and disorder, and would rather go without her M&S Victoria sponge than have someone think she'd let anything go to rack and ruin. Elsie Jenkins was a woman to whom appearances meant everything.

When he turned his attention back to her she'd moved on to talking about her new post man. "I don't see what was wrong with the old fella, he did a perfectly good job, but they decided to move him on to the Meadows Estate. Now we've got this new bloke who smells of cigars and insists on calling me duckie. I've got half a mind to complain, but no one would care."

Pete stood up, desperate to cut her off before she moved on to discussing the neighbour and her new boobs, "Shall we have a cuppa?" he asked.

As he'd hoped, she struggled to her feet and shuffled off to the back door, leading the way in to her cottage style kitchen. She put the kettle on and started arranging a selection of bourbons and digestives on to a china plate, while he put the flowers in a glass vase.

"How are you doing anyway, my dear?" she asked as she lit a cigarette. Her 40 a day habit had earnt her the nickname Fag Ash Lil years ago, and while he despised seeing her smoke, he had long since given up reprimanding her for it.

"I've been better, Ma" he said, leaning against the kitchen sink as he folded up her tea towel. Elsie raised a quizzical eyebrow as if to prompt him to continue. When he remained silent she reached for the kettle, poured the hot water into the cups and turned to face him.

"What's she done now?" she asked, automatically convinced that any hardship her only son might be experiencing must be at the hands of his shrew of a wife.

"To be fair," he replied, "it's not exactly Sarah's fault. It's a bit complicated." He spent the next five minutes explaining to her what had happened at the clinic, which included going over the basics of IVF with her again.

She'd never understood the desire to go through the whole rigmarole, she was firmly of the belief if you were meant to have children, then you'd have them. He knew she'd always wanted more children herself, if she could, she'd have had a house full; but as she said herself, the good Lord had decided one was all she was getting and she'd made the most of it rather than spending her life grumbling.

He'd clearly inherited her approach to procreation, but no amount of pleading or logical discussion had been able to persuade Sarah from pushing the boundaries and making something so that shouldn't have been. Considering where they found themselves today, he deeply regretted not putting his foot down.

Yes, Sarah had moaned and cried and cajoled and used every bit of manipulation known to man to get him to change his mind, but he should have stood firm. She couldn't have done it without him, of that he was certain. She would never have used a donor, even if she could have bank rolled the process on her own. Not only did Sarah want a baby, but she wanted her own baby. Their baby.

Elsie inhaled deeply, dropping ash over her floral dress in the process. She brushed it away automatically before finishing off their tea. "I told you, I said all this science malarkey was messing around with God's plan. I said, didn't I?"

She took a breath, and carried on before Pete had the chance to reply. "Now look at the mess she's gotten you in to, raising a stranger's baby. I ask you, of all the things! What if they're a coloured family? Not that there's anything wrong with them mind, the Jamaicans down the road are a lovely couple, but I wouldn't want to be raising one of their kiddies and trying to pass it off as me own. People would talk! Besides, I don't know where you'd go to get a curried goat. Waitrose might do them, I could ask the Mayor. And another thing…".

Pete couldn't listen to any more. "Please Ma, don't. This isn't Sarah's fault, she's distraught by the whole thing. I just don't know what to do. I can barely keep a straight thought in my head."

As she looked at him she was reminded of the young boy who had stood on this very spot, all those years ago, looking lost because he'd caught the love of his life round the back of the Church hall with another boy. That Maggie Anderson had a lot to answer for. If she hadn't been a monumental slut when she was a teenager all of this could have been avoided, and Elsie wouldn't have to deal with the likes of Sarah Smith. Despite the passage of years, she'd never been able to accept her as a Jenkins.

She handed him his cup of tea and lit another cigarette. It was against all her natural tendencies not to express an opinion, but she could tell it wasn't what he needed right now. She knew she could go on with herself at times, but she never meant to cause any harm or offend anyone. Well, most of the time she didn't anyway.

If she knew her boy, and of course she did, better than anyone, all he needed was to talk. He knew what he wanted, deep down, he just wasn't sure what that was at the moment. "Come, sit down with me for a bit. Tell me how you feel, but take them bloody boots off first." Pete obliged and they moved in to the front room.

He settled down on the Laura Ashely settee, leant back, closed his eyes and sighed. "It's all just too frustrating for words. I thought I wanted to adopt, but honestly Ma, I was thrilled when I found out she was pregnant at last. I don't know if it was the baby itself, or just the fact we could be done with all these blasted trips to the doctor. All I do know is that for the first time in years I felt happy, like a great big weight had been lifted. And now this. It's thrown it all in to a spin again and I don't know where I stand."

Elsie nodded sagely, as if this was the sort of problem she encountered on a daily basis. "What are the options?" she asked, unable to contemplate the possible routes her son may be forced to take.

Pete shrugged, "To be honest, I'm not sure, we've not really talked about it yet. We only found out this morning, and I came over here the first chance I got. I suppose she could terminate, which would just put an end to the whole thing, but then she's bound to want to try IVF again and I don't know if I have the patience for that. I said I would, but, I don't know. We could go ahead and she could have the baby, but I don't know what happens then. It's not ours, but I know she'd feel like it was hers. It's such a bloody mess!"

It was indeed a complex matter. Elsie couldn't imagine being pregnant with the child of anyone other than her husband, even if it had been put in there accidentally and without her knowledge. It would still be a foreigner inside her as far as she was concerned, and she'd want to get rid of it. Even in her own mind she could feel the conflict, she had never agreed with abortion, except in exceptional cases like rape and child abuse. It made sense then, why ruin everyone's lives? She wasn't sure if this was an exceptional case or not.

As far as she was concerned this baby should never have existed. Were it not for the abuse of science to create the thing that had been implanted into her daughter-in-law it wouldn't be there at all. Terminating it would probably be doing everyone a favour, but she wasn't sure Pete was ready to hear that. It would certainly put an end to any debate about what would happen were the child to be brought to term.

“My biggest problem,” admitted Pete “is that I just don’t know how to talk to her about it. Sarah’s never good at just talking things through, and I know we’re just going to keep arguing about it. She’s just so emotional. I want to go through our options, understand what they all mean and then take it from there, but she’s already shutting down on me. As far as she’s concerned it’s her decision, she’s already acting like it has nothing to do with me at all.”

It was a huge struggle for Elsie to see her son so emotional and at a loss. He was usually so calm and in control, always able to see a positive in any situation. She was rarely able to see things from Sarah’s point of view, but she could understand why she wanted to have the ultimate say over what happened. Like it or not, this was happening inside Sarah’s body, and she had to be the one that made the final decision as to what she was, and wasn’t, prepared to go through.

She felt powerless. Finishing her tea, she stood up, patted Pete on the knee and said, “You’re welcome to stay in your old room if you need a few days of quiet reflection. The bed’s already made up for you.”

With that, she left the room to finish the washing up and have another cigarette.

CHAPTER 19

It had been a few weeks since the appointment at the clinic when everything changed, and Sarah was feeling a little calmer. Of course, she still had her moments, and her and Pete had found themselves having numerous arguments about the whole thing, but she was crying less and she felt a little less hopeless. She'd feel better if he hadn't taken to sleeping in the spare room, but she hoped that would pass soon. It was just taking him longer to come to terms with everything than it had her.

Not that she was to terms with it, as such, but she was getting there. She hadn't told Pete, but she'd been back to the clinic and had another meeting with Dr. Harper to talk through how she felt. Although the clinic had provided her with contact details for a few counsellors, and had made it clear they would cover the expenses associated with any treatment she wanted to take, she'd felt more comfortable talking to someone she trusted.

As far as she was concerned Dr. Harper had been there from the beginning, and even though it was her clinic that was responsible for the mistake, she still felt she could rely on her and be honest with her. It had crossed her mind that Dr. Harper might have been partially responsible for what happened, but as far as she was concerned that made no difference. Not now. Nothing really did any more. All that mattered was finding a way to move forward and make everything OK.

During their meeting Dr. Harper had seemed distracted and very uneasy, but Sarah put it down to the fact she must be under a lot of stress too. This couldn't be an easy thing to deal with for anyone concerned, and Sarah refused to start labelling blame or shouting at people. That was Pete's job, though goodness knows she wished he'd step down from it now. The level of anger and hostility he bore towards everyone regarding this was making it so much harder to deal with.

Whilst she'd been talking to Dr. Harper, Sarah had steered the conversation round to the other woman, the lady who was carrying her biological child. She wanted to know how she was doing and what her thoughts were with regards to her pregnancy. Dr. Harper hadn't been able to tell her anything, hiding behind the well-worn excuse of patient confidentiality.

Sarah found it ridiculous, given the circumstances. Legally, she had no right to find out what was happening with her biological child, any more than this other woman had the right to demand answers of her. It just seemed wrong, and she couldn't help but feel the other lady would be feeling as confused and lost as she was.

As a result, she'd asked Dr. Harper to pass on her contact details to the other couple, to reach out to them and see if they wanted to meet to discuss what they were going through. The doctor had seemed reluctant, she clearly didn't want to get involved and seemed to think it might not be the best idea the couples coming together; however, Sarah had pressed her.

"I don't want you to pressure them, and I don't want their details unless they are happy to pass them on, but please, let them know that I'm prepared to talk if they are." She'd done everything bar getting on her knees and physically begging.

That had been a week ago, and today she was getting ready to meet Jenna Sanchez, the woman carrying her baby, for the first time. They'd already had the briefest of telephone conversations, but it was awkward. They both agreed they needed to see each other face to face, to know who it was they were talking to. It was such a deeply personal and unique situation, using the phone made it seem so impersonal and unemotional.

Sarah didn't want to make matters worse, didn't want to induce a situation where both of them spent an afternoon weeping, but she needed it to be what it was. She couldn't cope with it being robotic and practical, devoid of feeling.

Sarah felt guilty for not being honest with Pete and telling him what she was up to, but she knew he wouldn't understand. Though he kept saying he wanted to support her, he was still pushing for her to terminate the baby, and had even threatened to leave on a few occasions after he'd had a bit too much to drink with the boys. As things stood, he'd not started packing his bags so she was hopeful it wouldn't actually come to that.

For the time being though she didn't care what he thought, she needed to work out for herself what she wanted to do, what she thought was best. If he wasn't prepared to engage with that then she couldn't force him, but she refused to bend over backwards and make matters worse for herself just to make his life easier.

*****

Will sat in his office, reading through the letter he'd received from his lawyer. Despite what Jenna had said he'd decided to seek advice to find out where they stood. It was important for him to know what they could and couldn't do. He was a firm believer that you couldn't know what route to use to rectify a problem if you didn't know what all your potential options were. Legal advice just made sense as far as he was concerned.

Unfortunately, it appeared there was nothing they could do. While the baby might be biologically theirs, legally speaking they had no right to claim it. The host mother, as he kept referring to her, had all the legal rights. It was her body, she could even decide to have their baby terminated without asking their permission.

In fact, it appeared she didn't have to keep them up to date with what her plans were at all. She could do anything she wanted, and they would be none the wiser if she didn't want to divulge, and again, they couldn't force her. They couldn't even track her down and initiate contact, even though she was undoubtedly in the local area for them to be using the same clinic.

Not for the first time he wondered how easy it would be to get her details from Adrienne. He was convinced, given the part she had played in the whole situation, that he would be able to persuade her to drop him the woman's address, or phone number.

The part of him that wanted to be in control, that wanted to be doing something about this whole mess, was desperate to ask her. The rational part of him, however, knew that no good would come of it. The mystery woman would have every right to feel harassed, and would no doubt try and slap him with a restraining order, which wouldn't help their situation any further.

For the first time in his life Will felt completely powerless. He wasn't used to having no say or opportunity for input in a situation that affected him so deeply. Until now he had always been able to sway people round to his way of thinking, or create a strong argument for why his approach or idea was better. Here, there was nothing he could do.

It was just all so ridiculous. As far as he was concerned this woman had stolen his genetic material. He knew she hadn't done it on purpose, and that maybe stealing was taking it a bit far as she had as little say in the matter as he and Jenna had, but if she had the baby and planned on keeping it, that was stealing.

It was kidnap for God's sake and he found it incomprehensible that the law didn't seem to agree with him. Somehow giving birth to the child gave the woman more rights than he and Jenna had for paying for it to be produced in the first place. He knew the law worked both ways, they had their own rights with regards to Jenna's pregnancy, but it didn't make him feel any better.

He'd already made it clear to Jenna that he didn't want to keep this other woman's child, he wanted his child or no child at all. It wasn't a simple case of getting on with it as far he was concerned.

The sole purpose of procreating, as he saw it, was to create an heir. Someone to continue your family line, to uphold your name and to pass on your genes. A child was your legacy to the world, proof that you had been there, but that could only be the case if it was actually your child in the first place!

The whole thing was more than he could concentrate on, and he desperately tried to turn his mind to other matters. The problem was his other personal issue was no easier to solve. He and Adrienne had made the conscious decision to end things, and whilst that had made him miserable for a while, he had at least been able to concentrate on rebuilding his relationship with Jenna.

Now this spanner had been thrown in to the works he found himself wondering if he'd made the right decision not to fight for his other woman. The reality was this baby was his overriding reason for wanting to make things right with Jenna. It wouldn't be easy after all this time, but the thought of them bringing a child in to the world together had made it seem worth it. That somehow it was the right thing to do, and he certainly felt as though he owed it to her.

However, as things stood he had no idea what the reality of that child would be. Would she have the baby, and if she did, would she keep it? He had already come to the conclusion that if Jenna wanted to keep this other person's baby, then he no longer owed her any loyalty. It wasn't his child, and he was under no obligation to raise it with her. He could easily step out and start a new life with Adrienne.

He found himself wondering what things would have been like if Adrienne hadn't spotted him at the clinic, and he hadn't panicked. Without that sense of foreboding that he was going to get caught out, would he still have been on hand to support Jenna through that final attempt? Would he have taken her on holiday, if he hadn't had that overriding need to get away from all the complications that Adrienne could bring?

The fact that all of this uncertainty with regards to the baby, and what their future family would be like, had been enough to make him reconsider everything he had said and done over recent weeks. It made him realise nothing had really changed. Yes, he loved and cared for Jenna, but was it enough to entirely give up everything he could have with Adrienne? Especially now.

The real problem was Adrienne. Would she even want to consider moving on? The day she'd told him she knew everything, and had made the decision to walk away, she made it clear that she loved him and would wait. Again, it was only the thought of a baby being brought in to his dysfunctional marriage that had made her position untenable.

Now, the baby was a reality, but it wasn't as simple as that. If Jenna had this child, then it wasn't his, and he didn't have to be supportive in any way. It would be Jenna's decision, and she was old enough to own that for herself. He could walk away with absolutely no guilt or concerns for his wife. Adrienne wouldn't need to feel guilty either. For the first time in their marriage, he found himself hoping Jenna wouldn't do what he'd originally asked of her.

*****

Jenna selected her favourite silk scarf from the wardrobe, put it on and checked her reflection in the floor length mirror. Pleased with the result, she picked up her handbag and made her way downstairs.

Will was already in the office and she hadn't seen him that morning. He seemed to be leaving earlier and earlier, and staying later and later. It amazed her how quickly things had returned to normal, or at least their miserable version of it, once they had come back from the clinic on the day everything changed.

She found herself wondering if they would have remained in their renewed honeymoon period for longer had it not been for the bombshell that had been dropped on them. Will had been so happy about the baby and the new start it seemed to be affording them, when that was taken away from him, he'd started to switch off again.

When they did spend any time together the conversation was strained, as it had always been before their holiday. He didn't want to ask questions that might lead to discussion of the baby, even asking her how she was seemed loaded with potential pitfalls.

He'd once asked her about a shopping trip she'd undertaken and that had been awkward because she'd been looking at maternity clothes. It had only taken him one minute to clear out of the room, leaving her to wonder how long this would last for. As more days went by she'd concluded he could probably keep it up indefinitely.

Today was the first day she'd felt positive since they'd received that news. Sarah, the biological mother of the baby she was carrying, and the one who was carrying her actual child, had reached out to her. When Dr. Barker had phoned to pass on Sarah's contact details she'd been delighted. He'd seemed concerned about the potential for them meeting, but to Jenna it made perfect sense, and the fact that Sarah had obviously felt the same made her feel like she could automatically trust her.

No one else could possibly understand what Jenna was going through, she hadn't even tried talking to her friends about it. There was just no point. It wasn't the sort of thing anyone could begin to comprehend, and she was concerned they would just throw practical suggestions at her. It was all far too emotive to just put a solution on it.

Everything came with its own major complications and she felt it would be near impossible to make an actual decision about any aspect of this. Sarah was in the same boat, she knew they would be able to talk openly and honestly with each other and try to work out what was the best way to move forward. Together.

Of course, she wished things were different, she wished she could include Will in some or all of this, but he just wasn't receptive. He'd never been the most emotionally available of men, and in fairness this was a challenge even the most in tune of individuals would struggle to deal with. She just wanted him to be present, to hold her hand and look at her in that way he had whilst they were away.

Knowing that he cared what she was going through, and that he understood this was difficult for her too, would be a great help right now. Instead he hid, he pretended it wasn't happening and left her to deal with her own grief, in her own way, out of sight.

She was tired of feeling so alone though. It was a heavy load to carry and she didn't see why, after years of dedicated marriage, she should walk the away on her own. He'd made his feelings clear, she'd allowed him to talk through what he wanted to do and what he thought of the situation, but he hadn't done the same for her.

So far, she hadn't been able to verbalise anything and she felt it was all bottled up inside her, ready to explode at some point. It wasn't the explosion that necessarily worried her, but more where she might be when it happened. She was a walking, talking, ticking time bomb and she was constantly terrified about who might end up caught in the fall out should she go off unexpectedly.

*****

Adrienne sat precariously on the edge of her bath, leaning over the sink trying not to be sick. The emotional strain of the last few weeks had definitely taken their toll, and every day she felt increasingly worse. She'd been unable to eat properly and had long given up on a good night's sleep. For a while alcohol had helped, but now she felt she was relying on it too heavily, as every morning she nursed the hangover from Hell.

She desperately wanted to curl up in a ball and hide from the world. It was a strange feeling. Whenever anything had gone wrong before in her personal life she'd been able to throw herself in to work. It's why her career had taken off so strongly at a relatively young age, and she'd been proud of all she had achieved. Now work was as much of the problem as the personal mess she found herself in.

There was no escaping anything anymore, and she was left stumbling around trying to find a way out. To her distress, Sarah had continued to rely on her for support and guidance, stating that if she continued with the pregnancy she needed her to remain as her doctor.

Adrienne didn't feel able to tell her to seek attention elsewhere, but equally she wasn't sure she was best placed to provide her with the care she needed. She didn't want to be caught up in it all, but knew no matter how hard she wished things to be different, it was something she couldn't escape from. Not now.

This time last month things had been so incredibly simple. She had a man she loved, a job she was great at, and that was all she needed. She checked the timer on her phone and immediately looked down at the stick on her lap; now she had a married boyfriend, was facing disciplinary proceedings at the hands of the regulator and was having a baby of her own.

It honestly couldn't get much worse.

CHAPTER 20

The two women sat quietly at their table, nursing the drinks in front of them. They'd managed to avoid any awkwardness when they first met, despite both being unsure if they'd identified the correct woman to have coffee with. For anyone looking on, they might have seemed like friends, enjoying a quick catch up before moving on with the rest of their day.

Sarah studied the woman sitting opposite her coyly as she took a sip of her tea. She was older than she'd anticipated, but still stunningly beautiful. She felt slightly in awe of her. "I don't know what to say," she found herself admitting, inexplicably hoping Jenna would have the wisdom to know where they should start, and guide the conversation from there.

Jenna laughed nervously, "I know what you mean, there's so much I want to ask but it's trying to find the words, and knowing if it's appropriate." They smiled at each other, at least this was some degree of progress.

Sarah put her drink down with a purposeful air, "OK, how about we agree that nothing's off bounds? If the other gets offended, they have to say and we'll pick the bones out of it. I don't want you to feel like you have to walk on eggshells with me. I'm carrying your baby, I guess that makes us family."

She reached her hands across the table and took hold of Jenna's, giving them a gentle squeeze before letting go and picking her drink up again. It happened so quickly Jenna didn't have a chance to react, but she was left feeling uneasy. She'd never been comfortable with strangers invading her personal space, and always felt as though those who did need physical contact so soon after meeting were desperate to be liked. She surveyed Sarah and was reminded of an exuberant puppy, that longed to be loved.

While she knew what Sarah said made sense in theory, she also realised in practice it might not be quite so easy. Jenna accepted one of them had to make the first move, and it was clear Sarah was looking for it to be her. It would be easier when they actually got going, she was certain of it, but someone had to break the ice.

The only thing she really wanted to know was whether Sarah planned to keep the baby. Ultimately it was the only question that mattered, and the only thing she wanted to discuss; however, she knew it wasn't going to be possible to just blurt it out. You had to be diplomatic in some situations, and this was one of them.

Despite what Sarah said this did have to be approached with caution. Jenna was conscious of the fact that although fate had thrown them together in the most unusual of circumstances, they had to find a way to let the other in and develop a friendship. It was the only way to preserve both the lives they were currently carrying.

If Sarah was unsure about keeping the baby, the knowledge that Jenna planned to keep hers might be seen as pressure. It was all a nightmare, and impossible to really deal with if you didn't have the slightest idea what the other person was thinking or hoping the outcome would be. It was like a game of emotional poker.

She knew if she was going to be able to open up to this woman, this complete stranger despite the muddle they found themselves in together, she'd have to trust her. To do that she would have to know her, the way someone knew their best friend. It wouldn't be enough to ask some questions and analyse the results. This wasn't an interrogation.

"How long have you and your husband been married?" she found herself asking. She was conscious she sounded like a journalist interviewing a celebrity for some trashy magazine, but she had to start somewhere. She hoped allowing Sarah to talk about something that didn't seem entirely relevant, and wasn't difficult, would lead on to other subjects more naturally.

Sarah smiled instantly, she adored Pete and relished the opportunity to talk about him, especially now things weren't perfect between them. "Oh, we've been married for 17 years, but we've been together even longer than that. We were childhood sweethearts, totally inseparable from the minute we met at a youth club. I knew the second I laid eyes on him that he was the one for me."

Jenna glanced out the window, watching the traffic go by, struck by the fact Sarah's story sounded so similar to hers and Will's. "He was always so romantic", Sarah continued, explaining how he'd arranged a party for her and had proposed in front of all her friends and family, how they'd had the perfect wedding and how he bought her a bunch of flowers every Friday on his way home.

"He's not really changed over the years to be honest," she said, but her voice trailed off as she tried to forget he hadn't bought her flowers for a few weeks now.

Suddenly the waitress appeared at their table to ask if they wanted anything to eat. Sarah automatically picked up the menu and looked at it, eventually deciding to have a toasted tea cake. Jenna wavered, but concluded she might as well have something too, and opted for the fruit cup. It felt alien having something outside of her strictly planned menu, but to Hell with it. Everything felt alien these days.

She'd spent her entire adult life on some form of diet, and most of her teen years as well, come to think of it. Counting calories was a natural state for her thanks to her initial professional need, and then simply desire, to have the perfect body. Now her figure was going to take a battering anyway she might as well have some fun along the way.

"That sounds familiar", Jenna said once the waitress had taken their order and left them alone again. "Will and I met when I was just 18. We were at a party my agent was throwing, they were friends or belonged to the same Golf Club or something, I forget now, but we hit it off straight away.

"He wasn't like all the other men I'd known up till then, he was confident, but not cocky or pushy. He seemed so genuine that I fell for him there and then." She smiled, momentarily lost in nostalgia.

"Looking back, his English accent probably didn't do him any harm either. He was a real gentleman, and I couldn't help but be mesmerised by everything he said and did."

Conversation then flowed to careers, to the discovery that Jenna had once been a cat walk model who now dabbled with her own fashion line. Sarah was amazed, her companion was so nonchalant about her experiences and played them down, there was no way she could have been so reserved if it was her story to tell.

The people Jenna must have seen and rubbed shoulders with, the parties she'd probably been to, the stories she could tell. It took all Sarah's reserve not to question her about celebrity gossip. Her life as a substitute teacher was painfully bland in comparison.

By the time their food arrived they had discovered a mutual love of Louboutin's, though Sarah confessed she'd never owned a pair in her life, merely coveted them. Jenna decided to keep quiet about her closet full of pairs she'd barely worn, some of which had been gifted to her after shoots and runway shows.

She had worked hard for everything she'd ever received, including the freebies, and had made sacrifices to get them, but people always saw the material benefits of her work as something to be jealous of, and she didn't want to be seen as a bragger.

As Jenna picked over her fruit she realised how comfortable the conversation had been so far. It didn't seem as though she was talking to a complete stranger, but rather someone she'd known for years. It was easy to talk to Sarah, though she was mindful of the elephant in the room.

She wondered if the younger woman felt the same, if she also wanted to press about Jenna's plans for the baby, but was too concerned about how the question would be received to ask. She'd been in some awkward situations before, but nothing remotely prepared her for this, and she had no idea how to proceed.

Sarah rescued her from having to think of it any further by asking what Will thought of the situation. "It's hard for him," she answered. "Of course, it's hard for us both, but he's a man, his instinct is to find a practical solution, fix the problem and move on. He doesn't really comprehend that it's not as simple as that. You can't pop a band aid over this and hope for the best."

"I know what you mean," Sarah interjected. "Pete's exactly the same. He's not a big talker, I suppose most men aren't really, but he's completely closed about this. He's given me his opinion and as far as he's concerned that's the end of it. I don't really know how to handle it with him anymore, he just won't let me talk."

They sat in silence for a minute, weighing up how best to proceed. Taking a deep breath Jenna decided to go for the plunge, "I take it he wants you to terminate?" Sarah nodded, unable to say the words out loud. She knew this was coming, that it was a natural conversation for them, one that certainly had to be had, but she wasn't ready for it.

Although she'd done nothing but think about her options since the minute they'd found out what had happened, she was no closer to making a decision. She did hope that meeting Jenna would help her make that leap, but it was still too early for her to be swayed in either direction. Despite what Pete said about being supportive, she wasn't convinced he would handle it well if she decided to have the baby. She wasn't even sure what 'having the baby' really entailed.

If she gave birth to it, would it automatically be her responsibility? Would she be forced to keep it and raise this other woman's child, or would she be able to hand the baby over? Did the law dictate that she *had* to hand the baby over? She wasn't sure what she hoped the legal position would be, neither seemed terribly appealing in all honesty.

"Will is the same," Jenna said, her words jarring Sarah away from her thoughts. "He doesn't want to raise another man's child, and on some levels, I can understand. In an ideal world I don't want to raise a baby that has nothing to do with me, but plenty of people adopt, and I'm not sure there's any real difference."

Conversation then turned to Pete's initial desire to adopt, and why they hadn't. Now they found themselves where they were Sarah couldn't help thinking it would have been a much simpler and less painful process, not to mention more cost effective, had they just done what he wanted in the first place. She couldn't admit that to him, she'd never hear the end of it, but he was no doubt thinking it himself anyway.

Jenna admitted she'd have been happy to adopt, but it wasn't something her and Will had ever discussed either. They hadn't really discussed anything, truth be told.

"If you don't mind me asking, why didn't you and Will discuss all your options?" Sarah queried, desperate to understand the thought processes of this couple she was now linked with.

Jenna shifted in her seat and pushed her half-finished plate away. "We've been married longer than you and Pete, I suppose over time you become less one, and more like two completely separate entities.

"I don't know, maybe that's not fair, maybe it's just what happened to us. Either way, we were on different paths. Will had never been too concerned about starting a family, and for the longest of times I wasn't either. A pregnancy was never going to go down well with my career and I had worked far too hard to potentially give it up."

Sarah finished her tea cake, and wiped cream away from the side of her mouth whilst Jenna continued.

"As time went by we drifted further apart, and as I got older my career slowed, naturally. One day I realised there was a massive void in my life, and it was clear the only thing that was likely to fill that was a baby. Will had never been terribly keen on starting a family, it was something we'd just taken for granted we wouldn't do because it didn't fit with our other plans, but he was supportive of my need to. As I said, he's practical, he likes solutions, so he just threw money at the problem. To be honest, I think even if I had been in fine working order he'd have still suggested we try IVF to conceive."

Jenna hadn't intended to open up so much to this woman, but the words kept flowing and it seemed perfectly natural to tell her precisely how she felt. Sarah felt sorry for her. Despite the outward appearance that the gorgeous Jenna Sanchez had everything anyone could ever dream of, it transpired she probably had nothing of real value. Not the value she longed for.

Sarah counted herself lucky, what her and Pete had was not always perfect, she certainly didn't always appreciate it for what it was, but it was genuine. Their love was nothing but real and they always supported each other, even when it was difficult. Until now, perhaps.

She suddenly felt a pang of fear in the pit of her stomach. What if this was the one thing that could break them apart? What if they couldn't find a way to make it work, would they ultimately end up like Jenna and Will?

"Do you love him?" Sarah asked. She needed to know the answer to understand what Jenna was going through, what her thought process was and ultimately where her decisions might take her. The real question she wanted to ask was did Jenna love Will more than the thought of being a mother. Was her love for him enough to put this baby's life at risk?

Jenna bit her lip before replying, "Yes, I do. We've been through too many years together for me not to, but love is a bizarre construct that doesn't have anywhere near as much weight to these things as many people think."

Sarah was confused. As far as she was concerned love was everything. If you loved someone you could overcome any difficulties. She said as much to Jenna, who just laughed at her. "Sorry," Jenna said, "I don't mean to be rude, but I remember feeling that way once upon a time. Enjoy it whilst it lasts my dear, reality will bite you on the ass one day."

CHAPTER 21

Coop had already ordered the wine by the time Adrienne arrived, slightly late and very flustered. He'd been caught off guard when he received her text message that morning, begging him to meet her for lunch, but he was determined to play it cool. He had no idea what she might want to discuss, but he had his own agenda, and didn't want to look too desperate in his attempts to woo her back.

As a result, he barely acknowledged her before pulling open the menu in front of him. "The specials today are spicy pumpkin soup and something to do with veal," he said without looking up. Adrienne took a large gulp from the wine glass in front of her. She knew she would regret it, but she needed courage and fire in her belly more than feelings of virtue right now.

She found it hard to say anything, no safe topics of conversation came to mind, so she sat silently nodding while Coop briefly outlined the nightmare client he'd just had a meeting with, and how difficult Jenna was being. Apparently, she was refusing to discuss matters until she'd digested it all herself, though he clearly failed to comprehend what that actually meant. Adrienne found it hard to blame Jenna for her approach, but decided to keep her mouth shut.

Food ordered, they sat in silence for a few moments while he flicked through some messages on his iPhone. She sighed. It seemed liked five minutes ago he was sitting here confessing he was married, now she had her own confession to make. She had spent all morning trying to work out precisely how to tell him, what to say, but there was just no easy way around it. The words had to come out, and he'd appreciate her not beating about the bush.

After what felt like an age he looked up, "So, what was so urgent you had to see me today?" he asked, a slight tone of irritation in his voice. In that moment she was reminded of her father, always too busy with work to stop and smell the flowers. No matter what you were discussing or doing, you always felt you were on the clock. It was like having an appointment at the GP surgery; one patient at a time, only one symptom allowed, five minutes maximum.

Whilst she had hoped to ease in to the issue, the reality was there was no sugar coating to be done. She took another swig of wine and began, "I'm pregnant". The words out, she realised there really wasn't any more to say. This wasn't a debate. She was pregnant, those were the facts, the following conversation had to revolve around where they went next. All she'd had to do was get it started.

To his credit Coop didn't even flinch, he simply put his phone face down on the table and picked up his own wine glass. He sat quietly for a moment and Adrienne couldn't be sure if he was thinking over what she had just said, or if he was deciding if the wine was any good. He was so unreadable at times, it was like having dinner with a pro poker player. Eventually he asked, "What do you intend to do about it?".

The question caught her off guard, it wasn't something she'd given much thought to, though she daren't admit that to Coop. She noticed her palms were sweating and she began to feel light headed.

"Honestly," she said, "I thought it was something we ought to discuss, together." He nodded, but remained silent. She imagined he looked like this when he was considering an investment someone had just offered him; non-committal, ever so slightly intimidating.

"I confess," he said at last "that my experience with pregnant women is somewhat limited; however, I have been treated to a crash course over the last few weeks and have learnt something quite valuable." Adrienne met his gaze, unsure what he was going to say.

With no interruption from his companion, he continued. "When it comes to their bodies and their unborn children, women are the ones that make the decisions. There's no sense in trying to persuade them otherwise, it is just a frustrating waste of time. I make a habit of not entering into discussion until I know all the facts and what I am up against, so I would appreciate you telling me your thoughts on the matter."

Initially she felt wounded by his words and didn't like their current personal situation being likened to a business transaction. After draining her glass, she begrudgingly admitted to herself that she could see his point. While she valued his opinion, and needed to know where she stood with him, she was not going to be swayed either way by anything he had to say. She didn't think so anyway.

"My parents are Catholic", she offered as a response. When it became clear she was not going to break the silence that now lay between them, Coop picked up the conversation. "That's very nice for them I'm sure, but as I am not asking your parents for their input right now, I fail to see the relevance."

Adrienne was stung, "We don't agree with abortion", she replied aware she sounded surly, but felt this fact had been made obvious in her previous comment. Coop was not prepared to let her get away with it that easily. "I see," he said again. "By 'we' I assume you mean you, and not the Catholic population in general?"

She nodded slowly. It was true, she was not a fan of abortion, it was forbidden as far as her religious upbringing was concerned, but she could see in certain situations where it might be warranted. She definitely believed in a woman's right to choose.

"The problem I have with you using religious dogma at this moment is it makes you a hypocrite. You are a 36-year-old unmarried woman who has had multiple sexual partners. I say that not to insult, but to remind you of who you are as opposed to who your parents raised. You earn your money creating life, going against God's will and you are now pregnant with a married man's baby. I fail to see how much relevance your Catholic faith can possibly have in this discussion."

He took another sip of wine, clearly satisfied with the point he'd made, and looked at her expectantly. She was about to open her mouth when the waiter arrived with their order. She was relieved, she hadn't really had anything to say and was bound to blurt out something just for the sake of not sitting in silence.

There was a temptation to bring him completely up to date, tell him she might not be pregnant with his baby, but the reality was it wouldn't help her argument any. She was a Catholic girl, pregnant as a result of either a nameless one-night stand, or an affair. Neither were particularly good examples of her living a life dedicated to her faith. She was merely using it as an excuse, not a real reason.

She started on her meal, trying to understand precisely what he was getting at. Did he want her to have an abortion, and that's why he was mocking her?

"I'm not terminating," she said suddenly. "Regardless of religion or anything else, I'm 36. It might not have been planned, and it's clearly not ideal, but this might be my only stab at being a mother. I can do this alone, so I expect nothing from you."

She'd never planned to say that, it just slipped out. Isn't it what people said in these situations? You're off the hook, you don't have to be involved, keep your money. I am woman, hear me roar. It all sounded very good on paper but out loud, in the real world where it mattered, she wasn't so sure.

She was a single woman in a tiny city flat. She had a career she loved, though goodness knows what state that might be in a few months when the regulators had finished with her; how could she raise a child on her own with no income? It was too impossibly daunting a prospect. In the back of her mind she realised this was why she didn't want to tell Coop about the potential issue with paternity. It was one thing to say she didn't want help, but it was entirely another one to ensure no help would be forthcoming.

Coop picked up his knife and fork to start dissecting his steak. "OK," he said in between mouthfuls, "so, we're having a baby. I should probably talk to Jenna."

His response made absolutely no sense as far as she was concerned. Noticing her bemused look, he continued, "Jenna has wanted a child for the longest of times, and up until a few weeks ago I had very little to do with the process bar from the depositing of genetic material two years ago. To all intents and purposes this was going to be her baby, come what may."

Adrienne pushed her potatoes around her plate, unable to muster the energy to actually eat them.

"Sitting with her during that last IVF session something changed in me. The thought of creating a life appealed, and I confess I was ecstatic when I found out she was actually pregnant. For the first time I really considered what it would mean to be a father, and I re-evaluated everything in my life."

For the briefest of moments his eyes shone and he had a smile on his face. He seemed genuinely happy at the thought of Jenna carrying his child.

"However," he continued, "the baby she is having is not mine. We've not talked, but I know the path she will choose and while I do not wish to cause her harm for choosing it, I cannot stand idly by. I will not raise another man's child. She has made her choice, even if she won't openly admit it, and now I shall make mine."

He continued eating and Adrienne stared at him in silence.

On the one hand she admired how matter of fact he could be about the whole thing, calmly weighing up the options and the motivations of all people concerned; but on the other, it made her uneasy. How could he be so cavalier in his approach to his marriage? To simply walk away from the woman that had been by his side for 27 years?

He caught her eye again and laughed, "Oh come Ade, don't play the fool. You walked away once, and I'm not saying for one second you were wrong to, but you have walked back. Now the rules have changed slightly. Jenna remains pregnant, yes but that is now nothing to do with me. If she continues with her pregnancy, then I have no legal or financial responsibility to that child. My priority can therefore be yours and the child we are going to bring in to the world together."

Adrienne let out a long, deep breath and reached for another glass of wine; however, Coop pulled the bottle out of her grasp. "I think you have had enough, my dear, under the circumstances", he said as he poured himself a top up. She knew he was right, but at the same time more alcohol would make her feel infinitely better than she did at the moment.

Her plan for today had been to tell him about the pregnancy, but she had wanted to be honest over the potential paternity dispute. She had toyed with saying nothing at all, but she knew it would simply be her bad luck for him to somehow find out about the pregnancy anyway, so there was no point in keeping it a secret. Having worked on the basis she had nothing to lose, she didn't see how telling him it might not be his would change anything.

However, now he sat there saying he was going to leave Jenna so they could raise the child together, she suddenly felt unable to carry on with her full confession. Men always said they would leave their wives, but they never really did. They never left their wives for their mistress, there was always something that kept them tied to the status quo and a life of quiet misery.

Inadvertently her finding out about Coop and Jenna had provided him with a way out of his marriage, and a route straight to her door. Pouring herself a glass of water she took a sip, and fervently hoped the baby would look like him when it was born.

CHAPTER 22

The meeting was going a lot better than Jenna had anticipated. While she and Sarah didn't have much in common in terms of life experiences and even culture, they had found common ground through their unique circumstances and she felt they'd bonded. They had covered a wide variety of topics, from mundane chit chat involving favourite songs and places to go on holiday, to the more relevant.

By the time they made a start on their third round of drinks Jenna decided it was time to try and find out some more detailed and important information. "How long have you been having IVF?" she asked.

At first, she felt it was probably quite an irrelevant question and only asked as a way to get the ball rolling, but then she thought perhaps it was the best place to start after all. It would give her the opportunity to gauge how much this pregnancy, the baby, any baby meant to Sarah and her husband.

At least she would have a starting point and right now that's just about all she could hope for. Sarah leant back in her chair preparing to relive her story.

"Not long really, I suppose, compared to some. Pete and I had been trying for a while and it just wasn't happening for us. I came off the pill six years ago and we very much had the attitude of it'll happen when it happened; but it didn't happen. After two years, we started trying, properly trying, you know what I mean?"

Jenna nodded. She had enough friends that had been through the process to understand the distinction between spontaneous sex, and active baby making.

"I was charting my temperature every morning, using ovulation kits and researching optimum positions, but nothing seemed to work. I was convinced something was wrong, but Pete was reluctant to do anything about it for the longest of times. Finally, after another two years I managed to persuade him to talk to someone.

"So, we saw our GP who did some initial tests, but everything came back OK and he just said I probably needed to relax about it. So, we tried. We went on holiday, I stopped charting because I was becoming obsessed, but none of that made any difference either. Eventually I started researching IVF and that was about two years ago now."

Jenna found it interesting to hear someone else's journey, what had made them start on that path and what it had been like for them. She'd never spoken to anyone else about IVF and her own struggles with fertility. None of her friends even knew she was going through the process herself, she was too private to share it with them.

If truth be told, none of her friends were much more than acquaintances anyway. They were the sort of women you could call up to invite to a dinner party, gala or celebrity fundraiser, but you'd never phone if you had an actual problem. In Jenna's experience, if you needed someone to talk to, you made an appointment with your therapist.

"I take it this wasn't your first attempt them?" Jenna found herself asking, realising that Sarah seemed to feel more comfortable doing the talking than asking questions herself when it came to the more personal topics. Sarah nodded.

"When we first started Dr. Harper was reluctant to go full throttle at it given there was no real indication something was wrong with either of us. We tried intrauterine insemination for 18 months. It was Hell. We kept having to go back every month, Pete would give his sample and I'd lie there trying to be positive. Every month we'd do a pregnancy test, and every month it would come back negative.

"In the end Dr. Harper did some more tests and found my hormones weren't quite right. My egg supply was dwindling, and we were starting to run out of time. She suggested it might be worth considering being a little more aggressive, and that's when we started hormone treatment to get ready for implantation. This was the first cycle, so I'm lucky I guess."

Both ladies laughed. It was a bizarre situation. After both trying for so long, in their different ways, it *was* lucky to have finally managed to get a positive result. It's just 'lucky' wasn't entirely how either of them felt about the situation.

"How about you?" Sarah asked, leaning forward to take another sip of her drink. Jenna wasn't sure how honest to be; the full story was long and depressing. She didn't want to have to listen to herself telling it, let alone subject someone else to it. In the end she resolved that honesty was the best way forward. She couldn't ask this woman to trust her if she held back and told her half truths about any of her journey.

"We've been trying a while too. The truth is we left it too late to start thinking about family, we'd both been so busy with our careers that it just took a back seat. By the time we got around to it I was quite far down the dwindling path myself." She laughed nervously.

"I was 40 when we started IVF, so never really had the option of starting with insemination. We did the egg retrieval and Dr. Barker did everything he could. We ended up with 15 embryos and unfortunately, we've been working through each one of them over the past five years with no success. Until now."

Sarah put her hand on her stomach, "Is this your last chance?" she asked, practically whispering. Jenna lowered her head, "Yes. That was our last shot. Typical isn't it?" She laughed again.

"I am so sorry, none of this is even remotely fair", Sarah said as she reached out for Jenna's hand again. "I need you to know I've not decided what to do about the baby yet, but my instinct says I can't terminate. Certainly not knowing that this is your last chance to have the family you want."

Jenna met her gaze and instantly relaxed. This was the start of the only conversation they really needed to have. It was the elephant in the room, the question Jenna had been far too terrified to ask, but now it was there, she felt instantly better.

She squeezed Sarah's hand back, "Thank you. I know this isn't my baby, but there was just no way I could do anything to stop it from happening. Will wants me to terminate, but I just can't. I haven't told him yet, but he's under no illusion that I am not going to abort."

Saying it out loud for the first time made her realise just how strong her resolve was. It didn't matter what Will said or did, she wasn't prepared to listen to any of his cold hard logical reasons as to why having the baby made no sense. She didn't care what the outcome was, as long as this baby was OK. Will could do what he wanted after that.

"My Pete's the same," Sarah said. "He doesn't understand why I'm prepared to carry another couple's child. He keeps seeing it as this alien that doesn't belong to us, and he wants nothing to do with it."

Jenna completely understood. Although she couldn't agree with what Pete was saying, any more than she could agree with Will, she did accept why they might feel that way. It was a totally different experience for the men than it was for them.

Will had never been convinced about having a child in the first place, so she could completely accept why he was less than enamoured at the thought of her giving birth to someone else's, but for Jenna, there was no distinction.

This baby was growing inside her. It was there now and all things being equal it wouldn't be long before she could feel him moving inside her. Regardless of biology she knew she already felt a bond with this little hitchhiker inside her, and it seemed clear that Sarah felt the same.

It suddenly dawned on her that Will might have had a point though about seeking legal advice, it did make sense to find out what their rights were when it came to a real-life baby. While she would never have felt comfortable demanding that Sarah either carry her child or abort it, what would happen when the baby was eventually born?

Ultimately it would be Jenna's baby, would Sarah plan on keeping it and raising it as her own? Equally, would she be comfortable with Jenna raising her child? It sounded so callous, but surely, they could just swap when the time came? Giving birth was just a part of the process, it wouldn't make the baby you gave birth to automatically yours. Not really.

Jenna desperately wanted to ask the question, to probe a little further but she stopped herself. It wasn't the sort of conversation she felt comfortable initiating, besides she felt it was too early to be having it. Their relationship was in its infancy and too delicate to withstand making a terrible faux pas just yet. In a few weeks, or maybe longer, she could bring it up, perhaps more naturally than she could manage now, and it would seem less traumatic and invasive.

They moved the conversation on to comparisons of early pregnancy symptoms and delighted in the fact they both felt exactly the same. Sarah admitted she was struggling with mid-afternoon exhaustion and had taken to lying down on the sofa for an hour before getting dinner ready, while Jenna was being plagued by heartburn almost constantly. By the time they were ready to leave and head home nearly four hours had passed.

Sarah stood up first, put on her coat and gave Jenna a warm hug, "Thank you for agreeing to meet me. I've really enjoyed talking to you, perhaps we should do this again soon?" Jenna squeezed her back, "Of course, it's been lovely. Only Will knows I'm pregnant, so it would be wonderful to have a friend to share it all with, and who better than you really?"

They made plans to meet again in a few weeks' time, promising to speak before then anyway. With a successful first meeting behind them they walked out in to the sunshine together and then went their separate ways, hopeful for the first time that everything was going to work out OK in the end.

CHAPTER 23

Sarah was sitting in the front room watching one of her many evening soaps when Pete walked through the door. She froze, as though she had been caught in the middle of doing something she shouldn't have been. There was nothing unusual about her watching TV, Pete often took the mickey out of her for how easily she got hooked on mindless garbage; her reaction was purely a result of her meeting with Jenna. Ultimately, she had every reason to feel guilty.

When she first reached out to Jenna via Dr. Harper she knew she wasn't going to mention it to Pete, he'd have said it was a waste of time. Then, when they had spoken on the phone and arranged to meet, she rationalised not telling him because there was always an off chance that Jenna wouldn't show, and then she'd be getting herself in to an argument for no reason.

She'd never really considered the possibility that she would end up meeting this woman, and that they would talk about their individual responses to what had happened. Now of course that's precisely what had happened, and Sarah knew she had to come clean.

The problem was she couldn't come clean about one aspect of it without admitting she had kept other bits of it from him. Pete had always been so proud of the fact they didn't keep secrets from each other, and Sarah had always obliged by being open.

Except for the pregnancy tests of course, and the occasional white lie about how much an item of clothing had cost. She also might not be entirely honest about her monthly Stella & Dot purchases, but they were just minor things that could easily be brushed under the carpet. This was a bit bigger than a maxed-out credit card.

Pete had shouted out his customary "I'm home", before heading straight upstairs to grab a shower. It was one of the rules of her house, no workwear allowed near the cream carpets. He even had to wait for his post work cup of tea, or beer as it was more likely to be these days, until he was scrubbed and in a clean set of clothes. He was so used to it now he didn't even bother to poke his head round the door to see how she was; he just went straight upstairs, like a well-trained dog.

She breathed a sigh of relief, a brief reprise before she had to face the music. She got up and went to the kitchen to check on dinner and to pour Pete a beer, ice-cold from the fridge. After a long, hard day at work she knew this was likely to put him in a good mood, or at least a better one, and that's precisely what she needed him in for this conversation.

She'd given it a lot of thought since she got home from her meeting with Jenna, and had decided she was going to go ahead with the pregnancy. If this was Jenna's last chance to be a mother to her own biological child, then she couldn't be the one to take that away from her and, she reasoned, nor could Pete.

Although she didn't understand any of the legal implications of it all, like whose name would be put on the birth certificate, and who would be the legal guardians of each child, she didn't care. All she did know was that this baby belonged to Will and Jenna and she had every intention of giving it back to them.

Jenna clearly felt the same, and that was all that really mattered to her. The legal stuff could be worked out at a later date. They had plenty of time before anything was actually going to happen.

In her mind this was the best possible situation. It meant they could both have the child they wanted at the end, which was all that Pete seemed to care about. He kept going on about not raising another man's child, well this way he didn't have to. He would be raising his own child, so it seemed like a no brainer in her mind.

There was no logical reason for him to oppose it. The only slight drawback was the fact that she'd kept it from him in the first place, but even that she started to think was not the worst thing she could have done.

The sound of his footsteps carried over the noise from the bubbling pan of pasta and she turned around to greet him with a big smile on her face. He quickly surveyed the kitchen, the side table set for a romantic meal, complete with candles and he felt inexplicably anxious. Sarah was a reasonable cook, but she wasn't the type of person that would make an effort, unless there was someone relevant around to notice it. Pete did not pass as relevant on most occasions, so he was concerned where this was leading.

While he hoped it may be the overture to an apology about her more than unreasonable behaviour of late, he wasn't convinced Sarah had that level of introspection or maturity about her. She'd done something and he was being buttered up, that was the only explanation he could find, so he picked up his beer and headed for the table, like a lamb to the slaughter.

As he pulled out his chair he couldn't help thinking there had to be more to married life than this. He hadn't expected laughter and joy every single day, but a bit more of it every now and then wouldn't go amiss. It had all gotten so serious so quickly, and no one had ever warned him about that. He often wondered how different his life might have been if he'd taken an alternative path.

Sarah hadn't been the love of his teenage years, though he had grown fond of her in a short period of time. His Ma always referred to her as a rebound, and one that he should have bounced off of quickly, rather than shacking up with and then marrying.

He'd tried to explain, but deep down, he knew she was right. Sarah wasn't the one. For years he had wondered if Maggie would have been the one, but the reality was, there was an unknown one out there waiting for him. For now though, here he was and he had long ago made the decision not to dwell on it.

“I have a confession to make,” Sarah said as she placed a bowl of spaghetti Bolognese in front of him. He thanked her and then stayed silent, waiting for the bombshell that was about to fall on him. She was unsure how to continue. In her mind she would tell him she had something to tell him and he would say something back, there would be a brief interlude before she would have to continue with the actual confession itself. The fact that he kept quiet and started eating his dinner had thrown her.

After a significant pause he prompted her, “Well, you going to spill the beans?”. There was nothing she could do now, she had to say something, but she still hadn’t worked out where to start. “I’m going ahead with the pregnancy”, she said eventually, “it’s the right thing to do and I’m sure you’ll agree with me.” She blurted the last bit out in a frantic bid to stop him from getting angry with her and raising his voice. She didn’t want an argument, not tonight. There had been too many already over the last few weeks.

Pete shook his head, “I’m not going to agree with you, but I know it doesn’t matter whether I do or don’t, you’re going to do whatever the Hell it is you want, regardless of what I say. You always do.”

She was hurt by his comment, not because it was untrue, but because she hadn’t realised before this was the way he viewed her. She always thought she could do no wrong in his eyes, that she was the perfect wife and woman, but it would appear she had it wrong. How long had he felt this way?

Caught off guard by what he'd said, and the way it made her feel, she carried on eating in silence. "Look," he ventured at last, "I suppose my point is, it's not my place to tell you what you can and can't do. I want to, I desperately want you to do what I think is right, but it would be wrong of me to give you an ultimatum. It just doesn't work like that."

Sarah kept on eating, refusing to make eye contact with him, worried about where this conversation was now going. While she was glad they were talking, and she was even happier that he seemed to be taking the lead, this hadn't been the big confession she'd been planning on making. She needed to steer the conversation around so she was back in control, but she wasn't sure how.

"I've been doing some research," Pete continued. "If you want to have this baby, then the reality is it's going to become *our* baby. There's no way of getting in touch with the actual parents, and that's fine. We have automatic parental rights, and though we could give those up if you wanted to place the baby up for adoption, if you do want to keep it, that is your right. From what I can tell the law would be on your side."

She was amazed by what he was saying, and couldn't believe how quickly he had come around to the idea of them keeping this child and raising it as their own. In that moment she recognised the sacrifice he was prepared to make for her, and couldn't face ruining the moment by coming clean. He'd be furious, all over again. For the first time in weeks she felt there was a truce between them, and there was no way she was prepared to ruin that. She wanted to enjoy a little bit of peace whilst she could.

In her mind she rationalised her silence because it wouldn't make any difference to him right in this moment. He was prepared for her to continue with the pregnancy, so that solved the immediate problem. He would be psychologically preparing himself to be a father, which he would be – just come the time when a baby would be placed in his arms it would be his own biological one, rather than the one she was currently carrying.

At least, that was her plan and she saw no reason why Jenna wouldn't be in agreement with her about that. She smiled, it was all going to be just fine, nothing could get in the way of everything being perfectly alright.

CHAPTER 24

Jenna walked in to the kitchen and was caught off guard by the sight of Will sitting at the breakfast bar with a glass of Scotch in front of him. She couldn't remember the last time he'd been home before her on a work day and was slightly disconcerted by his presence.

She opened the fridge, pulled out a bottle of water and took a seat opposite him. "You're home early," she said, "tough day?" He nodded, "Something like that, I fancied taking the afternoon off. I thought you'd be home to be honest".

For an instant she felt guilty that she hadn't been available when he wanted her to be, but she shrugged it off. She had spent a lifetime being ready 'just in case', waiting for him to arrive when she anticipated him, only to be disappointed when he didn't show or ultimately had no need of her.

"I was meeting a friend," she offered and took a sip of her water, "it took longer than I anticipated." He looked down at his glass and said, "We need to talk". Jenna couldn't remember the last time she'd seen him look so serious and down. Even when things were bad, he was either optimistic it would all be OK, or he was furious because someone had done something he hadn't expected or regarded as being underhand.

This didn't seem to be a work situation though, and she couldn't fathom what he might want to talk about that required the use of Scotch. Then it hit her. He was going to come clean about Adrienne.

Her heart sank. Now was not the time to be having this conversation, and she didn't know how best to cut him off at the pass. She wanted to tell him about her meeting with Sarah, that she was confident that between them they could work out a plan that would ensure they all got what they wanted in the end.

For some reason the words wouldn't come. There was a degree of morbid curiosity about where his conversation might go. She was convinced it could only be Adrienne related, but was he coming clean in order to start a fresh slate, or was there more to it than that? More than once she had lain awake in bed whilst he worked late in his study, wondering if the complication with the pregnancy had been the death knoll for their apparently renewed relationship.

For her part, she knew that no matter how good it had seemed whilst they were away, and in the few short weeks after they returned, it was too little too late. Nothing would have induced her to pick Will over this baby, and that was all she really needed to know about the security of her marriage. He was never going to be the all-consuming love he had once been for her. Knowing that meant she was more than happy for him to walk away if he had to, whatever his reasons at that time were.

They looked at each other for a few seconds and she took a deep breath. One way or another things were about to change, and she mentally prepared herself for when the ground shifted. “I’m leaving you,” he announced with the sort of tone other men said ‘I’m just nipping to the pub’.

It was a statement, not an invitation to have a discussion and there was no indication that anything she could say would change his mind. Will was not the sort of man who said things on the spur of the moment. She knew he would have sat and thought about this long and hard, would have weighed up the potential implications, the financial cost of a divorce and would have finally come to a cold and calculated decision.

Something had clearly happened that meant Jenna was now officially surplus to requirements. It amazed her how little she cared. In fact, there was an utter sense of relief. She was going to be freed from all her obligations, she wouldn’t have to play the part of the devoted, yet utterly neglected wife. In many ways, she would finally get her life back and have the chance to be her. Or the new version of her that motherhood would no doubt create.

Again, she wondered if she should tell him about Sarah, but she worried he’d change his mind. That knowing they would be able to raise their baby, together, would be enough for him to stay with her. It wasn’t a risk she was prepared to take now she was so close to freedom. Now she realised that she was desperate for the freedom she’d always feared he’d give her.

"Are you not going to ask why?" he queried, confused by her current lack of response. He had anticipated her screaming at him, demanding some form of explanation, perhaps even throwing things. Pregnant women were prone to fits of emotion, Jenna certainly had form back in the earlier days of their marriage, and has a result he had removed all sharp objects on display to be on the safe side.

Instead, she gave him what he felt was a pitying look and simply said, "You have your reasons, I'm quite sure they are none of my concern. When are you going?".

This was not what he expected at all. Of all the possible ways he'd played this conversation out in his head he'd not planned for her to be reasonable. He wasn't sure if reasonable was actually the right word, she seemed switched off, on automatic pilot, almost as though she didn't care what his reasons were.

Maybe she wasn't grasping the seriousness of the situation. For one awful moment he thought she might have misunderstood his words to mean he was going away for a few days. He decided to clear things up and give her the explanation she hadn't asked for.

"I've been seeing someone, for a while now actually and I think it's time I stopped living two lives. It's not fair to you, it's not fair to her and frankly I just don't have the energy for it anymore."

There, he had done it. He'd told her what she would need to know to make it clear what his intentions were, and why there was no point in trying to talk him out of it.

He didn't want to crush her, that would never be his plan, but he didn't want her to think there was any hope for them. That somehow, she could persuade him to stay out of pity for the poor pregnant lady he had once loved.

Jenna stood up and straightened her dress. "Well, it's about time I suppose. Adrienne does deserve better, and I'm sure now you are able to give her your full attention your relationship will flourish. I honestly wish you both all the best, but if you can excuse me, I would like to grab a quick shower before I meet Martina and Erika at The Boat House. Apparently, Cordelia is in fits about her 50th Birthday party, and we're staging some kind of intervention."

She took a second to push her stool back in and then walked calmly out of the room, leaving Will with no alternative but to stare after her with his mouth open. She smiled to herself as she went upstairs. The silly buffoon, he had genuinely thought she'd no idea, that somehow this revelation was going to come as a shock to her and shake her to her very core.

That was the problem with men like Will, they were so concerned with their own view of the world, so proud of their mini victories and constantly congratulating themselves on their innate superiority that they failed to see the people around them already had all the knowledge they hoped to shield them from.

Of course she had known, just like she had known about all the other flings and dalliances he had occupied himself with over the years. It had taken her a while to realise there was something different about Adrienne though, that she was potential mistress material rather than just a bit of fluff he liked to take out and spoil every now and again. As loyal as Alice was to Will, she was equally as loyal to Jenna. Women talked.

Over a short period of time Adrienne had become a regular companion for him, even curbing his desires for other women. Until the temp last summer that is, though she was nothing more than a minor blip on his radar. Jenna found herself wondering if Adrienne knew about the temp, and whether she would be hurt if she ever found out. However, that was not her problem, and Adrienne would either ultimately be oblivious to Will's wandering ways, or she would have to find her own method of dealing with them.

She sighed, almost feeling sorry for the younger woman she'd never met. It was one thing Jenna being able to take all of this in her stride, she knew Will. She had essentially grown up with him, seen him develop and become the man he was today, while Adrienne believed she had landed the perfect finished article.

Over the last 25 years of marriage there was nothing Will could do that would surprise her. Actually, that wasn't true. His behaviour on holiday had taken her off guard, she couldn't have predicted that in a million years.

Now it made even less sense the way he'd behaved when he found out she was pregnant. He had genuinely seemed to want to stand by her side, and for a moment she'd dared to believe that he may have ended things with Adrienne. She didn't for one second believe that would be the end to his philandering, but merely the end of actual romantic entanglements that could pose a threat to their married life.

She could only assume that the problems with the clinic and the knowledge that things were going to be more complex than they'd originally hoped had caused him to rethink his plans, and had sent him back in to Adrienne's arms.

She stripped off, turned on the shower and stepped inside, letting the hot water wash away her troubles.

CHAPTER 25

Sarah pulled her car on to the driveway and was immediately impressed by the house sitting in front of her. It was exactly how she imagined Jenna's home would look, a Georgian property with columns flanking the grand front door and ivy creeping over the exterior. It gave the perfect image of countrification, whilst still being so close to the city.

Turning off the engine, she stepped out of her car which looked battered and pathetic next to the immaculate silver Audi already in situ. By the time she reached the door Jenna was already there to greet her, and gave her a big hug. "Welcome," she said as she invited her in and pointed her in the direction of the kitchen immediately to her left.

The visitor couldn't help an audible "Wow" escaping her lips as she took in the kitchen. It was easily the size of the entire downstairs of her and Pete's pokey two-up two-down. Putting her bag on the marble worktop, Sarah was in awe at everything she saw, and desperately hoped she'd be given the guided tour before she had to leave.

As Jenna pottered around finishing off making a pot of tea and placing some Mr. Kipling's on a china plate, Sarah got comfortable on one of the high stools at the breakfast bar. "This place is just amazing," she said, at last. Jenna smiled awkwardly, she loved her home, but she was always uncomfortable when she had visitors.

Her friends from the club would often try to find faults with her décor or the general upkeep. It was a game they all seemed to play with each other, but one Jenna never really understood the rules for. However, those who did not fit in her wealthy circle of friends would ultimately be jealous of what she had achieved. She never felt as though she could find someone she could just be comfortable with. People always had an expectation, and she had to play her role suitably.

Jenna pulled up a seat so she could join her guest, and offered her the cake laden plate. "How are you?" she asked, as Sarah helped herself to an almond slice. In between mouthfuls Sarah launched in to a tirade against Pete, and more specifically her mother-in-law.

"No matter what I do, it's not good enough. But then, she's always been like that, it's just this pregnancy has made her even worse. Which I swear Jen, I just didn't think was possible."

After 30 minutes had passed and Jenna had made another cup of tea, Sarah was still talking at her, reliving a diabolical trip to the baby store and an argument over a tulle bassinet.

"Honestly Jenna, you'd love it; translucent, three-dimensional French lace with accents of satin charmeuse. I favour the fluted dome, but Pete said as it was over six foot we'd need planning permission to put it up! Honestly, he is such a philistine, it breaks my heart."

The older woman found herself nodding along, struggling to think of anything to reply with, and thankful she was unable to get a word in edgeways regardless. Part of her wanted to shake Sarah, in the hopes it would bang some sense to her, but she controlled herself. She found it hard to believe Sarah was capable of thinking an argument over nursery furniture took precedence over everything else that was going on in their lives.

Finally, Sarah stopped, picked up another cake slice and asked what was going on with Jenna. Now it was finally her turn, she wasn't sure what to say. There was a huge part of her that just wanted to pretend everything was completely alright; and the other part of her strongly believed that maybe it genuinely was.

"Will's moved out", she found herself saying matter of factly. Sarah's face was a picture, utter shock with a hint of terror.

"Oh my God," Sarah exclaimed, "what happened?".

Jenna realised it was customary for people in this situation to say it was complicated, and wave their hand airily, trying to dismiss a difficult conversation. The reality however was that nothing could be simpler. Will had needs, for a long time he'd decided Jenna hadn't been able to meet them, so he'd found someone else who could.

"I'd known for a long time," she admitted. "Wives are never quite as clueless as men seem to think they are. Rightly or wrongly, I decided to let it go. Adrienne seemed to make him happy, but for whatever reason, hadn't been able to take him away. He'd decided to be unfaithful, but he'd wanted to stay married."

As she said the words Jenna couldn't decide if she came across as understanding, or a complete idiot. Why did it not bother her more that her husband wanted to be with someone else, but wanted to still have her, too? Should she have had more self-respect and demanded he choose her, and only her? That's what their vows had implied he'd do. That's what a married man should do.

She always told herself that she cared, that she loved Will deeply, and therefore didn't want to push him to making a decision, which ultimately might not be in her favour. Now though, she wondered if she just got herself in to such a rut, and didn't think she deserved any better. Perhaps she only stayed because of the baby, or the idea of a baby. If they'd separated, or divorced, would he have allowed her to carry on with the IVF?

Of course, she'd never know the answer, though she could guess. If he'd walked out, whether voluntarily or pushed, her chances of motherhood would have gone with him. Yes, there might have been other options available to her, but time was not necessarily on her side, and she'd never liked the idea of having to start all over again with the process.

Sarah sat open mouthed for a moment, trying to take it all in. Jenna could see she was processing the knock-on effects, and was wondering what would happen about the babies.

"I never got the chance to talk to him about you", Jenna said. "As soon as I came home from seeing you, he announced he was off. We've not spoken much since, and mainly through our lawyers, but he's made it clear he has no interest in this baby." As she spoke she placed her hands on her stomach.

It was true, Will had no interest in what Jenna did with this pregnancy. If she wanted to keep the baby, that was her decision, and had nothing to do with him. He didn't want to have a conversation with her about the clinic, and had even said if she wanted to pursue compensation he'd leave it entirely to her, and she could keep everything she won. It was her loss, not his.

Deep down she knew she should talk to him about Sarah, and the fact their biological baby was going to be a part of their lives, but she couldn't bring herself to. Something had fundamentally changed in him, and he'd decided to shut down on her. The truth was she didn't have the energy to force him to have a conversation about something that should have been important to him. If he didn't care, she didn't want to try to persuade him to.

“I haven’t spoken to Pete, either” Sarah offered. She didn’t have the same barriers as Jenna did, but for some reason it still seemed like an impossible conversation to broach with him. Things still weren’t good between them, although he seemed to have ended the outright hostility that had been present for some time.

There was a part of her that wanted to tell him, that knew it would make things easier if he knew everything was going to be OK, that she’d found a solution without his help. The other part of her was terrified how he’d react when he found out she’d been talking to the woman carrying their baby for weeks, and hadn’t once thought to mention it to him.

Jenna couldn’t pretend to understand what Sarah’s reluctance was to discuss things with her husband, but she was determined not to judge her. She must have her reasons, and obviously she knew her husband better than anyone else. No doubt it would all work out OK in the end.

“I have to ask”, Sarah said at last, “does this change anything for you? I mean, you being alone now?” There was a part of her that hated herself for even thinking it would change anything, but she had to be sure. She had to ask the question, and she hoped Jenna would understand. Thankfully, the look on her face said that she did.

“Of course not,” Jenna replied with a smile. “The truth is Sarah, I’ve always been on my own with this.

It's now just going to be obvious, rather than hidden behind closed doors."

*****

After a pleasant evening watching box sets and snuggling up on the sofa, Sarah and Pete decided to go to bed. As he made his way upstairs he tried to remember the last time he'd enjoyed being in her company quite so much. For the first time in ages they'd laughed, they'd joked with each other and they'd just had fun. It was so nice not to be embroiled in conversations about pregnancies, babies, nurseries or what school would be best.

Sarah had equally enjoyed the night, and already decided if he tried to pester her for sex, she probably wouldn't turn him down. With everything he'd done for her, she felt she owed him a little bit of a reward. She realised it probably hadn't been easy living with her for these last few weeks, but he'd been really quite supportive recently and she did genuinely appreciate it.

As usual Pete did the rounds, making sure all the windows were closed. By the time he was finished in the bathroom, she was already lying in bed, staring up at the ceiling with a look of puzzlement on her face.

"What's on your mind?" he asked as he climbed in next to her.

"Oh nothing," she replied. He recognised the tone in her voice, and had been married to her for too long to accept that "nothing" was the genuine answer. There was something, but whether or not she wanted to talk about it here and now was another matter. He knew better than to press her, he wasn't sure he wanted to get in to a big saga now, not when he'd finally felt talking to her didn't need to start World War Three.

He gave her a peck on the cheek, told her he loved and rolled over, anxious to get to sleep as he had another early start in the morning. These plans Sarah had for the nursery all cost more money than he'd ever imagined, which meant he was having to step up his game when it came to booking in jobs.

No sooner had he closed his eyes and started to relax than he felt her sit up next to him. There was a short pause and then she nudged him. "It's just, something Jenna said made me think, and it's been bothering me ever since."

Sighing, Pete pushed himself back to a sitting position, and got himself comfortable against the padded headboard. He had no idea who Jenna was, and had little doubt this was going to be the most pointless and confusing conversation ever.

However, he also knew if he didn't show willing Sarah would never relent, and what could be dealt with in five minutes, would actually turn in to a full-blown argument that would see him spending the rest of the night on the sofa.

"What did Jenna say?" he asked, hoping he sounded suitably curious to not arouse her displeasure. Immediately Sarah wriggled herself up to sit next to him, "Well," she started, "she was telling me how Will had left her for his mistress, and it turns out that the mistress is actually called Adrienne. And I just thought that was a bit odd, given it's the same name as Dr. Harper, and it's not exactly all that common a name. I mean, how many Adrienne's are there in the area?"

Pete wasn't sure if he was meant to give an answer to that question. Surrey was actually quite large in terms of population, and whilst he didn't know for certain how popular the name Adrienne was, he was sure more than one person had it.

Besides, he wasn't convinced Dr. Harper lived in Surrey. The clinic was in the middle of London, so it was quite plausible she actually lived in Bexley or Enfield or Ealing. Hell, she could bloody live anywhere!

Unable to give a definitive answer he simply shrugged, which Sarah took as enough encouragement to carry on. "Just what if it's the same Adrienne? Maybe Jenna doesn't know, and if it is the same woman then, well that complicates things a lot doesn't it?"

Not for the first time in recent weeks Pete felt as though he was coming in half way through the conversation, and needed to be caught up. "Who the Hell is Jenna and what does it have to do with our doctor?" he asked, hoping the explanation would be simple so he could still manage a relatively early night.

Sarah was silent. In the excitement of trying to solve the mystery as she saw it, she'd jumped in to this conversation without thinking it through. Now he'd asked the question she immediately regretted it, and started to panic. How on earth could she explain who Jenna was without actually explaining who she was?

Unable to think of a suitable answer immediately she cried pregnancy, and ran off to the en suite under the pretence of needing a wee. Despite managing to buy herself a few minutes she was no closer to having a solution by the time she got back in to bed, and it was clear Pete was not in the mood to drop it.

"Sarah, answer me" he tried again with a determined tone to his voice. "Who is Jenna?"

*****

Ten minutes later Pete was dressed. He stormed out the room and started collecting his things from the bathroom whilst she followed hot on his heels. "I'm sorry," she called as she walked behind him.

"I wanted to tell you, but I just couldn't find the right time, and then I met her and we got talking, and she really is very lovely Pete. Such a sad story, she's been trying for years and…". He walked back in to the bedroom and slammed the door in her face, cutting her off mid-sentence.

Undeterred she opened the door and leant against the door jam, ensuring he couldn't shut it again. "Please, let me explain," she begged. He turned around and glared at her, a look on his face she'd never seen before. Pete didn't get angry, so she wasn't sure how to handle him when he was like this. She rummaged around for the right thing to say, but he beat her to it.

"Explain? Explain?" He shouted, his face inches from hers. "What on earth is there for you to explain? You somehow got in touch with this woman, met up with her and decided our fate, all without bothering to consult me. You've had me labouring under the impression we're going to raise this unknown baby, because we had no alternative; when in fact you already had everything planned out and sorted. I'm fed up of it Sarah. I'm fed up of you thinking you're the one in control and no one else matters. To Hell with you and your stupid baby!"

She felt routed to the spot, physically unable to move, as though his words had winded her and she was struggling for breath. He reached on top of the wardrobe and pulled a hold-all down and threw it on the bed. He then moved round to the large chest of drawers on the other side of the room and started grabbing handfuls of underwear.

"What are you doing?" she asked, panicked. He didn't look up, but carried on grabbing items from his side of the bed. "What does it look like I'm doing?", a bitter tone now invading his voice.

When he'd filled the bag with shirts, trousers and clean overalls he picked it up and walked towards her. For a moment she contemplated blocking his way, refusing to allow him to pass until they had the chance to talk things through properly, but the look in his eye deterred her. The way he was behaving in this instant she wasn’t sure what he was capable of doing, so she stepped to one side.

As he made his way down the stairs he called out, “I’ll be at Ma’s. I don’t know how long for.”

And with that, he was gone.

CHAPTER 26

Pete lay on his back, staring at the ceiling, trying to organise his thoughts, and his life. It was a struggle at the best of times, but he found it even harder cramped in to his boyhood single bed, complete with Batman cover. It had been late when he'd arrived at his Ma's the previous night, but she'd been awake, having her last cigarette of the day when he'd knocked gently on her door. They'd barely spoken, she just gave him a reassuring hug, and let him disappear up the stairs without the need for explanation.

He was the first to admit his Ma wasn't always the easiest of people to be around, she had a head full of opinions and absolutely no filter, which either made her seem exceptionally wise or bigoted, depending on the topic of conversation. One of her greatest strengths though was knowing when it wasn't time to talk. She could be practical when needed, and right now, that's precisely what he wanted from her.

The way he'd behaved with Sarah had been a knee-jerk reaction to finding out she'd gone behind his back. He was genuinely hurt that she'd kept something so important from him, and he couldn't begin to understand it. Was she that scared of him that she honestly felt she couldn't approach him about this? People were always remarking how understanding and patient he was, especially when it came to Sarah, so it made no sense to him at all that she would be nervous.

He could accept things hadn't been perfect of late, but a large part of that had been her doing, not his. Maybe he could have been calmer and more supportive after they got the bad news at the clinic, but he had tried, and things had been better of late. There was absolutely no reason for her to keep something this monumental from him. For weeks he'd been struggling to come to terms with the realisation that his biological baby could be …

Well, that was the problem, to be honest. It could be anything. The woman could have miscarried, or chosen to terminate. She might have felt the same as him, that there was something unpalatable about bringing another couple's baby in to the world and raising it as your own. The thought had upset him, and he didn't like to dwell on it, but the alternative had seemed so much worse. One day he could be at a school event, or in the supermarket, and his child could be standing next to him, and he'd never know. Or would he?

Would there be a fleeting moment of recognition, as this stranger's child ran past him, or begged and pleaded for a chocolate bar in the checkout queue? He couldn't imagine how that moment would feel, and he worried he'd always be on tenterhooks, panicking that it could be just around the corner. He'd never know either way, whether it was a possibility or something he didn't even need to worry about.

That was the real problem, the entire uncertainty of it all, and he'd found it impossible to balance everything in his head. It was an utter head fuck, he despised Sarah for her fundamental inability to see things from his point of view.

To think that Sarah hadn't thought it was worth telling him, talking it through with him, and trying to alleviate some of the agony she'd managed to save herself from, pained him more than anything. He would have done anything for her, Hell, he had done everything she'd ever asked of him, yet she didn't feel he was worth a conversation and a touch of honesty.

For the first time, as he continued staring at the same patch of flaking plaster above him, he wondered if his marriage might be over.

*****

Adrienne rolled over and spooned up behind Coop, enjoying the simple pleasure of him being next to her every morning. She closed her eyes, and was asleep again within minutes. He, on the other hand, lay as still as possible, trying to take shallow breaths for fear of waking her again.

It had been three weeks since he'd walked out on his old life, and more importantly, away from Jenna. He wasn't at the point where he could say he regretted it, but he was rapidly realising things weren't quite as amazing as he'd expected them to be in the new life he'd chosen for himself.

Living in Adrienne's apartment was the biggest issue. He was so used to having space, and all the luxuries money could buy. Although Adrienne didn't do badly for herself financially, she seemed to view the purchase of coffee machines, or quality bed linen as an extravagance. Whilst many would regard her home as perfectly acceptable, he firmly believed that by living with her he was slumming it. She lived far too comfortably within her means.

He'd already suggested, more than once, that they move to a hotel until they could find something more permanent for their growing family. Adrienne, however, wasn't keen on the idea. She didn't want someone coming in and cleaning around her every morning, or spending weeks living out of suitcases. Not when they already had somewhere perfectly suitable at their disposal.

Unfortunately, their definition of what 'suitable' meant wasn't the only issue. After two years together, he'd assumed how they had been with each other was how they actually were. However, it hadn't taken long to realise that in reality, both of them had been on their best behaviour as they shared space for limited periods of time. Living together was definitely a whole new level, and had revealed some flaws in their compatibility.

Underneath her professional exterior and the aura of control and calm, Adrienne was actually a slob. She left dirty clothes strewn across the floor, thought nothing of rinsing a cup or item of cutlery quickly under a cold tap before reusing it, and dropped food crumbs around the flat with such efficiency he swore she was Gretel in a previous life.

Her slovenly ways actually made his skin crawl, and he longed for his pristine home which Jenna lovingly tidied in preparation for the twice weekly visits from the cleaner. It was clear now precisely how much he'd taken for granted, and it wasn't just the creature comforts and higher quality living conditions.

After a bad day at the office, Jenna always knew what to do. Without him having to say anything she had always known what he needed. Sometimes she'd probe gently and find out what had happened, other times she would quietly hand him a glass of his favourite Scotch, and leave him to it. Adrienne, on the other hand, badgered him, determined to know everything she could about his life now it was officially linked to hers, despite his requests for her to leave him alone.

He felt stifled. That was it. It seemed ridiculous that he should feel trapped by a situation he chose for himself, but that was the reality, and as he lay there pretending to be asleep, he desperately started looking for a way out.

*****

Sarah had been awake for hours, unable to sleep without Pete by her side. She'd lain there for a while, trying to doze off after she'd eventually stopped sobbing, but had given up at 3am and gone in search of solace via the fridge. A plate of cheesecake and three cups of tea later, she was still emotionally drained, and now felt a little queasy.

All night she'd been trying to work out what Pete was going to do next. The look on his face made her think he was entirely capable of anything. She no longer believed he wouldn't leave her, that there was no way he'd file for divorce. However, there was still a part of her that prayed he wouldn't.

She didn't want to trivialise anything, but what she'd done wasn't that bad in the overall scheme of things. It's not like she'd had an affair with his best friend, or something. All she'd done was handled a very delicate situation a bit badly. Given the circumstances she didn't think it was entirely fair to assume she could have done better. Equally, she had the added handicap of having to deal with pregnancy hormones, which meant thinking straight was even harder than usual.

No, there was no way Pete would leave, let alone divorce, his pregnant wife. He knew that would be a scandal amongst their friends, and he wouldn't want them to be the talk of the town. He'd need a few days to have a sulk, but eventually he'd see sense and come back to her. She'd apologise, of course, and admit she'd been in the wrong, but only about not telling him sooner. She should have done that, but she wasn't sorry for getting in touch with Jenna in the first place.

If she hadn't done that, if they hadn't started talking and built a relationship with each other, she was adamant that there would have been no good outcome to this horrible situation.

The clinic weren't going to do anything to help them, instead they were too busy covering their own asses, and hiding behind what the law did and didn't allow them to do. No, this was the only chance they had of getting their own baby at the end of the whole nightmare, and as far as she was concerned, that was worth Pete having his feelings hurt for a while. She clung to that hope desperately, knowing that now, hope was all she had left.

CHAPTER 27

Since the day she found out about Coop being married, no day had started well for Adrienne. There was that briefest moment, the gap between sleep and being completely awake, where she was safe. When she could roll over, wrap her arms around him, and feel everything was going to be OK. However, it never lasted for long, and by the time her brain had fully woken up, she was again left whirling everything around in her mind as the feeling of anxiety increased.

Every night she went to bed hopeful of getting more than two hours consecutive sleep, and praying that tomorrow would be better. It never was. Today certainly hadn't been.

After the first few days of her 'mutually agreed' suspension she had found it harder and harder to impose any form of routine. Mutually agreed, the idea made her laugh. The reality was Greg had insisted on it, and although she had understood that it made sense, she also thought she'd be better off at work, doing what she did best, and carrying on with her normal patients. Mutual wasn't precisely the word she would have used.

In fact, the more she thought about it, the more annoyed she was. At first she'd been given a couple of days off, then she'd been allowed to return and it had been business as usual. The investigation was ongoing, but she was allowed to see new and existing clients.

Then one day that had changed. They'd decided she would be better off being absent. At first she'd just accepted it, but the more she thought about it, and she had very little else to think about during those long, boring days, the more unfair it seemed.

The reality was she was no more to blame than Greg was, yet he'd been allowed to stay on. He was a partner, of course, so he had more sway. She'd tried talking to Coop about it, but he wasn't great at listening. Her problems with the clinic were too tied up with his issues with Jenna, and he had no interest in them at all. He wanted to forget about the whole thing, and simply suggested she enjoy the time off, especially at this stage of her pregnancy. It was easier said than done.

Each day she'd get up, and wander aimlessly around the apartment, thinking about all the things she should be doing, but somehow unable to summon any motivation to get on with things. By the end of the first week she'd stopped showering or getting dressed, and spent all her time in the same pair of pyjamas. Everything suddenly seemed like too much effort.

Of course, there were times when she pushed herself beyond her comfort zone, and forced herself to remember that there was an entire world going on out there, whether she wanted to be a part of it or not. She'd gone shopping, well, ordered online, and she'd made meals for Coop, hoping it would please him. It didn't. Nothing ever seemed to be good enough, no matter how much effort she put in to it.

Today though, she'd been forced to kick herself up the backside and get out properly in to the real world. Greg had called and asked her to come in to the clinic as soon as possible. He didn't offer any explanation, just simply that he needed to speak to her urgently, and face to face.

She knew it wasn't going to be good, but she had no way of preparing herself for how bad it actually was. When she arrived at the clinic, Kate pretended to be busy with some files, and refused to make eye contact with her. Instead of hanging around, soaking up the icy atmosphere, Adrienne went straight to her office, and within seconds Evelyn poked her head around the door and demanded she come in to the staff room.

Greg was already waiting, with a pile of papers in front of him and a man she didn't recognise. Just thinking about it now, fresh tears welled in her eyes, and she reached for the box of tissues on the coffee table in front of her. It was impossible to understand how she'd found herself in this situation, when just a few short weeks ago everything had been perfect.

Her job was going well, she felt certain Greg and Evelyn would take her on as a partner within the next few months, so her career and financial future were sorted. Things might not have been perfect with Coop, but the only problems she thought they'd had was not being able to spend enough time together. How wrong she'd been.

Now, of course, everything had fallen to pieces, and she was left with nothing. The last shred of hope she'd been clinging to that things would be OK, given time, was taken away from her today when Greg made it clear the clinic wanted to wash its hands of her, with immediate effect.

She had no idea how he could know everything, but it was obvious someone had said something to him. He knew about her relationship with Coop, the fact she'd found out on that fateful day he was married, and that's what led to the alleged error in the lab.

Alleged.

That word had hung in the silence between them, whilst the clinic's lawyer started pulling out a non-disclosure agreement for her to sign.

Alleged? There was nothing alleged about the error. It was precisely that, nothing more, nothing less. Something that shouldn't have happened, and wouldn't have happened if her mind had been entirely where it was needed. Alleged? To suggest that there was any attempt at malice, or even conscious thought about what happened, really insulted her.

It had been a total accident. Hadn't it?

Adrienne knew that under the circumstances she might not have been painted in the most flattering and professional of lights, but she was not a vindictive woman. The thought that anyone could suggest she was capable of causing all of this on purpose hurt more than the reality that her career was entirely over.

Now, as she sat alone in her flat, she wondered how on earth she was going to explain her current situation to Coop, who could be home at any moment.

A fresh wave of sobs caught in her throat as she reminded herself that her career had always been everything to her, and now she'd managed to throw it all away, purely because of a man. She felt so utterly exhausted.

Whilst it had been a long and emotionally draining day, she knew she felt like this mainly because of the pregnancy. Although the morning sickness was making her feel terrible physically, and that was taking its toll on her, she'd realised that her biggest problem with getting through each day was the fact this pregnancy hadn't been planned.

If it hadn't been for her strong desire not to be one of those women who aborted the results of their lax birth control methods, she wouldn't be sitting here feeling like this right now. She honestly didn't feel she had much choice but to go ahead with the pregnancy, and as a result almost felt as though it wasn't something she had actually chosen. It was the default option, rather than the desired one.

She remained convinced that once the baby was actually here, she'd feel better; that she'd just adapt to the role of mother without too much of a fuss. Now was where the problem lay. She had no bond with her non-existent bump, and no real interest in anything to do with the pregnancy. She found herself wondering if there was such a thing as pre-natal depression. Maybe that was something she could start researching tomorrow, she thought. She certainly had plenty of spare time on her hands now.

It hit her again, another wave of pain. She'd lost her job. There was no discussion, no debate, not alternative options. Greg and Eleanor had decided she was surplus to requirements, that the best thing they could do for their practice was to cut ties with her. Without her involved they could make a good case for common negligence. They wouldn't have to go in to the finer details involving her, or Coop or Jenna. They had plausible deniability, without her.

She sighed, fully acknowledging the feeling of depression that had settled over her. She felt entirely trapped and had no idea what to do. Once Coop had decided he was going to leave Jenna he'd acted very quickly. She was still amazed he'd kept to his word. She'd half expected him to go home to break the news, and then chicken out, feeling sorry for the woman standing in front of him.

He hadn't talked about what happened, but simply phoned her that evening to say it was sorted and he would be contacting his lawyer first thing in the morning to start divorce proceedings.

Now they were together, spending every night making small talk over her home cooked meals. Or at least they did when she could be bothered to cook.

Most nights she just heated something in the microwave, or forced him to order in.

A huge part of her wanted to deny it, but things had definitely changed between them. She wasn't sure if it was just the pregnancy and the fact that he perhaps found her less attractive, or that she was too tired to perform bedroom acrobatics the way she once had, but his attentions had definitely cooled. On some levels she wanted to ask him what was wrong, wanted to tease it out of him, but she was scared that once prodded, he would admit he had made a terrible mistake.

There was no way she could handle that level of honesty, so she kept her mouth shut in the hopes he would too. She'd already lost count of the times he'd told her "Jenna doesn't do it like that", or "Jenna would have known how to handle that". To date she had never reacted, instead saving her tears and frustrations for when she was alone, which was becoming more and more often.

She was convinced Jenna wouldn't have cried and being told that would have sent her over the edge. More and more often she wondered why on earth he had embarked on an affair in the first place, if Jenna was as perfect as he made her out to be.

One day she might pluck up the courage to ask, but it wasn't going to be any time soon.

PART THREE

"The moment a child is born, the mother is also born. She never existed before. The woman existed, but the mother, never. A mother is something absolutely new."

- Rajneesh

CHAPTER 28

Sarah and Pete sat at separate ends of the couch, not looking at each other and deliberately not touching. It had been nearly five months since he'd gone to stay with his Ma, and Sarah was starting to wonder if he was ever going to make it back to their home.

Dr. Bevan crossed her legs and looked at them expectantly, "This is your fifth session and I'll be honest, we're not making as much progress as I would have liked by this stage. Neither of you are really opening up about how you feel, and I think that's a mistake. These sessions are your chance to say what you feel, in a safe and neutral environment, you should use them as such."

Pete looked down at his folded hands in his lap and let out a little laugh. Sarah turned to look at him quickly and Dr. Bevan leaned forwards, eager to encourage him to speak his mind. "Pete," she said, "I understand it was you who wanted the opportunity to talk today, so please, say what's on your mind."

Sarah turned her body towards him, waiting expectantly for him to start speaking; however, she was met with silence. "Honestly Pete, you are so infuriating!" she said with pure venom in her voice. You drag me down here and then we sit in silence. We could do that anywhere for free, and yet you accuse me of wasting money!"

Dr. Bevan was on the verge of asking her to refrain from accusatory and threatening language, but it seemed on this occasion it was goading Pete in to responding. He lifted his head up, shifted in his seat and began talking.

"Forgive me if after years of being together the idea I have the right to speak, and that you will actually listen to a bloody word I say, is a little novel." He paused, "To be honest, it's hard to know what to say. I don't know where to begin. My head hurts."

Dr. Bevan nodded, "That's a good start Pete. What's troubling you the most? We could always start there." Pete thought for a moment, it was hard to say precisely what bothered him most about the whole situation. The fact was, he didn't know anymore. Not that long ago the only problem had been Sarah trying to get pregnant. It had been a long and hard journey, finances aside it had taken an emotional toll.

Then of course she did get pregnant, and for the briefest of moments he felt relieved. The kind of relief that hits you all of a sudden and makes you realise just how stressed you were in the first place. It was the relief that said it was over, that it had worked, that they could just move on to the next stage of their lives. That's all he wanted, to put the IVF journey behind them.

He had always thought the pregnancy would be the easy bit; well, maybe not easy, pregnant women weren't easy to be around, but easier than what he had already been through. For the briefest of moments, he'd started looking forward to being a father, rather than just a sperm donor.

Hearing that things weren't going to be as simple as he'd hoped had of course hit him hard. He knew it had hit Sarah hard too, but the problem was they didn't deal with it together. She completely closed down and didn't want to talk. In retrospect, perhaps he pushed his own agenda too hard, and forced her to shut down on him. In some respects, he couldn't really blame her for that, but it made it impossible to deal with things properly, or at least as a married couple should.

"I feel alone", he ventured. "Sarah has been on this journey for so long, trying to achieve what she wants, and I've just been tagging along. It's not been my journey, not really. Then to find out the baby she's carrying isn't ours, that was just an impossible thing to handle, but again, I've had to handle it on my own. She just hasn't wanted to talk about it. I feel completely shut out and like my opinion doesn't even matter."

Dr. Bevan scribbled something on her notepad then turned to Sarah for her input. "I don't think that's fair, we've done all of this together. He agreed to the IVF, he was at every appointment, he helped with the injections. This *has* been our journey. As for the baby, well I tried to talk but he lost his temper and walked out. I really don't see how this is any of my fault at all."

It was true, she didn't understand how he could be so callous and needy about the whole thing. She was going through this, it was her body that was growing a whole new human being, she needed support and love and he couldn't grow up enough to be able to give it to her. Besides, she had tried her hardest to make the situation as easy as possible, reaching out to Jenna and trying to come up with a plan that would suit everyone.

In fairness, it was a good plan and one that ultimately would cause him very little distress. All he had to do was support his wife through pregnancy, which he would have had to do if the baby she was carrying was theirs anyway, and then hold her hand whilst she delivered. OK, so the baby they went home with wouldn't be the same one they met at the end of labour, but that was a small detail she believed he should have been able to get his head round. No matter when she chose to tell him about it.

Pete was struggling to hold his temper, something he was finding increasingly difficult when it came to Sarah. He had always been very calm and collected when it came to her whims and occasionally crazy ramblings. Over the years he'd found ways to deal with her, and for the largest part managed to shrug off anything crazy or insensitive she had to say. Now he felt like he no longer had the energy for it.

"The way I see it," he said at last, "is Sarah believes because this is her body she is the only one going through this. I understand how it must be hard for her, and she ultimately has the say in what she does with her body, but she needs to accept that this is my life too. She keeps making decisions on her own, and pretending to be hurt when I don't react the way she expects me to."

Sarah pulled a face that indicated she felt Pete was being unduly harsh and unfair, yet again. This whole process was ridiculous, they were never going to agree on anything and she didn't know how to push things forward.

The reality was if they couldn't get past this then there was every chance they were going to have to get a divorce, and she couldn't bear the thought of that. She didn't understand people walking away from their relationships at the best of times, but it was unforgiveable in her mind when there were children were involved.

"I think Pete fails to understand that at the end of all this there is going to be a baby. Our baby. I know it's unconventional the way it will be joining our family, but the fact is it will be ours in the end and he is going to be a father. He needs to understand that."

Sarah didn't want to keep bashing him over the head with the same point, but it was important. There were only eight weeks to go before her and Jenna's due dates, realistically their babies could be here in as little as five. The time for coming around to the idea and getting on board was rapidly dwindling, and he needed a good kick up the backside as far as she was concerned.

Pete shifted to the edge of the sofa and leant his arms on his knees, exasperation showing on his face. “I get that biologically we are going to have a baby at the end of this, despite what you think I’m not some stupid plumber that can’t figure basic shit out Sarah! The point is that this entire thing has been about you, not us, and I’m struggling to understand how I can move forward and raise a child with you. I don’t trust you to include me in our child’s life, to allow me to have a say and be a part of its upbringing. It’s like it’s The Sarah Show and I don’t see it ever changing.”

It was true, ever since they’d embarked on this journey she had been gradually moving away from the young girl he had fallen in love with. Every day she become more obsessed with getting pregnant, and now she was, she was impossible to talk to. Somehow she had turned in to this thing in front of him that he didn’t recognise, and was not sure he was in love with any more. He couldn’t say those precise words, but that was what he was thinking.

“Excellent, I feel we’ve made progress here today,” Dr. Bevan interjected, glancing at the clock on the wall. She closed the file on her lap and reached for her diary, a clear indication that the session for today was over. “I think we should aim for another session next week, how does Thursday at 2 sound for you both?”

Pete sighed. He knew he'd promised Sarah he would give everything he could to make these sessions work, and he had genuinely hoped they would help, but the more time went by the less convinced he was that they were having any impact. If anything, he was probably feeling less inclined to make their marriage work.

Talking about what had happened, and how he felt wasn't going to change the reality that he was constantly falling out of love with his wife. He despised what she had become and he was not convinced having a child was going to be enough to patch up the broken pieces. He was concerned that you'd always still see them there, like cracks in a tile that people were too cheap to get replaced.

"Yeah, sounds good to me", he found himself saying while Sarah just nodded along. He stood up, put on his coat and left without saying goodbye to Sarah. He just wanted to get back to work where the conversation was easier and nothing was expected of him that he couldn't easily deliver.

*****

Will was already sitting at his desk by the time Alice came in to the office at 8am. In all the time she'd worked for him, she'd never known him to be in before her, and it caught her off guard. She poked her head round the door and asked if there was anything she could get him.

He looked up, startled by the intrusion and gave her a smile, "A coffee would be nice", he ventured and with that, she disappeared. He returned his gaze to the pile of papers before him that he'd already been staring at for two hours, but still nothing was registering.

For the first time in his life he was unable to concentrate on work, purely because he felt so bloody miserable. He pushed the papers away and spun his chair round so he could face the full-sized window behind him. Staring out at the expanse of city lying below him, he picked out his favourite landmarks and tried to recall the underground stations lying between them. It helped him refocus.

Before long though, his mind drifted back to the real problem – home. Or, to be more, specific, Adrienne. The entire situation was infuriating, and he genuinely didn't know how to set everything right again.

For the first time in his life he felt he'd done the right thing by saying he would stand by her when she announced the pregnancy. He couldn't very well leave her to fend for herself when he had gotten her in to such a difficult predicament. Of course, if Jenna had been pregnant with their actual baby, then the outcome would have been entirely different, but she wasn't, so it didn't do to dwell on that.

He'd been so excited to be a father, which still amazed him after so many years of being ambivalent, at best. However, things weren't working out with

Adrienne how he had imagined, and for the first time in his life he realised that Jenna had provided him with more than he'd ever realised. Now, he felt as though he had no one to turn to. He knew Jenna wouldn't be interested in listening to his worries; in fact, as soon as he packed his bags she had refused to answer the phone to him, instead making him communicate via their lawyers.

It had been five months since Adrienne had been sacked, and since that time she'd totally shut down on him. For the first few days she wouldn't even leave their bed. It had taken him a week to persuade her to have a shower. In the end he'd physically dragged her and almost thrown her in to the cubicle with her pyjamas still on. The whole time she was under the water she refused to wash, and instead sat there sobbing hysterically. Finally, he'd had enough of listening to it and had left for the office before she had time to drip dry.

Nothing had turned out how he'd imagined, and it grated with him. The last few months hadn't proved any better, and he had long run out of patience for Adrienne's prolonged despondency. Now she was refusing to leave the apartment, wouldn't answer her phone, had cut off contact with all her friends and had wrapped herself in a cocoon of paranoia. He knew she was struggling to come to terms with the path her life had taken, but his sympathy had long worn out.

Jenna would never have behaved like this. She would have had the common sense to realise life went on, and no amount of moping and feeling sorry for herself would change that. It was then he realised how much he missed his wife, and potentially what a huge mistake he'd made. Now he found himself wondering how difficult it might be to get his old life back.

Remembering how Jenna had been so nonplussed by his confession regarding Adrienne, he was convinced there was very little his wife needed to forgive him for. Surely the fact that she hadn't over reacted at the time meant she had already come to terms with his behaviour, and therefore had forgiven him long ago? Yes, it might be hard for her to accept him back initially, her primary concern being what the members at The Club might say, but he knew cold hard logic and pragmatism would win her over in the end.

The biggest issue was what to do with Adrienne. While he had no doubt some people would automatically assume she was his responsibility, he most certainly did not feel the same way. She had entered in to all of this with her eyes wide open, and had made her own decisions as an adult. Sadly, things had not played out the way either of them had envisioned, but that was life, and the key to success was learning how to roll with the punches.

If she was unable to do that, then he couldn't force her, and he was most certainly not willing to wallow in self-pity alongside her, no matter what anyone else thought on the matter. He had tried to move on, tried to engage her with hopes for their future together with their child, but she had replied with a wail and had merely climbed back in to bed.

No, he had done everything he could to support and encourage her to accept her new life, and she had made her decision. Now, he had to do what was right by him, and he realised, in that moment, that Jenna was the answer to all of his problems. He would return home, forget about the whole sordid affair, and move on. That way he would be able to concentrate on work again and everything would return to normal.

He was confident if he assured her he was able to accept the baby she was carrying as his own, and raise it as such, then all would be well. The truth was, no one else need know what had happened, so he didn't need to worry about people talking behind their backs. Jenna was such an intensely private person that she would never have told any of their mutual friends about the IVF, or the problems that had caused them. It would just be assumed that this baby was theirs, and that would be the end of it.

So confident was he that he could handle Jenna, that the only thing that required his attention now was how to deal with Adrienne. The reality was that now he had emotionally distanced himself from her he believed he had no ties with her, other than the weight of expectation, and therefore he could just walk away. Not for the first time he wondered if he'd be able to file for custody of their unborn baby, his rightful heir, citing her as an unfit mother. It was all such a complicated mess!

He smiled as he thought how easy it would be to leave. He could simply pack his bags and move out without any financial responsibility. In fact, it would be the cleanest of breaks, and by the end of the week he anticipated being back in his own home and completely stress free. He acknowledged Jenna might need some reassurances from him to feel really confident in taking him back, but he was more than happy to provide those. This little foray in to an alternative life with Adrienne had taught him that the grass was most definitely not always greener. He didn't have the stomach for complicated personal relationships, and instead wanted the reliable and steady woman back by his side, where she had been for nearly three decades.

Adventure, excitement and sexy lingerie were one thing, but they wouldn't last forever, and they brought with them a whole level of complication he didn't desire. He was confident he'd be able to persuade Jenna he would remain faithful from now on, and dedicate himself to family life and all that entailed.

CHAPTER 29

Jenna slid in to her seat in the booth as gracefully as you could when you felt you were smuggling a beach ball under your top. Pregnancy suited her, and despite her fears that her aging body may not carry it well, she had experienced no real problems. Frequently she congratulated herself on having always maintained a healthy diet and strict exercise regime, she was sure it was making all the difference. In reality though, even if she had the worst pregnancy on record, she wouldn't have been able to complain. This was too hard fought for to whinge about backache or swollen ankles.

Sarah on the other hand wasn't fairing as well. As she looked across the table at her she could see puffiness had seeped in to every part of her body; she must have put on at least 16 pounds Jenna thought, horrified. No wonder she was struggling to get around and had developed the clichéd pregnancy waddle many weeks ago. Jenna felt mean for mocking her, even if it was just to herself. This separation with Pete had hit Sarah far harder than Jenna's own impending divorce had touched her.

Despite the fact the two women were both living the exact same experience, it was Sarah who the bad things happened to. It hadn't taken Jenna long to work out that Sarah was undoubtedly very high maintenance. If there was a symptom to be had, Sarah had it, and usually far worse than anyone else had ever experienced it.

"Counselling was a disaster, again", Sarah said as soon as she had settled herself properly. "I honestly don't know why we're bothering; he won't engage, and when he does he's just mean to me." Jenna listened patiently as Sarah recounted her visit that morning to the marriage counsellor, but already knew in essence what she was going to say.

The problem wasn't that Pete wouldn't talk, it was that Sarah wouldn't listen. Somehow over the years she had failed to develop the ability to turn her own thoughts, feelings and emotional responses off long enough to find out how someone else was experiencing something.

There were moments when Jenna wondered how she coped with Sarah, and whether she was going to be stuck with her for the rest of their lives. Would this experience mean they formed an inseparable bond that would stretch to the end of time? Did giving birth by accident to another person's child ingratiate you in to their lives forever? Would they both become 'aunty' and spend Christmas and school holidays together, marvelling at their unique and extended family set up?

Jenna couldn't help but think that after the dust settled they would probably go their own ways. They would both become so caught up in raising their own child, in the joys and perils of motherhood that anything else would be regarded as an unwelcome distraction.

She certainly found herself hoping that would be the case. She liked Sarah, had become attached to her on some levels, but everything was so complicated and the entire relationship was based on an extreme set of circumstances that no doubt meant it couldn't last longer term.

In reality though it probably was something they should talk about at some point, but there were so many other things they hadn't really touched on since their first meeting. Any time they had met or spoken on the phone their conversation was usually dominated by Sarah's dramas, which meant little time was left for anything else to be covered. Jenna reasoned there was only eight weeks left before these babies were likely to make an appearance, so it made sense that some of the more practical aspects of their future had to be forced in to the light.

"I saw Dr. Barker this morning," she ventured, stopping Sarah mid-rant about Pete. Sarah looked up, keen to hear the latest news on her unborn child. "Is everything OK?" she asked. Jenna nodded, "Yes, no problems, baby is fine, it was just a standard check-up; but he did suggest that we both come in for a consultation together." Sarah raised an eyebrow and failed to see why this would be necessary.

"From what I understand the clinic thinks it might be better for everyone if we were taken in to deliver at the same time", she continued. Sarah shook her head, "I don't want to be induced. I want everything to be natural. I've already written my birth plan. Besides, I want to be there when you give birth to my child."

Jenna sighed. No conversation was easy with this woman! "I understand that," Jenna said "but think about it for one minute, please. What happens if I go in to labour before you? It could be a couple of days, it could be a week or so, nobody knows. If that happens, who looks after your baby? Technically, legally, I'm the mother. I'd have given birth, so it would stay with me."

The scrunched up look on Sarah's face made Jenna immediately frustrated. "Sarah, we talked about this. Legally the woman who gives birth is recognised as the mother. There is nothing we can do about that! But I digress. If I deliver first that's goodness knows how many days where I am caring for your child. I want to breastfeed my baby when the time comes for him or her to be born, so do I breastfeed yours to ensure I have a milk supply?"

Sarah turned pale and was clearly uncomfortable with the conversation. Jenna felt guilty, she didn't want to have to pile it on high for her, but the fact was these were important issues that weren't just going to resolve themselves. They were things that should have been talked about weeks ago, but Sarah always clammed up and changed the subject back to her and Pete.

"I assumed you'd just hand her over when she was born," Sarah said like a sulky teenager.

Jenna nodded, "I could, but that doesn't solve a whole host of issues. How are you going to cope with a newborn whilst heavily pregnant? You can barely walk as it is, imagine having a baby strapped to you all the time as well as a bump! And what happens when you do go in to labour?"

It was infuriating, there were so many combinations of events, none of which they could even begin to plan for if things were left to take their natural course. Jenna didn't want to be induced any more than Sarah did, but so far none of this pregnancy had been what she'd envisaged in her fantasies, so as far as she was concerned it made very little difference. If they came out of it with two healthy babies, and walked away with their own biological child at the end of it, Jenna was happy to chalk it up as a win for both sides.

"I know, you're right," Sarah admitted. "I haven't really wanted to think about it. The whole thing terrifies me." She hung her head, and began to cry. "This has just been so hard on me. Being pregnant, it's exhausting, and now with this thing with Pete. I just don't know what I'd do if I had to raise the baby on my own. I have so much I have to worry about, and I have no one I can turn to for support! I'm not as strong as you." With that tears welled in her eyes, and she started rummaging in her bag for a tissue.

Jenna rolled her eyes and reached across the table and squeezed Sarah's hand. "I know, I know. It's got to be so hard for you, but I have some advice that I really think's going to go help." Sarah dabbed at her eyes and looked up, waiting to hear her soothing words.

"You need to suck it up, buttercup." Jenna said, with more passion than she'd originally intended. Sarah was shocked, and leant back in an attempt to distance herself from the harsh words being inflicted on her.

Jenna carried on, "This sucks, there is no argument about that, but you're about to have a baby. You are about to be a mother, and the second that happens the world is going to stop revolving around you. You need to quickly find a way to shut up and deal with the crap that's thrown at you, or the rest of your life is going to be very difficult. Now, shall we order?"

Jenna unfolded her napkin on to her lap and signalled for the waiter to come over. She was pleased with herself, it needed to be said, even if Sarah looked like she had just been slapped round the face.

For too long people had looked at this woman in front of her as though she was a delicate little flower that needed to be nurtured and protected. In fairness, Sarah had done nothing to dispel that myth but had instead actively encouraged and cultivated it. The little woman who knew nothing and was dedicated to the idea of the idyllic family life.

Well, whatever floats your boat, but Jenna knew she was stronger than anyone had ever given her credit for, she just needed to be reminded and told to tap in to it. Pete wouldn't be in the position he was if he'd attempted to stand up to her once in a while, of that she was certain.

Sarah blew her nose and pulled out the mirror from her bag to check her make-up was still intact. Jenna smiled, fix your face so the outside world suspects nothing and carry on carrying on. It was what got Jenna through every blip and bump in the highway so far, and she knew it would work for the younger woman sitting opposite her.

The rest of their lunch date was relatively unremarkable. They discussed the weather and the rumours that snow was on the way and quickly moved on to how their nurseries were coming along. By the time they'd finished and split the bill, Sarah had agreed to a joint appointment, and was open to discussing induction. Deep down Sarah knew it made sense, besides the thought of Jenna's boobs being anywhere near her perfect baby made her feel sick.

*****

Adrienne sat on the sofa, staring in to space, willing herself to get up and do something. The simple truth was she'd already expelled all her energy for the day by simply getting out of bed. Doing anything more than that would just be overkill.

She'd managed to get her hygiene routine down to two showers a week, and only one hair washing. That was trial enough, and on that one momentous day she still couldn't find the energy to use the blow dryer, instead letting her hair drip on to her shoulders whilst time worked its magic on her locks.

Resigning herself to the fact she wouldn't be getting up and 'doing' anything, Adrienne collapsed back on to the sofa and slowly drew her legs up, wrapping her arms around them as best she could thanks to her growing bump.

Sighing, she closed her eyes for a moment, blocking out the misery of her small apartment. It had never appeared miserable to her before, but now it felt like the loneliest, most pathetic place in the world. Since she'd been forced to leave work, she'd barely ventured outside, finding comfort and security instead in her self-imposed prison.

No one could hurt her here, or at least that's what she kept telling herself when Coop tried to persuade her to venture outside. The reality was staring at these walls was a torture all of its own, and was probably doing more harm to her than anyone else ever could.

Opening her eyes again, she looked around her. There, on the coffee table was a pile of trashy magazines Coop had tried to throw away, suggesting she place more stimulating reading out for her guests. The guests that never came. Jenna apparently favoured tasteful art books featuring landscapes or modern architecture.

Her eyes fell on the front door, which she would sit and stare at for hours every evening, waiting for him to walk back through it. He was staying out later and later each night, ‘working’. Of course, she had no proof he was doing anything other than what he said he was, but she couldn’t shake the feeling he’d used the same excuse to Jenna when he was in actual fact with her. She was always conscious that what he did with her behind Jenna’s back, he could do behind hers.

Finally, she managed to pull herself to her feet, and trudged over to the small kitchen which was in desperate need of a clean. Glancing around, her eyes fixed on the leftovers from last night’s meal. In an unusually positive frame of mind, she’d used all her energy and determination yesterday to cook a big pan of pasta in tomato sauce. Of course, it hadn’t been as nice as the one Jenna used to make, and ultimately, she’d crawled back in to bed with an empty stomach, leaving Coop to watch his football match. Before he’d moved in she hadn’t even realised he liked football.

Leaning against the counter as she waited for the kettle to boil, Adrienne was amazed how quickly everything had changed. Just a few short months ago she felt she had everything she could ever want, and now it had all fallen to pieces. Admittedly, she didn’t really have Coop back then, but the reality was she had him more then than she did now.

They hardly ever spoke these days, not least because she had very little to add to any conversation thanks to her lack of external stimulation. He would talk briefly about work, but always said he’d been thinking about it all day, he didn't want to talk about it all night.

It was impossible now to think back to what they used to talk about, in the days before they'd been thrown together like this. Remembering their many stolen nights together, Adrienne laughed out loud when she realised for the first time that they'd never really talked at all.

With such long gaps between visits, they'd made the most of their time together, by grabbing quick, but lavish meals, and spending the rest of the time in bed. Conversation had never been terribly high on the agenda, and there was never much opportunity to have anything bordering on a deep and meaningful anyway.

Looking back, it struck her as strange now that she'd never realised how shallow their entire relationship had been. From the start the romance of it all had been enough to completely blow her away, and from there, she'd been swept up in the fun and excitement of it all.

Her entire time with Coop had been novel, something different and entirely unexpected. He had shown her things she'd only been able to dream of, and had treated her with nothing but love, care and attention; or so she'd thought. Now, as she remembered all the gifts he'd give her she couldn't help feeling as though she'd been bought off.

Anytime she'd started querying why she couldn't see him for longer, or speak to him whilst he was away, a new box would appear and she'd have another expensive piece of jewellery to add to her growing collection. The nagging feeling had never really gone away, but it had been quietened enough that she never pushed it any further.

Rage started to build inside her from nowhere. She found it incomprehensible that she, the always sensible and cool-headed Adrienne, could find herself pregnant by a man she barely knew. It might not seem that way to anyone on the outside looking in, but she definitely didn't feel she had any idea who this man was in her life. More importantly, she could no longer tell what he was, or wasn't capable of.

Deep down she knew she had no future with him, but it was one thing knowing that, and another thing to do anything about it. Obviously, she wasn't worried about what would happen to him if she attempted to throw him out. She was more worried about what would happen with their baby. Her baby.

He'd hinted more than once he had concerns about her suitability as a mother, certainly with her current mood swings and general state of depression. Nothing terrified her more than the thought he would try to gain custody of the child once it was born. She was under no illusion that was the only reason he was still with her, his last-ditch attempt to be a father, now he'd realised that was what he'd wanted all along.

More than once she'd contemplated telling him that the baby might not be his. Not purely in an attempt to potentially get rid of him, but more out of a desire to do the right thing. She hated the idea that after escaping the risk of raising another couple's baby with Jenna, that Adrienne would be tricking him in to the same situation. He might be an entirely selfish and egotistical bastard, but he didn't deserve that, and the guilt weighed heavily on her every day.

It was mainly the not knowing for certain, in either direction, that put her off saying something. As she lay awake each night, staring at the ceiling, she'd turn the conversation over in her head. She'd play out what she could say, and no matter what words came to her mind, she sounded like a stupid little slut who couldn't keep her legs shut.

It was an image she didn't want Coop to be left with of her. She'd rather be able to say with 100% certainty that the baby was, or wasn't his, than spend the next four months having to admit she had no idea.

CHAPTER 30

Sarah opened the front door and briefly glanced at the pile of letters on the doormat before stepping over them. She had little doubt the majority of them would be bills, and they could always wait until later. There was no point in rushing to pick them up, Pete wasn't here to judge her anymore.

She dumped her mountain of shopping bags on the floor and struggled out of her coat before carrying her hoard upstairs. While her friends had all found their own hobbies, from adult colouring to paper quilling and knitting, Sarah had always felt left out. She'd never been much of a crafter and despite her best efforts culinary skills had somehow managed to completely bypass her. Instead, she had dedicated her spare time to becoming an expert shopper.

Over the years she had developed a knack for finding the best bargains and instinctively knew what the right price was for any fashion item, whether it be shoes, handbags or the latest designer dress. Invariably her tastes far exceeded her means, but she made a rule to not always allow that to stop her from getting what she wanted. Credit cards definitely came in handy for that. While Pete had often joked she was a closet shopaholic, Sarah maintained she exercised a huge amount of control over her retail desires.

Since he'd left her to fend for herself though that self-control had waned somewhat. At no point in her life had she ever lived alone, she'd gone from her family home and the watchful eyes of her parents straight in to married life. She had transformed from young girl to housewife seamlessly, transitioning from performing one role to the other without missing a beat. The problem was that as a result she had always conformed in some way or another to how she was expected to behave.

It was never said out loud, but she knew whilst she had Pete to think about, or more specifically his potential reactions, she wouldn't overspend. She'd managed to keep a lid on her retail therapy if for no other reason than to avoid potential conflict when the bank statement appeared and she had to explain an extortionate store charge. Now, essentially left to run free for the first time ever, she felt like a kid in a toy shop. As she surveyed the shoe boxes piled up in her wardrobe and the mound of bags from Mothercare, The Baby Boo Boutique and Mamas and Papas she had to admit she may have gone slightly overboard.

Five weeks after he'd left her the card statements started to arrive, and at first, she didn't think anything of them. She'd always dealt with them in the past and never had any problems, but a few weeks later she realised she had less money than she was used to. She had underestimated just how much Pete used to give her for housekeeping, to get the food in and buy the occasional take away. As soon as he left the house those weekly deposits to her bank account had stopped.

When she first realised she'd phoned him, querying where the money was and asking whether it had just been an oversight on his part. She understood how busy he was, she'd said, so could see how he could have forgotten, but he made it clear it was perfectly intentional. He'd asked, rather curtly she'd felt, that surely, she didn't need his money to buy her food.

She'd been on the verge of telling him she was carrying his baby, so he should support her, but instead, she kept her mouth shut and silently sulked until he reminded her he was still paying the mortgage. He'd sounded exasperated when he explained he was still giving her half of the money for all the other household bills, despite the fact he wasn't living there anymore. As far as he was concerned there was no reason she should be out of pocket.

In an ideal situation that would continue to be the case, but now she had nothing left and the letters were beginning to get nastier. She clearly needed him for more than she'd ever realised before, and was deeply regretting not being a better wife. Though, she did still struggle at times to understand precisely what more she could do for him.

As she unpacked the last of her new belongings she resolved to phone him in the morning and arrange a meeting so they could talk, properly, without that stupid therapist interfering and patronising them. She had to win him back, get him back in to the house so things could return to normal before she lost her mind and her credit rating.

*****

After lunch Jenna had felt emotionally drained and decided to take a drive to the seafront to unwind. She'd walked down to the promenade and sat watching the waves disappear in to the distance as the tide went out, marvelling at the power of nature and the pull of the moon.

She had spent so much of her youth playing on far more exotic beaches than this, but somehow the man-made boulders and miles of shingle appealed to her more. There was a beautiful ruggedness to the landscape in front of her, and as far as she was concerned it seemed more natural without the perfectly tanned bodies and the scores of surfers littering the waves.

There were times where she missed her life in the States, but she'd been away for so long she wasn't sure she really understood what that life meant any more. Times had changed and people moved on. The truth was she had spent so much of her career leading a nomadic existence that this was the first time she'd ever been able to really call anywhere home. She had lived in the UK for eight years now, and was as settled here as she would ever be.

She had contemplated packing up and disappearing once the babies were born and the two women had settled in to caring for their rightful children, but now it was far more complicated than it had once been. At first, it would have been a great idea and entirely possible. Will had made it clear he had no interest in their baby, and was instead throwing himself into his new life with Adrienne. She was let off the hook, she could disappear in to the sunset and raise her child, alone.

Comparing then with now, Jenna realised how much better that outcome would have been. His decision to back away made things far simpler, she wouldn't have to be concerned with the wants, needs or desires of anyone other than her child when the time came. If she wanted to pack up and move to Italy, France or Norway, she could.

The fact was she'd had choices, but now she felt obligated to say. Will had never told her that Adrienne was pregnant, and when she found out it had all made sense. She'd often found herself wondering how he could go so quickly from being desperate to have this baby with her, to packing his bags and filing for divorce.

She knew the mix-up had complicated things, and that they would never agree on the best way to proceed, but it had never seemed enough of a reason to go to that extreme. Even with him not realising how easy it was to resolve. However, Adrienne being pregnant with his biological heir, now that was something he would want to protect, especially if he no longer saw value in what it was he was giving up with Jenna.

He'd been quick to initiate divorce proceedings, in fact his wheels had barely stopped spinning on their once mutual driveway by the time the letter arrived for her. She was happy with things the way they were, there was infinitely less tension in her life now that she was Will-free. It never ceased to amaze her precisely how much better she felt, and that mere months ago she would never have believed it was possible to feel this way.

Jenna had never considered herself cut out for single life. She came from a family where appearances were everything, it was little wonder she'd found herself embarking on a career where nothing else mattered. Her father would have been mortified at the thought of his baby girl being left to fend for herself, abandoned by the man he had trusted to keep her safe.

It would have completely passed Papa Sanchez by that Will had done nothing to nurture, protect or encourage Jenna in all of their years of marriage. She had to admit he didn't hinder her, he didn't put limitations on her and he didn't force her to be the little woman that so many other men might have done; but not putting a foot on her head to keep her down was not the same as giving her a leg up. He could take no credit for any of the things she'd managed to achieve in her life, but then he had never attempted to, in fairness. She didn't have to jealously guard her accomplishments.

The few friends she had spoken to about their break up simply didn't understand. They would have been mortified if their husbands had shown them up in such a way, leaving them to be with another woman. Even worse, a younger woman. It seemed to make no difference to them that all their husbands were currently seeing other women, and though it was on the surface a closely guarded secret, the entire community knew. Their whole marriage was little more than a pretence, and it was one that Jenna was very glad to finally be done with.

She was the only emotional support she'd ever been able to rely on anyway. The way she saw it, she was missing nothing by no longer being with Will. In all of this the only emotion she felt was pity. Pity for poor Adrienne who had come out of this the worst off of them all. It would be easy to blame the other woman, but the reality was she knew Adrienne had no idea that was the role she'd played, not until that fateful day.

Whilst she knew Will was not a bad man, the way he had treated this young woman was appalling. He had used her as his go to, had clung to her and was now only with her for what she represented to him. Jenna knew it, Will knew it, but she was convinced Adrienne had no idea. There would come a point where he would reject her, and he didn't think the younger woman would be strong enough to withstand that. She felt a tinge of guilt as she thought about it, but quickly pushed Adrienne to the back of her mind again.

Checking her watch, she realised she'd been out far longer than she'd planned and decided to head back to the house. The drive home didn't take long, just 40 minutes but she found herself feeling increasingly tired as time went by.

She was still unable to get a good night's sleep, though now she firmly believed it was more to do with her growing bump and the impossibilities of getting comfortable than the fact she was lying in bed alone. In all honesty she relished the space in her King sized bed and struggled to imagine a time when another person, other than her child, would occupy the space next to her.

When she arrived at the house she noticed his van was already on the drive so she didn't bother to get her keys out of her bag. She opened the front door and made her way to the kitchen to get a bottle of water. Looking around she couldn't see any trace of him, which surprised her. She was sure he'd be in the front room watching the news by now.

She glanced out the patio windows to check he wasn't in the garden and then moved to the bottom of the stairs. "Hi, I'm home" she called out, wondering if he might be in the shower. On second thoughts, he probably wouldn't hear her if he was, so she started to make her way up.

"I'm in the nursery," his voice replied and she picked up the pace, eager to find out what he was doing. She reached the doorway and was immediately blown away by the sight that met her gaze. This morning the room had been entirely bare, but now it had a fully erected feeding chair, changing table, wardrobe and cot, all sitting elegantly on a deep cream carpet. She leant against the wall, totally overwhelmed and unable to say anything.

He turned around and smiled at her, "Surprise!" he said as he got up off his knees and came over to give her a peck on the cheek. "I know how much this place has been bugging you, so I wanted to help out. Hope you like it." He looked sheepish, as though he might somehow be in trouble for doing the nicest thing anyone had ever done for her.

She grabbed his hand and looked in to his eyes, genuinely touched by the kindness and generosity he had shown. Smiling she said, "You are amazing, thank you so much. I honestly don't know what I would do without you, Pete. You're my Guardian Angel."

*****

He put his key in the door, and was immediately surprised to realise for some reason it wasn't working. He checked the bunch in his hand, making sure he was inserting the right one in to the lock, and tried again. Still it wouldn't work.

Shaking his head, he started banging on the painted wood in front of him, furious that he was going to have to confront Adrienne instead of simply being able to sneak in and pour himself a glass of Scotch. It had been a long day and he really couldn't be bothered with any dramas or baleful looks from the world's most depressed woman.

A minute or two had passed before Adrienne opened the door, peering through the small gap afforded by the security chain. "Let me in," he demanded as he glared at her, bored of the paranoia that had clearly led her to suddenly changing the locks without telling him.

"No," she said quietly, and moved to close the door on him. He quickly managed to place his foot in the small gap, and held the door open against her weight.

"What the actual fuck, Ade?" he shouted, not caring for once if his voice attracted the attention of others. What was happening made absolutely no sense to him; this morning he had left her lying on the bed, barely able to summon the strength to lift her hand to wave a careless goodbye as he walked out the room, now she was barring his entry to their home.

"You don't live here, anymore" she replied, barely loudly enough to be heard over his now heavy breathing.

"What did you say?" he asked, his voice getting gradually louder, and laced with annoyance.

Taking a deep breath, Adrienne stood up straight and thrust her chin out. "You. Do. Not. Live. Here. Anymore." She said again, louder this time, and slowly so as to avoid any confusion.

All morning her thoughts had been chasing each other round her head. She was furious the way that her life had turned out, and how everything had seemingly been destroyed in such a short space of time. However, she'd realised something as she sat staring at her trashy magazines, nothing was as out of her control as she thought it was.

No, she wasn't going to get her job back. No, she was never going to be able to forget what had happened. No, she couldn't change the fact that for a while she had been The Mistress. There were all things that had been and gone.

Now though she could change the way she felt about her future. Nothing said she had to be with Coop. She didn't have to live here in this apartment with him, waiting for their child to be born. Certainly not when there was a 50% chance it wasn't even his. She was subjecting herself to a life she knew was ultimately going to cause her misery, and logic said there was no reason she had to.

Something hit her this morning and made her realise she could do it all by herself. Coop always made her feel inferior to Jenna, this wonderful woman who had it all; but for a while, at least, he had chosen to betray Jenna for her. That meant she was better than Jenna. Or if not, she certainly wasn't any worse than her.

She was not inferior. She was strong. She could do anything she put her mind to, and she could certainly raise her child, on her own. At no point had she thought she was reliant on Coop for money; she merely thought she wanted him.

Now though, she realised he was never really going to be there for her. He was only capable of emotionally supporting himself, and anyone else was either there to support him, or was surplus to requirements.

It had become increasingly clear that she now fell in to the latter camp, and she was sure it was only a matter of time before he kicked her to the curb. Things had been bad of late, but she had far too much self-respect to have him walk out on her.

For hours she'd been waiting for him to come home, and had desperately been trying to psych herself up for this confrontation. Changing the locks had been the first practical thing she could do. She'd then packed up all his things, which hadn't taken as long as she thought it would. They might have been living together, and planning a life moving forward, but he still didn't seem to really be here with her.

She'd arranged for a taxi to come and pick up a suitcase full of his clothes, and had sent them off to the Hilton for him to collect. She hadn't cared whether it was where he wanted to stay, or if it fitted in with his plans; she just wanted him out of her home and her life as soon as possible.

It had been her biggest fear that if she had let him come in, he would be able to persuade her that she was over reacting. That she was imagining how bad things were, and that everything was her fault any way. The last thing she wanted was to be in a position where she was going to be stuck with him, not now she had realised it was he who was actually making her miserable, not the situation itself.

"I'm done," she said through the gap. "You don't love me, I don't love you. We just thought we did. This baby's not even yours. I slept with someone else when you were on holiday with Jenna. You're free to do whatever the Hell you want, just leave me out of it."

With that, she slammed the door in his face and threw herself, sobbing, on to the sofa.

CHAPTER 31

Jenna woke naturally and rolled over. She was unsure what time it was, and even less sure she cared. She had no immediate place to be, so was in no rush to get up and start her day. Not for the first time lately she found herself thinking of Sarah. Wondering how she was, what she was going to do and how it would all play out for her in the end.

On top of her genuine feelings of concern about this woman she had been thrown in to this whirlwind with, there was a deep-seated sense of guilt. No matter how often she told herself she had nothing to feel guilty about, there it always was, lying just beneath the surface. She hated herself for lying to her, which made her laugh. If Will was in this position she knew he wouldn't regard it as lying, it would simply be failing to tell the entire truth. Factual omission was not the same as out and out fabrication.

Regardless, she felt guilty for not being open about her relationship with Pete. Not that there was a relationship to confess to, not in the sense that many people would consider to matter; they weren't lovers. However, she wasn't sure that salved her conscience. She also couldn't appease her guilty mind by reminding herself that this situation was borne out of a desire to help Sarah.

Although it hadn't been long, it was now hard to recall how it had all started. One minute, Pete was just a name to her, one she heard frequently from the mouth of Sarah; the next, he was sitting opposite her in a café at Euston station.

When he'd called the first time she'd been caught completely off guard, but his gentle and friendly manner had put her at almost immediate ease. He hadn't mentioned how he'd managed to get her contact details, but she'd assumed Sarah must have at last come clean about their fortnightly visits. When she considered how much Sarah knew about her, and the friendship they had developed, it did make sense that the biological father of the child she was carrying would want to meet her himself, and she'd agreed to see him.

It wasn't until later that day when Sarah phoned herself that Jenna realised it might not be quite as simple as that. It didn't take long to discover that whilst Pete knew the truth, it hadn't come intentionally from Sarah, and equally had not been received well. Whilst her immediate thought was to cancel the impending meeting for fear Pete might not prove as friendly in real life, she still kept her word and said nothing to Sarah.

In the end, she'd gone ahead with the meeting, rationalising that this relative stranger was not going to harm a pregnant woman in a public place, no matter how angry he might be with his wife.

No matter what his initial plans might have been for, the reality was they got on like a house on fire. As they talked and laughed, Jenna could immediately see why Sarah had fallen in love with him so quickly. There was a charm about him you often saw in people, but was rarely genuine in anyone else.

Jenna warmed to him straight away and it wasn't long before the conversation was flowing naturally. He confessed quite quickly, without any prompting, that he'd obtained her phone number from Dr. Barker at the clinic. It made sense, she thought to go down that route, rather than asking Sarah for it – at least now she understood why he hadn't wanted her to say anything about them meeting up.

For some time, she just let Pete talk; it seemed to be doing him good to get off his chest his feelings about what had happened. It was also nice to be able to have a proper two-way conversation about it all, instead of just listening and being allowed to "umm" and "ahh" occasionally in response. Despite the topic of discussion, Jenna found she was quite enjoying spending time with him.

As she'd been talking to him, Jenna had resolved to tell Sarah everything first thing in the morning. She knew Pete wanted to keep it quiet; however, she felt uncomfortable keeping such a big secret from the woman she was desperate to be entirely honest with. The last thing Jenna wanted was any animosity between them both, and she knew this would be enough to drive a wedge between them.

However, Pete admitted he had another reason he wanted to talk to her. It wasn't simply about getting to know the other woman involved in this sticky situation, as he described it. No, he wondered if she knew that Dr. Harper's name was Adrienne.

He hadn't had to say anything else, in that moment everything started slotting in to place. For some reason she'd never been curious about who Adrienne was. Whilst many women would have taken to social media to practice their stalking skills, Jenna had refused. She had no interest in seeing what her rival looked like, or what she did. She much preferred her to be nothing but this almost imaginary figure lurking in the background of her marriage. It wasn't about refusing to acknowledge her existence, it was almost as though Jenna didn't regard her as being important enough to feel threatened by. She was nothing; let her simply remain a name.

Between them her and Pete discussed what might have happened. Had Adrienne not been aware that Will was married? Perhaps she'd known, but hadn't realised his wife was coming in to her clinic for treatment. They both found it hard to believe, but it was plausible.

If that was the case, had something happened to make her realise? Had she been the one responsible for the mix-up with their embryos? If so, was it an accident, or had she done it on purpose? There were so many questions, and whilst a large part of her wanted to have the answers to all of them, she also reasoned that now was not the best time. None of this was going anywhere, and there would be plenty of opportunity to make the clinic pay later down the line.

The one thing the revelation had done was immediately make Jenna felt less guilty about meeting up with Pete in secret. If Sarah wanted to keep her in the dark over something as important as who Adrienne was, then two could play that game.

She smiled now as she thought back to how well they had got on during their first coffee date, and that it had eventually turned in to a long lunch one instead. It was only because Jenna had somewhere else she needed to be later on that day that she'd made any attempt to move. She could have talked to him for hours, and it was quite clear that he felt the same.

Their parting was awkward; as still a relative stranger she wasn't sure if it was a hugging situation, so had refrained, whilst he'd gone in for an embrace. Thankfully, they had both laughed it off and she made her way home, slightly disheartened that she would probably never see him alone again.

A few days later though, he had called, and they'd agreed to meet for lunch again. Both of them were in such need of someone to talk to, someone who understood and didn't place any pressure on them. It made a welcome change. He seemed to have no issue with keeping their meeting a secret from Sarah, and she most certainly didn't feel she owed her any explanation any more.

She was struck by his honesty, and admired his candour greatly. He seemed confused, but deeply hurt, and wasn't afraid to show it. The whole thing had knocked his feet out from underneath him and had unfortunately forced him to take a long hard look at every aspect of his life.

He admitted he cared deeply for Sarah, but wasn't convinced that love was necessarily the right word. He had always wanted to stand by her, but she was making it increasingly difficult. That said, he didn't want to be a part time Dad and knew that his child, no matter how it came in to this world, deserved far better than that.

Being able to talk to Jenna about how his actual child was doing seemed to be a great help for him, and for the first time she felt resentful of how Will had behaved, and how easily he'd been able to dismiss her, but more importantly, his biological child.

After that second meeting, her and Pete had met up every other night for a week; just talking, laughing and reminding each other that life didn't always have to be complicated. They got on and very quickly became firm friends. One night when Pete was complaining about being a nearly 40-year old man living at home with his Mum, sleeping in a single bed under his old Batman duvet cover, she offered him one of her spare rooms instead.

It had been the most natural thing in the world, a solution that caused her no problems but would hopefully solve one of his. She hadn't even stopped to think about it, the offer tumbling out of her mouth before she knew what was happening. It wasn't until later that night, hours after he'd accepted, and she was lying awake in bed that she found herself in turmoil.

What on earth would Sarah think if she ever found out? Again, Jenna laughed, of course she would find out, women always did, and of course she would be hurt. She'd have every reason to be, but somehow Jenna managed to push this to one side by repeating her mantra that she was doing nothing wrong. She was just trying to help. Besides, she owed Sarah nothing.

For the largest part she did believe that, she and Pete were just friends. They confided in each other, they helped each other, they were there as company and a support network. On the surface it's probably the least torrid thing a man and woman could do together, it certainly wasn't an affair. However, Jenna also understood the subtle reality no woman could ever articulate properly, the simple truth that conversation was far more intimate than sex ever could be.

Sarah would no doubt be able to forgive a sexual dalliance, though understandably would make Pete suffer for it. Turning to, and relying on another woman in his time of need, was something else entirely. It was emotional, not physical, and that was a betrayal many women could never get over. While she could accept Sarah's potential wrath should she find out the truth, she also couldn't judge Pete for not turning to his wife. She'd made herself completely unavailable emotionally, as far as his needs were concerned, and that was unacceptable in Jenna's opinion.

She had struggled back and forth with this internal conflict for weeks, despite her initial hard line on the matter, but never seemed to get any closer to finding a resolution that sat well with her. All she could think was that Sarah had to be told at some point, and that the responsibility for that confession should probably lie with Pete.

However, from a purely selfish perspective she didn't want to rock the boat with the woman that was carrying her child, not when they were so close to the finishing line. It would have to remain a problem without answer for some time, and she would continue to try and push it from her mind.

A knock at the door disturbed her from her thoughts and she struggled to a sitting position as Pete came in with a cup of tea. He placed it on her bedside table and perched himself on the edge of her bed. It was an unusual feeling having someone consider your needs, wants or desires and she was still getting used to this morning ritual. Never before had the offering of a morning cuppa seemed so romantic, purely because it was the every day.

"How did you sleep?" Pete asked, concern etched on his face, "You look tired." Jenna pushed her hair from her eyes, propped a pillow behind her back for support and winced in pain. "I'm OK," she replied, "it's just getting harder to find a position that accommodates this bump."

Pete looked at her expanding belly and asked, "Can I?" She nodded, this had become part of their morning routine too, Pete would place his hand on her stomach and marvel at the kicks and flips his child was doing in there. It was a wonderful thing to watch, to be able to witness him bond with his unborn baby, and she was glad to be able to facilitate it.

He frowned, "Awww, Nugget's not playing this morning?" he asked, used to early morning acrobatics instead of this foetal version of the silent treatment. Jenna looked down at his hand, then back at his face, "No, I don't think he is. Actually, I've not felt him move since last night."

CHAPTER 32

As Jenna lay on the bed in the examination room waiting for the Midwife to arrive she surveyed the décor gloomily. Why did they always have to make such rooms so clinical, she wondered. Of course, it was a hospital, a degree of medicalisation was necessary for practical reasons if nothing else, but blinds with a bit of colour wouldn't go amiss. She also failed to understand how garish floral-patterned cubicle curtains lent anything to the atmosphere of the room. Simple block pastels would have been far more relaxing and aesthetically calming.

Pete paced the room, stopping occasionally to read an ear-torn notice on the importance of proper handwashing protocol or the benefits of breastfeeding. Watching him move from poster to poster made her feel better, it was like watching a bumble bee trying to decide which flower to settle on.

It was also reassuring to see he was as nervous as she was. Too many people in situations of potential crisis had a tendency to pretend all was OK, to brush it off, to belittle the tension and write it off as overreaction. Jenna appreciated the fact he was in the same boat mentally as she was, it confirmed to her she wasn't just being neurotic, that this could be something.

She hoped more than anything it wasn't, but she was too realistic to put much stock in hope and blind faith. She had to know, for certain, then she could deal with whatever it was. There was no point in theoretically assuming all would be OK just because it would be tragically unfair if it wasn't. In her experience life had an unnerving habit of being tragically unfair at times.

There was a light knock at the door and the Midwife appeared, full of smiles and energy despite being 12 hours in to a 13-hour shift. She introduced herself as Maggie and quickly read through Jenna's maternity notes, whilst simultaneously asking her to explain again why she was here this morning.

Minutes later Jenna had lifted her top and Maggie was listening to her bump with what looked like an ear trumpet. In all her standard appointments her usual Midwife had used a high-tech Doppler to check the baby's heartbeat; this contraption looked archaic in comparison and caught Jenna by surprise.

Maggie caught her looking at the Pinard horn she had pressed against her stomach and said, "These are far more accurate for listening in on little one. The Doppler's pick up too much other noise, it can be misleading". She then turned her head and moved the device, continuing to search for the sound she needed to hear. Suddenly she stood up and smiled, "Sometimes these babies can be so awkward. I'm just going to go and get the ultrasound and do a full check for you. Hang tight for me."

With that, she left the room. Jenna and Pete looked at each other, "That can't be good," she said, a hint of panic in her voice. Pete came over and sat on the edge of the bed, she shifted slightly to the right to give him more room. Considering they were designed to cater for pregnant women Jenna marvelled at how narrow the beds actually were. You'd never get a good night's sleep on one of those, she thought to herself.

Pete took her hand in his and stroked it with the other, desperately trying to find a way to calm and reassure her. Jenna was reminded of the way her Gramps used to stroke his mares when they were being shoed, their head over his shoulder, he'd rub their strong necks and whisper banalities in their ear.

"Let's not go jumping to any conclusions right now," Pete said, "it won't help. She'll be back, and we'll take it from there, OK?" In this very moment Jenna wished she could be reassured, wished she could buy in to the belief that the baby was being lazy, that maybe a growth spurt accounted for the lack of movement.

Perhaps this midwife, who seemed very lovely, was actually a trainee and had no idea what she was doing. There would be comfort in all of that, a degree of hope that all really would be OK, but she couldn't buy it. None of that seemed likely, and the realisation that something might be very wrong started to lay heavy on her.

"We ought to phone Sarah," Jenna said, conscious of the fact that whilst this was physically happening to her, it was also Sarah's baby they were discussing. Pete nodded, "It can wait," he said. "Let's see what we're dealing with, and then we can make a plan. Right now, just breathe and let me worry about Sarah."

She took a deep breath and closed her eyes, trying to shut everything out but the sound of her breathing. This was Hell, she concluded. This not knowing bit. Fearing that something was wrong and waiting to hear the verdict. She found herself wondering if this would be the hardest part of her day, or if things were about to get much worse.

The door opened again and Maggie returned with an ultrasound machine and a tall man in a white coat. While Maggie busied herself getting the equipment set up, the man introduced himself. "Hi Jenna, my name is Dr. McCarthy and I'm one of the consultants on the maternity ward. I understand you're experiencing reduced foetal movements at the moment?"

Jenna nodded, trying not to be infuriated by this constant repetition of her reasons for being there. So far this morning she'd explained it to the midwife on the phone, again to the lady at reception when they'd arrived, gone through it with Maggie and here we were with a fourth person. It seemed overkill as far as she was concerned, but she rationalised she was probably being a little ratty due to her anxiety.

Dr. McCarthy started feeling her stomach, pushing far harder than was comfortable, but Jenna tried not to react. "When was the last time you felt your baby move?" he asked without looking at her. "Last night was the last time I definitely remember, about 6pm" she replied, wincing as the pressure he was placing on her uterus increased. He picked up the ear contraption and placed it on her stomach.

"Movements normal up to that point?" he asked casually.

Jenna wasn't entirely sure what he meant, the baby had been moving on a regular basis, but movements on the whole had reduced. She explained that the baby had been less active than before, but her midwife had said that would be normal as living conditions became more cramped.

Dr. McCarthy nodded and turned to Maggie, "We ready?" he asked. She nodded and handed him the bottle of gel to put on Jenna's stomach, "Slightly cold", he said as he poured a big dollop just above her pubic line.

With his other hand he moved the screen closer to him, completely obscuring Jenna and Pete's view. Jenna found herself wondering if this was intentional, a deliberate ploy to shield her from something she might not want to see. A few seconds passed, but to her they felt like an eternity, lying there, waiting to hear what was happening.

It was a bizarre feeling, waiting for someone to confirm what was going on inside you. She couldn't help but feel she should know, instinctively, and was disturbed by the fact that an external third party would be the first to be aware of her fate. Their fate.

Maggie and Dr. McCarthy looked at the screen, and then at each other. Something unspoken passed between them and Jenna felt the blood drain from her face as the hairs on her arms stood to attention. Ice coursed through her veins and she held her breath. It wasn't intentional, she felt as though she no longer had control over anything. Her brain seemed to be processing everything faster than she could keep up, and was already going in to survival mode.

Pete was still holding her hand and she could feel the sweat breaking the surface, but she wasn't sure whose sweat it was. Her heart started racing and she felt sick. Dr. McCarthy handed her a wad of paper towel to mop up the gel that had been smeared all over her abdomen, while Maggie turned off the monitor and pushed it away from the bed.

The tall man looked down at her and took her other hand in his, "I am so sorry Jenna, there is no heartbeat". The words hung there, none of them moving or speaking. She felt Pete squeeze her hand and whisper an "oh God", before standing up and trying to put his arm round her. As the enormity of those four words hit him it was clear he no longer had the strength to stand, and he collapsed back in his chair instead.

Jenna was relieved, she didn't want the comfort but was physically unable to move, pinned to the bed by shock, so would have been unable to shrug him off. She wriggled her hand free from Dr. McCarthy and continued wiping her belly, struggling to a sitting position once she was satisfied she was clean again.

She lifted her eyes up to look at the Doctor and Maggie, opened her mouth to seek clarification, and instead found herself asking for more paper. She returned to wiping her stomach, even though she was now completely dry. Her mind whirled, and suddenly landed on the scene from Macbeth where Lady Macbeth is sleepwalking, shouting "Out, damn'd spot! Out, I say!" In that moment she felt she would never be able to stop feeling the sensation of that cold gel on her stomach.

"The baby is dead?" she found herself asking, to no one in particular. It sounded so cold as it bounced off the white walls, but she needed to understand. He hadn't said they couldn't find a heartbeat, he said there wasn't one. So that meant the baby had died, surely, but no one had said that. The words had to be said, she needed to hear them.

Dr. McCarthy nodded, "Yes, I am afraid so. We have no way of knowing why at this time, and we may never know, unfortunately for some women it is an incredibly cruel twist of fate no one can control."

Jenna was no longer listening, she felt as though she'd been placed under water and all the once vibrant sounds around her had become muffled. Instinctively she looked at Pete, his usually smiling face suddenly looked grey and tense and she wasn't sure he would ever recover. The last few minutes seemed to have had aged him dramatically.

In that moment she burst into tears. She wanted to mourn for the baby, the little innocent life that had done nothing to deserve this, the little hitchhiker she had grown to love the way a biological mother should love her child, but all she could think about was Pete. This man had become her rock, her best friend and she loved him dearly. The guilt she felt at losing his child, the child he had spent weeks bonding with and worrying about, was overwhelming. She felt she had somehow betrayed him, and he would never be able to forgive her.

Then her thoughts turned to Sarah and how she would cope with the news. The whole thing was an incredible mess and there was no logical way to understand how to move forward. Who had the most right to grieve? The actual parents who had relied on science to create this little miracle in a lab, or the woman who had been kept awake by this tiny person's frequent kicks in the ribs and never-ending heartburn for months. There was no answer, there was no magical equation that could unequivocally balance who was going to be the most distraught by this loss.

The doctor mumbled something about giving them some time alone and he quickly made his exit from the room. Maggie, however, stayed with them. Jenna was her responsibility and she refused to leave her at this tragic time. She might not be able to offer any meaningful support this second, but she certainly couldn't do anything if she wasn't here. She pulled up a chair and sat next to Jenna's bed, leafing through her maternity notes.

Jenna looked at her, "What happens now?" she asked. It was something she had to be aware of, there must be a procedure, but she wasn't convinced she was ready for the answer. Maggie leant forward and put her hand on the bed, positioned perfectly so Jenna could hold it with minimal movement should she wish.

"At some point, you have to give birth," she answered, trying to sound authoritative, without being callous and unfeeling. It was a difficult balance, all she wanted to do was break down with this woman and cry for her loss, but that could wait until she got home.

"There's no rush," Maggie continued, "and you do have options". Jenna nodded, focussing on the practicalities for the time being. There was a huge comfort in following procedures, understanding the way things were. It was far less complicated than trying to comprehend what was actually happening. She could always worry about that when it was all over, and she was back home, no doubt alone.

"I want a c-section," she said. "Just get it over and done with." As far as she was concerned that would be the less traumatic way of dealing with it. Knock her out, get this baby born and be done with it. She was just the vessel that was supposed to keep it safe, it had nothing to do with her after that. She had no right to see it or have anything to do with it. She just wanted it removed and returned to its rightful parents. They could then decide what to do while she lay in bed recovering.

Maggie leant forward again, “I’m sorry Jenna, we can’t do that. You have to give birth naturally unless there’s a medical reason to suggest it wouldn’t be safe for you.” Although Maggie kept talking, explaining the relative benefits of a natural birth as opposed to a caesarean section, the speed of recovery and goodness knows what else, Jenna was not listening. She was immediately lost in the horrific thought that she would have to go through hours of labour knowing that at the end of the agonising process there would be a dead baby brought in to the world. It was barbaric.

Why on earth would these medical professionals, who had sworn to do no harm, insist on putting a woman through such a thing, when she was already going through the worst time of her life?

CHAPTER 33

Maggie sat in the office, her back to the door and her arms wrapped tightly around herself, trying to provide a comfort she knew would never come. On any other day she'd say she had the best job in the world, despite the paperwork, red tape and the crippling exhaustion. Today though, as she watched the clock tick past the hour she should have finished, she didn't know how she would possibly continue to put one foot in front of the other. Let alone do anything more meaningful.

Helena came in behind her, placed a reassuring hand on her shoulder and passed her a steaming hot mug of tea. There was no need for words; everyone on duty knew what was happening in room 5. Maggie lifted her head and a half-smile briefly spread across her lips before she took a tentative sip from the chipped mug cradled in her hands.

"When do you finish?" Helena asked as she surveyed the patient status board on the wall. Maggie looked back at the clock, "Now", she replied, before returning to her tea. Helena nodded, "You staying?" It was a question, but Maggie knew it was more rhetorical than quizzical. Jenna may have come in at the end of her shift, and under any other circumstances she would have handed her over to the new midwife on duty, but she couldn't today. No, she wasn't her responsibility any longer, from a practical point of view, but Maggie could never leave. Not now.

"Nikki is on for me, but I just – ", she stopped, and shrugged. Helena straightened her pony tail and picked up a pile of folders before saying "We're all thinking of you; you'll get through it chick, one step at a time". With that, she was gone, on to tackle the woman in room 10 who refused to believe she was still only 4 centimeters dilated.

Maggie took another sip of her tea and unfurled her legs from beneath her. She never knew how much time to give people in these situations. She was only too well aware that 10 minutes might never be enough, but two could be far too many. In the brief time she'd spent with them Maggie had been struck by how devoted Pete seemed to be to his wife, which was a relief. She genuinely felt if they would just talk once the dust had settled, they might get this through together. What they would be left with wouldn't be how they came in, but any luck, it would be strong enough to endure.

She stood up, took another swig from her mug and physically dusted herself down, trying to prepare herself in some way for the emotional and physical battle that lay ahead of her. She took a deep breath and made her way back to room 5.

*****

Sarah curled back up in bed with her cup of tea and a pack of Jammy Dodgers. She'd always been so fussy about eating in bed, hating the thought of finding crumbs under her pristine silk quilted coverlet. In fact, it had always been a rule in her house, their house, that no food was allowed upstairs. Now, as she sat munching her way through the contents of the pack, she wistfully thought back to the last time she'd woken next to Pete.

In that moment she would give anything to have him sat next to her, dropping crumbs everywhere. She swore that once their baby was with them, and Pete was back home where he belonged, she would be far better. She would relax and stop being so uptight about all the little things that clearly didn't matter. Who cared about crumbs when everything else was perfect?

She sighed. Although it dominated nearly every waking hour, she still had no idea how she was going to get him back. She wasn't naïve enough to think that a simple phone call and apology was going to be enough; she would have to show him she had actually changed and was making an effort to be the type of person he wanted to be with. No, she would have to do something far more meaningful than that if it was going to make an impact with him.

Taking a deep breath, she placed her cup back on the bedside table, and then opened the drawer. Where once it had been full of IVF and early pregnancy leaflets, now it was crammed to the brim with unopened bank statements, bills and final demands. If she was being honest with herself she had no idea how much money she owed. It had been weeks since she'd started transferring money out of their savings pot to pay for shopping, and now she knew it had dwindled to a few hundred pounds.

Her steadfast belief that she could somehow pay it all back before Pete realised what had happened had finally abandoned her, and she accepted she needed help. Whilst a large part of her wanted to run to her Mum and Dad for help, she knew she'd done that once too often over the last few months, and their generosity was running out. Now she'd come to the end of the line and had to face the music.

Picking up her phone she selected Pete's number and pressed call, determined at last to be honest and open, and beg for his forgiveness and help. She was surprised to find his phone was diverted to voicemail, and hung up before leaving a message.

*****

Will had decided to take the day off work so he could spend time working on Jenna to let him come back home. At first, as he sat on his perfectly made hotel bed last night, he'd been surprised by Adrienne's actions. Never in a million years would he have imagined she could behave in such a way.

However, as the shock wore off and he thought about things more clearly, he was annoyed. He was annoyed that she had been the one to end things first. He had been rejected. By her.

He wasn't entirely sure whether he believed her about the baby. It seemed odd that she would suddenly decide to tell him now that it might not be his. In all the time he'd known her he never got the impression she was the one-night stand kind of girl, and certainly wasn't stupid enough to get pregnant from a meaningless bar fling. Though, what did he really know about anything anymore?

Everything with Adrienne was far too complicated, he rationalised it would probably be for the best if he just walked away from it all completely. Even if the baby were his, it would be a small price to pay for getting his life back to normal.

For the fifth time he picked up his personal mobile and called Jenna. With each unanswered ring he became more and more frustrated by her stubbornness. As more time passed whilst he listened to the anonymous voice of the answer machine his blood began to boil.

He'd already determined to leave a message this time, to ensure she paid attention to him and didn't continue to dismiss him out of hand. At the beep he said, "Listen here Jen, I need to talk to you. Stop being so stupid about this and have lunch with me. I shall collect you from the house at 1.30pm." With that he hung up and went to grab a shower.

*****

When Maggie reappeared in room 5 she saw Pete and Jenna sitting on the faded blue arm chairs, holdings hands. She placed two plastic cups of weak, but sweat tea in front of them and settled herself on the bed. Every inch of her was desperate to ask how Jenna was, but she knew it would appear trite if she actually asked.

"I've brought all the paperwork with me," she started, "so we can go through everything as and when you're ready. There's no rush, and I'm here to answer all your questions." Jenna took a sip of tea and initially recoiled at the taste, but carried on drinking anyway. Finally, having steadied herself, she asked, "What do we have to do now?"

Maggie slowly began to explain their options, reminding them that at some point, their baby had to be born. "You can go home, if you like, and wait for labour to start naturally. It could happen soon, or you may have quite a long wait, there's no telling I'm sorry to say."

Pete looked at Jenna, trying to gauge how she might be feeling about that option. When she said nothing he asked, "I know you say it can take a while, but is there anything we ought to be aware of if it doesn't happen soon?" Maggie nodded, glad he was starting to ask questions, it was a positive sign.

"The longer it takes for the baby to be born, the more his physical condition will deteriorate in the womb." Maggie always found this a difficult point to try to get across. In this situation a family would already be struggling to come to terms with their shock and grief, but it was important they understood what waiting could mean.

"There's no knowing how your baby will look when he is born come what may, but the longer we wait, the harder it may be to see and hold him, from your perspective. Equally, if you would like a post mortem to try to explain cause of death, the results are more likely to be conclusive the less time there is between …" she faltered, but Pete nodded, clearly understanding what she was trying to get at.

"OK," Jenna said, "and if we decided not to wait, what happens? Will you induce me now?" She asked the question because she had to know the answer, but she wasn't entirely sure she knew what she hoped the response would be.

Maggie took a breath, and began. "Again, you have options. You can decide to be induced, but that doesn't have to happen immediately. You can go home, take some time to be alone, maybe talk to your friends and family, prepare yourself. We can then make an appointment for you to come back in and we can get started. Or we could …"

Jenna raised her hand to signal her to stop, "That's fine," she said. She turned to look at Pete and took both hands in hers, "We need to speak to Sarah. Let's go home, and get everything sorted. Then we can come back whenever they tell us to." He stared in to her eyes and nodded his approval, “OK” was all he managed to reply.

“When should we come back?” Jenna asked, a look of determination plastered on her face.

CHAPTER 34

They drove back in silence, neither of them had the energy to start a conversation, let alone maintain one. Once Jenna had opened the front door they both moved their way in to the front room, taking up their usual seats, and continued their silence.

Ten minutes passed before Pete broke the quiet by asking if she wanted a cup of tea. She looked at the large clock on the mantelpiece, saw it was 1.15pm and was taken aback by how late it was already. The day seemed to have been going on forever, and had only just started at the same time.

She turned to look at him and replied, "To be honest, I think I'll have a glass of wine. It seems that sort of day." He smiled, she definitely had a point. "I'll join you," he said as he made his way back to the kitchen.

A few minutes later they were sitting together on the sofa, both cradling a large glass of Pinot Grigio. Suddenly, Jenna laughed, and Pete raised a quizzical eyebrow in her direction. "I've not touched a drop since the second I found out I was pregnant," she placed her hand on her dome-like belly, "It feels weird drinking now". He squeezed her hand and couldn't find the words to say.

After taking a long drink from her glass, Jenna placed it on the table in front of them and turned to face Pete. "We need to work out what we're going to say to

Sarah, and when" she said, desperate to come up with a plan so they could move forward. "She has to know, and sooner rather than later. I just don't know how much to actually tell her."

Pete sighed, and placed his glass next to hers. "You can tell her whatever you like, I honestly don't care." He didn't add that now the one thing that could have persuaded him to return to his wife had been taken away from him, he had no intention of going back. Now wasn't the time, and Jenna didn't need to hear it. Jenna thought for a moment, before speaking again. She completely understood his position, and knew what he wasn't saying; however, things were a little more complicated for her. Although she was also grieving for the life that had died inside her, she was well aware her actual baby was safe and sound, growing inside Sarah.

The thought of doing anything to jeopardise that terrified her, and she didn't know how best to proceed without making matters worse. She found herself walking a very difficult tightrope, wanting to confide in the man who had undoubtedly become her best friend, and knowing he had his own demons he was battling with in the same moment.

He had known Sarah far longer, and more intimately than she had, so she turned to him for advice on how best to handle it with her. Though it was the last thing she wanted to do, she knew realistically she would have to be the one who picked up the phone and broke the news to this poor woman that her child had died. As she played that over in her head she had no idea how she would find the strength to do it.

She would have loved nothing more than to pass the job to Pete, but that approach would have brought far more difficult issues to their door. Why on earth would Pete know before Sarah, to be able to tell her in the first place? While the first option seemed far too difficult, the second one was impossible.

Pete was about to speak when a knock at the door interrupted him. Jenna glanced towards the door, more out of habit than a genuine attempt to see who it might be. She made to stand up, but he put his hand on her knee and told her to stay where she was. There was silence again as he padded up the hallway towards the door. She heard him work the catch and then the unmistakable sound of Will demanding, "Who the fuck are you?"

*****

Before Pete had been able to say anything, Will barged past him, glanced in to the kitchen and then followed the hall down to the front room, where Jenna was now rising to greet him. "Who the fuck is that?" Will barked again as he came face to face with his wife for the first time in nearly six months.

If she was taken aback by his unannounced intrusion, Jenna didn't show it, instead merely replying, "Hello William. Do come in and sit down." She gestured to the arm chair at the corner of the room which had always been his spot of choice on the rare nights he was home long enough to enjoy it. He scoffed, and began pacing up and down staring intermittently at Jenna, and then back at Pete.

Jenna returned to her seat, and picked up her glass of wine, taking another sip before providing Will with the answer he sought. "This," she said at last, "is Pete. He is the biological father of the baby I am carrying and …"

"What the fuck is he doing in my house?" Will demanded, not giving Jenna a chance to finish what she was saying.

She sighed before carrying on, "This is no longer your house Will, and you know that. You filed for a divorce and left me to get on with things. I owe you no explanation about anything any longer. Now, I'd like it if you could leave, Pete and I have something important to discuss."

Furious at the way he'd just been spoken to and conscious he had been ridiculed in his own home, in front of a man he did not know, something inside him snapped. Feeling every bit the cuckold, and embarrassed by the situation he suddenly found himself in, he chose to follow the age old Cooper approach to conflict resolution: hit first, ask questions later.

In one seamless motion he turned, took a step towards Pete and swung for him. The blow caught the younger man square in the jaw and sent him sprawling backwards in to the wall, knocking a vase of flowers to the floor in the process. Initially caught off guard, Pete quickly regained his composure and was on his feet again before Will had time to recover himself from the original punch.

Now the tables had turned and Will found himself held against the wall, with Pete's hand around his throat, as his other clenched in to a fist and was raised level with his face. He barely made out the sound of Jenna whimpering to his right as he closed his eyes in readiness for the inevitable collision with his nose.

"Stop!" Jenna screamed, and Will could feel the pressure lessen slightly on his neck.

"My waters have broken."

*****

Sarah pushed her way in to the changing room and shut the door excitedly behind her. As she took off her coat and discarded it on the floor, along with her bag, she started to look at the options she had laid out before her. The new season had brought with it some amazing colour combinations, and she was impressed to see the maternity fashion lines had followed industry trends.

As she rummaged through the 15 dresses she had in front of her she had a nagging doubt. With only eight weeks left before this baby was due to make an appearance, it might be a slight waste of the money she didn't have to buy an entirely new wardrobe at this moment. She could, she attempted to reason, just wait it out in what she already had, and then treat herself to new clothes once her perfect body had returned.

Of course, she had a point; however, new clothes were new clothes. Eight weeks could turn in to ten weeks if the baby was stubborn and decided to stay put. Besides, new clothes always made her feel better, and it was important for a pregnant woman to be calm and happy. It was good for the soul, which meant that ultimately it would be good for the baby.

Pleased with her logic, she even managed to dismiss the minor problem of cash flow. She'd checked, she still had money in their mutual savings account, and because Pete hadn't answered his phone this morning, she hadn't yet been able to come clean about her financial problems. That meant it didn't matter if she added a few extra hundred pounds to the deficit when she did eventually come clean. He'd never know the difference anyway.

Pulling off her normal clothes she threw them on the floor, on top of her bag, muffling the sounds of her phone as it rang repeatedly.

CHAPTER 35

Jenna felt the contraction start to take hold and she took a deep breath. As the pain surged through her body she breathed out slowly, telling herself "It will be over soon, it will be over soon". It had always been her plan to have as many drugs as the hospital would allow her. When it came to thinking about what labour looked like for her, she had imagined lying in a pristine white hospital bed, full of epidural and vaguely aware something was happening whilst she occupied her mind with a good book.

While she genuinely hoped she would be a stereotypical earth mother, she'd never felt the need to prove her worth or strength by delivering naturally. She'd long since come to the conclusion that getting pregnant was ordeal enough, she didn't need to subject herself any further to prove her maternal worth. Equally, she had made peace with the possibility of having a c-section and causing permanent scaring to her otherwise perfect body. It wasn't a big deal at all, not in comparison to having to labour for hours and physically expel a human being from her body.

It wasn't that she was lazy in any way shape or form, she just didn't see the need to do it when there were alternatives. Pregnancy was hard enough and physically draining, why start your time as a mother to a real live human being feeling sore and exhausted from the ordeal? Now though, she felt differently.

Yes, she had desperately wanted to be taken down to theatre, put to sleep and have someone else take care of what needed to be done. She had howled at the thought of being part of the process, and on some levels would have much rather woken up a few hours later, safe from prying eyes and able to recover on her own. However, now as she prepared for the peak of yet another contraction she realised it was right to do it this way.

She didn't care for the medical argument that it would be better for her, physically if she was able to deliver naturally. Lists detailing the risks of c-sections and surgery compared to a vaginal delivery meant nothing to her at the time, when they had been read as part of the process to encourage her to make a decision and come to terms with what was happening.

However, the idea of being present, completely present, for the birth of this baby, suddenly meant everything to her. He deserved to be welcomed with loving arms, and his journey in to the world should be cherished for what it was, even if it was nothing like anyone had ever hoped or planned.

*****

As another contraction reached its crescendo Jenna felt an uncontrollable urge to push. She leant back against the weight of Pete who was standing behind her and let out a low, long moan. Jo, the midwife who was now in charge of her care, appeared by her side and felt her uterus, looking at the monitor to the side of the bed and instantaneously checking the time. Jenna met her gaze and was reassured by the gentle smile offered.

Jo stood up, "Are you happy where you are Jenna, or would you like to get on the bed?" It seemed like a ridiculous question, she could never be happy anywhere in this situation, but she also knew now was not to the time to start biting back. She wanted to reply, but the contractions were coming so thick and fast now there was no time to gather her senses before another one took hold. She barely had time to gather breath, let alone formulate a thought and speak it.

In the brief lull between pushing and the next wave she merely shook her head, hoping that Jo would understand her silent plea to leave her where she was. Moving was just too impractical, and she didn't want to be distracted by attempts to coordinate her legs. She'd been standing for so long at the side of the bed she felt rooted to the spot, and wasn't sure she had time to learn how to move again before the baby would be with them.

With the next contraction she automatically crouched to the floor, feeling her pelvis open and encouraging gravity to do its thing. Pete, still behind her started to rub her lower back, the pressure counteracting the pain inside her and making things feel slightly easier than they had. To get a better grip on her he settled down to sitting behind her and she leant back. The next thing she knew she was sitting on the floor, leaning against him for support, with her knees bent.

Jo crouched in front of her and started laying out various mats to help clear up the inevitable mess. “On the next contraction I’m going to need you to give me a really good push Jenna. Hold it for as long as you can, I can see the head and we need to get him moving a bit more now.” As the contraction came Jenna tried hard to do as Jo asked, but she felt herself holding back. One small push and the contraction died away, leaving her a moment to catch her breath.

Instinctively Jo knew what the problem was and put her hand on Jenna’s knee, “Sweetheart, he’s going to be perfect. Don’t worry. Let’s do this so we can meet him and say hello, OK? Come on, here’s another one, now push for me.”

Jenna pushed back against Pete and anchored herself to him, riding the wave of the contraction and putting all her effort in to pushing. She could feel the blood rush to her head as she held her breath, forcing herself to hold on for just one more second through the intense pressure and in to a stinging sensation she had never experienced before.

“Keep going, keep going, keep going”, she could hear Jo saying as she gradually ran out of air and strength. She was rewarded with a “well done” and a pat on the leg as she closed her eyes and rested her head on Pete’s shoulder. He placed his hand on her forehead and gently wiped her hair, stuck with sweat, away from her eyes as he whispered in her ear, “I am so proud of you, you’re doing brilliantly. You can do this.”

She wanted to cry and scream back at him "No, I can't", but she didn't have the strength. This wasn't meant to be how this happened. She'd never really given much thought to how all of this would work, it was so alien it would have been impossible to predict accurately, but she had dreamt of the moment she'd hand over the perfect baby her body had nurtured to its rightful parents. Now that moment was being taken away from her and she had no idea what she was going to be left with.

A feeling of trepidation weighed upon her at the thought of what was about to come in to the room with her. She had seen bodies of the dead before when she'd attended the funerals of her relatives, but the thought of looking at, or even cradling a dead baby, filled her with a sense of dread unrivalled by anything else. A baby shouldn't arrive in to the world not breathing. It should know love, and this poor tyke would know nothing. Would never have been touched, or held or kissed. She wanted to scream, to believe in a God she could blame and plead with, but she was empty.

All she wanted was time to process what was happening, but she knew that time was all but over. Under other circumstances she would have welcomed the momentum that her body had built up, and the speed with which she was being carried along, but now she was wishing she could stop everything and take a break.

She wasn't ready, but the reality was that even in the haze of what was happening, she knew she never would be. There was nothing that could prepare any human being to welcome this moment, and nothing could ever make them accept it. Time suddenly felt as though it was standing still, and as Jenna pushed with her body and listened to the encouragement of the other two people in the room, it suddenly happened.

Where there had been an intense force inside her, something that completely took her over, in an instant it was gone. There was no pain, no pressure, no fear; nothing but an overwhelming feeling of peace and accomplishment. Instinctively she listened out for those first cries, the sign that she had done her job and a whole new life was begun, but in that moment, she remembered they would not come.

The silence was deafening.

*****

As the taxi pulled up outside the house Sarah fished around in her purse for some cash. Handing it over, she asked if the driver would help her to carry all her bags up to the front door. She loved having a large pregnancy bump to use as an excuse to not have to do anything for herself these days. Half smiling, she realised how much she was going to miss it when the time came to actually have this baby.

Within minutes she was back inside, and surrounded once again by bags. She sighed as she contemplated taking them all upstairs to sort them out in to their rightful cupboards. At least this time she hadn't bought too many new things for the baby. The reality was she'd already bought one of everything that seemed to be available on the High Street.

She waddled down the hall and in to the kitchen, putting her bag on the kitchen counter and pulling out her phone. The battery had died hours ago, and she was desperate to try and get hold of Pete again. Plugging it in to the charger, she put the kettle on and rummaged in the cupboards until she found another pack of biscuits. Her emergency stash, though she hadn't yet decided what the emergency was.

After a few minutes the phone was charged enough to turn back on, and she noticed she had numerous missed calls; three from Jenna and five from an unknown number. Realising she had a voicemail, she picked the phone up to retrieve it.

The automated voice on the other end told her she had six new messages. She only made it to the second one before she dropped the biscuits in a state of shock.

*****

Jo wrapped the lifeless body in a blanket, and carried him over to the cot on the other side of the room. Pete sat with his arms still wrapped around Jenna whilst another midwife busied herself tidying up around them.

Suddenly Jenna exhaled, as though finally realising she had been holding her breath. After taking in a lungful of air, her next breath out turned in to a sob and she wailed. The scream was primal and spoke to the pain she felt deep in her soul. Pete clung to her, and buried his face in her hair as their bodies shook in agony together.

After a few minutes their crying calmed, and they both started to catch their breath. The new midwife gently took Jenna's hand and asked if she wanted to get in to the bed. Between her and Pete they managed to pull the broken pieces Jenna had become to a standing position, and guided her to the edge of the bed. Swinging her legs up, she collapsed back on to the two hard pillows waiting for her.

A steaming mug of extraordinarily sweet tea was thrust in to her hand as someone, she assumed, Pete continued to stroke her hair. "You need to drink, my sweet", a female voice said and Jenna closed her eyes, wishing everything would just go away, but knowing it wouldn't.

Jo returned to her side, a tiny bundle in her arms. "Do you want to see your son?" she asked, and Jenna stared up at her, frozen in fear. Pete stood up and immediately moved towards the window, trying to distance himself from the one thing he knew he couldn't stand. "No," he found himself saying. "I can't, I just can't." Another sob caught in his throat, and he collapsed on to the chair behind him.

Jenna held out her arms to take the baby she had carried for 32 incredible weeks. As she looked down on his tiny face, she let out a gasp which made Pete look at her. “He’s perfect, so incredibly perfect.” She paused and held out her hand, trying to persuade him to come closer.

“He’s got your nose, and lips. Pete, please, come and meet your son. He needs to be loved. You have to come and love him.”

CHAPTER 36

It had been a week and Pete sat opposite Sarah, an array of brochures spread before them on the coffee table. Anyone looking in would be forgiven for assuming they were planning a party, surrounded with images of balloons and flowers; however, the photos depicting tiny coffins told the real story and painted a much more painful reality.

Leaning back Sarah exclaimed, "I just don't know which one to pick. I shouldn't have to do this!"

Pete sighed, more from sheer exhaustion than frustration. "I know, I know", he offered, "but we have to do this. It's the only thing we can still do for him." He paused, "I like this one," he said, handing over a picture of what, to all intents and purposes, looked like a wicker baby crib, complete with blue ribbons. "It looks comfortable."

She didn't even glance at the page, and instead shoved the brochure back at him. "Comfortable? What the Hell does that matter? He's dead you idiot, comfort isn't exactly an issue!"

In an instant Pete was back on his feet and pulling his coat on. "I can't do this anymore. I've tried to be supportive, I've tried to give you time. I've tried to bury my own feelings so I can be there for you, but he was my son too and God damn it, I'm in fucking agony as well. Stop being such a bitch, just for once in your life Sarah!"

With that he stormed out of the room, and a few seconds later she heard his van roll off the driveway and speed down the road. He literally couldn't get away from her fast enough. Burying her head in her hands she began sobbing, gently at first, then increasingly hysterically until she could barely catch her breath.

Finally, she stood up, grabbed a tissue and dabbed at her face, trying to stem the tears flowing down her cheeks. It was all just so unfair, and she still couldn't get her head around what had happened, nothing made the slightest bit of sense, and that's what she found so hard to accept.

This time last week she had woken up, and everything had been the way it should have been. It was the before-time, when Grayson was still safe. Now, just seven short days later she was planning a funeral for the baby she never got to see open his eyes. No one should ever have to go through that. Ever.

Every night she replayed the moment she found out as she lay in bed, unable to contemplate sleep. From there she remembered walking in to the delivery room to find Jenna cradling her child. All the midwives were crowded round her, offering their support, encouragement and condolences.

No one had given Sarah another thought, she wasn't offered any sympathy. No, in their eyes, Jenna was the grieving mother and she was just some pregnant friend that had dropped by to, what, gloat? In that instant her resentment was born. Resentment towards

Jenna for killing her son, and resentment towards the baby Sarah was still carrying. Apparently, you couldn't grieve for your dead child if you were busy carrying someone else's.

Jenna had, of course, played the martyr. After spending time with Grayson, she had graciously handed him over so Pete and Sarah could be alone with him. It had felt like she was doing them a favour, like somehow Jenna had some right to be devastated by what had happened. This had nothing to do with her – this was not her baby and she had no right to feel anything other than ashamed.

The autopsy had revealed the placenta had stopped working, though there didn't seem to be any clear-cut reason as to why that would be the case. Having done some research Sarah had found that Jenna's age might well have been one of the contributing factors. It didn't matter to her that, theoretically at least, anything could have caused it, or that it could have happened to anyone else; the simple truth was it had happened to Jenna, and that was all she cared about. That made it all her fault.

Her simplistic view of the world dictated that Jenna should be held solely accountable for the pain Sarah was now suffering. If she hadn't left it too late to have a baby, then her age wouldn't have been an issue. If she hadn't been such a crappy wife, then her husband wouldn't have felt the need to have an affair with the doctor who then cocked up their implantations. It was all her fault, and she now found herself wishing there was a way she could make her pay. Thoughts of revenge were the only things keeping her going at the moment, and she clung to them fiercely.

Pete had suggested they invite Jenna to the funeral, but Sarah had refused, strongly believing the other woman had no right to be there. Her grief had stripped away any compassion she could have felt, or understanding how this might have affected her one-time friend. Whilst Pete had tried to get her to see things from another perspective, Sarah simply couldn't and wouldn't entertain the idea that going through labour the way Jenna had been forced to would have taken its own emotional toll.

*****

Jenna sat in the booth by the window, their old favourite spot, and watched the world carry on its daily business. She always found it amazing that no matter what personal tragedy anyone was labouring under, one thing was always certain, nothing else would stop. Not even a breath would be missed or a heartbeat skipped. Time kept on ticking and the wheel continued to turn.

On some levels she found it comforting, the monotony of inevitability trudging on ad nauseam. On others, it was hard to come to terms with the reality of the anguish routed so entirely in her being and its parallel with the hustle and bustle of everyday life. When the maître d met her at the door and asked if she was well, her forced smile gave no indication of her desire to scream 'of course not', at the top of her lungs.

How could she be well? Her body, her actual self, had caused the death of a perfect baby. She had failed in the one thing she was charged to do for that soul. She could never be OK again, and her punishment for that was to live with the anguish that such innocent and commonplace pleasantries would bring for the rest of her days.

As she unfolded her napkin and surveyed the wine list, more out of habit than desire, she wondered, not for the first time, what she was doing here. When Will had phoned and asked to meet her she had immediately blown him off. It had taken her a few days to even come clean about what had happened with Grayson, saying the words seemed to add a whole new level of reality that she hadn't been quite ready to embrace. She'd just made excuses; a headache, a hair appointment, a meeting with a designer.

The biggest problem was the fact she thought there was something for her to 'come clean about'. For her, at least, it felt like she had done something wrong, something she had to confess to. Sarah's reaction hadn't exactly helped, and she couldn't shake the feeling that all of this was entirely her fault, and she should be held accountable.

Eventually she'd run out of excuses and stamina, and he'd caught her off guard. Having ignored his last three phone calls, she found herself answering him when he called on that Friday. As she heard the intrusive sound of the ringtone she realised if she didn't answer it she might not carry on. Out of the blue his call had become a lifeline, a reason to get up and leave the pills unopened on the counter.

She remembered answering and his voice immediately saying, “It’s today isn’t it, the funeral?” Those words had been enough to knock the wind out of her and she collapsed, in a broken heap on the cold, tiled kitchen floor, unable to move and barely able to breathe.

He’d stayed on the line, occasionally muttering platitudes like “It’s OK”, “you’ll be alright” and “take a deep breath”; then, within what felt like minutes he was at her side. Even to this day she had no idea if he’d come through the unlocked front door, or if she’d let him in. It didn’t matter, for once he’d come, and she hadn’t had to ask.

For hours he held her, and when she finally slept he stayed by her side, ensuring she wasn’t alone. It was the first sleep she’d managed since Grayson, and thankfully it had been dreamless. When she woke she had heard voices in the hall, and realised Pete and Will were arguing. It wasn’t much of an argument, Pete being respectful of Jenna’s home and need to sleep, Will unsure of confronting this man he still hadn’t worked out. Instead it was a confused war of words and emotional prevarication.

She’d no idea how long it had been going on for, but it seemed to be over within minutes. Pete thanked Will for being there, but politely asked him to leave, and Will had acquiesced. It was all very grown up and gentlemanly. If she'd been less fuggy headed from sleep she may even have been able to find it all slightly amusing. Instead, she'd been left baffled.

They hadn't spoken for a while after that, she wasn't sure how to approach him following an act of unwavering support she'd never anticipated from him, and she assumed he was unsure if his continued concern was welcomed. Eventually though he had phoned, and asked yet again if they could meet. He clearly wanted to talk to her, and she felt, after his recent actions, she did at least owe him some of her undivided attention.

However, now she was sitting here, waiting for him, she started to question if she was doing the right thing. It would be so much easier to simply brush him away and direct him to her solicitor. She knew whatever he wanted had to relate to the divorce in some way. He had decided to avoid their legal teams for some reason, and she felt he deserved her trust, at least in this.

She felt his presence before she heard or saw him. Whenever Will walked in to a room people stopped, they always had. He simply commanded admiration. It probably helped that the majority of people in the restaurant knew who he was, and how much he was reportedly worth. That always gained attention and faux respect, though at times like this it was a hugely unwelcomed distraction.

After a few moments he was by her side, and clearly wanted to greet her with a hug. She moved herself in to a position where she could stand, held her arms out and accepted his overly enthusiastic greeting. Every inch of her wanted to push him away, but she knew it would cause a scene whilst all eyes were on them, so instead she limply returned his squeeze, allowed him to kiss her cheek, and then thankfully returned to her seat.

He slid in opposite her and picked up the menu before meeting her gaze. Eventually he reached over the table, took her hand in his and said, “I trust you are feeling better, my dear?” The way he worded it she couldn’t help feeling it sounded less like a question and more like a request. Unsure how to answer she simply nodded, and eased her hand away from his grasp. In all the years they’d been married they had never managed to have a suitable conversation about their feelings and fears, she saw no reason why they should attempt to embark on it now that the end was nigh for them.

Once their food had been ordered Will leant back and said, “Are you not going to ask how things are with Adrienne?” Jenna smiled, this was it. This was what he wanted, and now she was to play her part in his silly little game. For a moment she was tempted to tell him precisely what she was thinking, but instantly thought better of it. No good would come from the honesty burning away inside of her.

Instead she nodded, “Tell me, how are things?” and she too leant back, ready to listen to the tale he wished to share. The next 10 minutes passed in a haze of half-listening as Will recounted the trauma that had been Adrienne's fundamental inability to get a grip on reality, as he described it. She murmured in the right places, and did all she could to sound as though what he was saying mattered in the slightest to anyone other than him.

"However, I didn't invite you to lunch to talk to you about Adrienne", he said at last. Jenna's heart sank, having been subjected to his ridiculously long and self-serving monologue she immediately realised there was probably worse to come.

"Please," she found herself saying, "just get on with it. I don't have the patience for games and would rather spend the time dealing with whatever it is, than dodging the issue by exchanging awkward small talk."

Will was taken aback by the directness of her comment. Jenna had always been the type who could listen patiently, say the right things, soothe the soul, and who would never dream of pressurising someone in to speaking before they were ready. This was his floor, and he was not used to her dictating the direction and speed with which conversation should be had.

He moved the remaining half of his steak around the plate, before putting his cutlery down and taking a long drink from his wine glass. "You know me well enough to understand why this is hard for me to say; however, it is clear that with the benefit of hindsight, I have made a grave error."

Jenna looked at him dispassionately and waited for him to continue, not feeling in the least inclined to offer any encouragement for what seemed like his latest confession. He coughed slightly, more from nerves than need, “Adrienne is not for me, and I was foolish to allow myself to be seduced by a younger woman and all the trappings she had to offer. I am sorry, and I hope now that this distasteful situation with the baby has been resolved, we can move on and get back to where we belong.”

As he finished his little speech he genuinely looked as though he expected some kind of reaction from her. Jenna looked at him, her mouth slightly open, trying to weigh up what her response should be. Did he honestly think that such words were going to carry any weight with her, that somehow his realisation that he had been wrong, that he had acted poorly and made a grave error of judgment, was enough to make her fall at his feet and offer him forgiveness?

Surely not, no apology had actually been offered, instead he was approaching her with what seemed little more passionate than a business deal. The remerging of two entities, back in their rightful place after a period of estrangement and disagreement. While the thought that everything he had put her through with Adrienne could just be swept under the carpet was ludicrous, the comment that irked her the most was the thought that the ‘distasteful situation with the baby’ had been resolved.

He was well aware how deeply affected she'd been following the death of Grayson, and that as a result she had still been left bereft of a child, whilst suffering the hormones and physical issues associated with new mothers. To think that somehow that equated to a resolution was the most insulting thing he had ever subjected her to in all their years of togetherness.

Will took her silence as confirmation she was thinking what he'd said over, and he seized the opportunity to continue. "The reality is, we know where our baby is. I don't care how you came to find this Pete, but his wife is pregnant with my child. Our child. Together we can ensure that our baby comes back to where it belongs. With our legal team, we can blow any arguments they have for keeping it out of the water. We'll completely destroy them, and then we can be a family."

Jenna sat with her mouth slightly open, stunned by what he'd said. She was still struggling to come to terms with how she felt about how things had played out. Although she was still desperate to be a mother, there was a part of her that genuinely felt as though she owed Sarah understanding and patience. She genuinely hoped Sarah wouldn't want to raise another person's baby, but she also knew that grief could do strange things to people. There was no way she could guarantee she wouldn't want to keep the baby if their roles had been reversed.

The reality was, if the clinic hadn't made a mistake, if both couples had left on that day pregnant with their own biological children, then the same thing might have happened. Jenna might still have lost their baby. She would still be left sitting here, no longer pregnant, with a fully decorated nursery waiting for an inhabitant that would never come.

Knowing now that Adrienne wasn't pregnant with Will's baby, left Jenna feeling used. Would he be sitting here with her, having this discussion about moving on with their lives, and reconciling, if Adrienne hadn't dropped her bombshell? Would he still be interested in using the full weight of the law (which, she knew, wasn't on their side anyway) to get their baby back, if he still thought he had his own child on the way with Adrienne?

Now things hadn't worked out the way he'd anticipated them to, Will was trying to salvage something from the wreckage. The problem was, Jenna wasn't sure she wanted to be salvaged. Yes, it would be easy to go back. It would solve some problems, she wouldn't have to think, she could just put on her old life like a comfortable pair of slippers. The real issue was, she was done with sleepwalking her way through her life. She wanted to be happy, even if it had to be hard fought for.

She hated herself for admitting that a part of her was slightly tempted, but looking at Will, she couldn't bring herself to do it. His attempts to turn this in to a legal argument, without stopping for one second to think about the people who were caught up in it all, and how they felt, made her feel sick. The way he could just disregard everybody was appalling.

In that instant Jenna found herself faced with a moment of clarity, it hit her like a bolt of lightning. She placed her napkin on her plate, stood up with her coat in her arms, leant over to Will and whispered in his ear, "Go fuck yourself, you arrogant, self-centred prick".

With that, she turned her back on him and left, her head held high.

CHAPTER 37

Pete was asleep on the floor in the nursery when the phone rang and woke him up. Since Grayson's death he'd realised this was the only place he could find enough emotional peace to be able to close his eyes, and eventually drift off. He didn't understand it, and if he was honest he hadn't really tried, but occasionally his mind did wander curiously over why it helped.

Perhaps it was simply a safe place – it was full of happy memories, which weren't all immediately tied to Grayson. This was never meant to be his room, and Pete hadn't built any of it for his son, but he was reminded of him in here. Just not in a threatening way.

Despite everything he still had hope that in the not too distant future the room would have its very own occupant, and Jenna's life would be complete. It wouldn't make any difference to him, whether Jenna did or didn't become a mother was nothing to do with him, but he desperately hoped that somehow everything would work out in the end. He was jerked away from his thoughts by his mobile ringing loudly next to his ear.

He rolled over and groaned as he realised the havoc the hard floor was playing on his back. Reaching out for the phone he saw an unknown number and answered with a curt, "What?". He assumed it was a sales call, the only call any tradesman was guaranteed to get on any given day, and was in no mood to be talked at by a pushy prick who no doubt earnt more than him.

"Mr. Jenkins?" a pleasant female voice asked at the end of the line. He grunted, now jumping to the possibility this was one of Sarah's many creditors chasing for the extortionate amounts of money she owed them.

"It's the midwife on Ward 28, calling about your wife. We need you to get to the hospital as soon as possible. I don't want to alarm you, but she's being prepped for theatre and we need to deliver the baby. You need to get here as quickly as possible."

Pete bolted upright and staggered to his feet, half listening to the voice still talking to him. He ran downstairs, hung up and pulled on his boots. He immediately tried Jenna's mobile, but it went straight to voicemail. Not sure where she was or what she was doing he didn't want to panic her, so he instantly decided not to leave her a message. Instead he scribbled, 'Gone to the hospital, call me ASAP', on a post-it and stuck it to the fridge, hoping she'd see it the second she came in.

With that he grabbed his car keys and was out on the main road in seconds, hurtling towards the hospital.

*****

Will stayed in the restaurant for a long time after Jenna left, totally blindsided by her parting comments and unsure what to do next. He'd been so sure a simple explanation of what he'd done wrong, and a request they move forward together would be enough to make her see sense. They'd been married for so long, and were so inextricably linked throughout the years that he couldn't understand why she would be so willing to throw it all away.

He'd made mistakes with other women in the past and she'd always been forgiving. It wasn't a case of taking him back, she had never sent him away; it just made no sense that she would now refuse to accept him home. A large part of him wondered if it might be the hormones talking, that somehow despite the fact it was not her baby she'd lost, she was reacting emotionally to this situation. Women were like that, he reasoned, completely unpredictable, even volatile, and impossible to understand.

Looking for a way to absolve himself of any responsibility for how Jenna might be feeling he found himself questioning, not for the first time, why this Pete had seemingly taken up residence in her life. It only just dawned on him that at their last meeting this stranger had asked *him* to leave, rather than the other way around. How had it not occurred to him to find out what was going on between them before?

Was Jenna not interested in getting back with him because she was romantically involved with this Pete? Perhaps they were playing some long-game, tricking the other woman into delivering the child, and then somehow running off with it so they could raise it together. It would make sense, and offer an explanation as to why she hadn't been interested in pursuing a legal option against the couple.

Whilst he sat in quiet contemplation of the women in his life he finished off three brandies, and was no closer to any form of conclusion. Reluctantly accepting it would now be unwise to drive himself home, he called the office to request Tom come to collect him. Alice answered and seemed relieved to hear from him, asking if he was OK.

"Of course, I'm OK," he barked at her, then steadied his voice, immediately feeling guilty for taking his frustrations out on her.

Alice had always been there for him, and whilst he knew she was paid handsomely to do her job, she'd never made him feel like her loyalty was merely a financial transaction. He genuinely felt her support, and would be utterly lost without it. She didn't deserve to be treated as poorly as he had done over the years, like she was an afterthought or simply part of the furniture.

He shifted in his chair, uncomfortable with the parallels between his treatment of staff and the women in his personal life. "Sorry," he continued, "I'm fine Alice, thank you. I just need a lift. Can you ask Tom to come and get me?"

Once he hung up he checked his watch and winced at the time. His knee jerk reaction, after years of conditioning, was to panic about the mood that would await him at home. For the longest of times it had been the cold ambivalence of Jenna, quickly followed by the accusatory and jealous whinging of Adrienne.

Now, for the first time in 30 years he was heading home to an empty hotel room and no one to demand answers from him. The prospect both thrilled, and terrified him.

*****

Sarah sat in bed, shaking. Earlier in the day she'd been shopping, but had started to feel exceptionally unwell. Her head had begun pounding and her vision had become blurred, which caused her to be violently sick. The shop assistant immediately phoned an ambulance, and it wasn't long before she found herself on a busy maternity ward.

After various checks and people coming and going she'd been told she had pre-eclampsia, and had then been moved to a private room, away from the comings and goings of the overcrowded day unit. At first, she'd liked the peace and quiet, but then she realised how dull and boring it was when you had nothing but your own miserable thoughts to occupy yourself.

The room had been so still, but as soon as her blood pressure had spiked again it had filled with doctors, consultants and midwives. Never before had she been surrounded by so many people, and yet felt so lonely. She was being poked, prodded and talked at. No one was sitting there, holding her hand or asking her how *she* was. No one cared about her at all, and she was scared.

The next thing she knew she was being wheeled out of her room, down a long corridor. The porter pushing her bed was talking to a nurse, or midwife, she wasn't sure which, about a backlog in A&E. As she sat there, the centre of her own universe, she was reminded of shopping. She was always infuriated when retail assistants talked to each other whilst serving you, as though you were an inconvenience to their day by coming to their checkout and wanting to hand over money. That was bad enough, but this was so much worse.

Now, here she was, terrified, and being told they had minutes to deliver her baby or they could lose them both, with a porter who only cared for his busy workload. She had a frightening thought this could be the last conversation she ever heard, and started crying uncontrollably.

The woman by his side looked down at her, and squeezed her hand. "Don't worry love, you'll be fine, they know what they're doing and they know how to do it quickly. Your husband is on his way, and will be here when you wake up. It's going to be just fine."

With that, the bed crashed through a set of double doors and she was suddenly in what felt like a walk-in freezer. A tall man leant over her and introduced himself as the anesthetist looking after her today. He sounded like he was welcoming her on board a flight, and she found herself wondering if she would ever be able to make that trip to Rome.

More people spoke to her, asking her questions or giving her information, but she couldn't take any of it in. She felt like she'd lost the ability to comprehend English. Were it not for the fact she was already panicking about everything else, she'd have worried she was having a stroke.

Before long she felt a sharp scratch on the back of her hand and the soothing voice of the pilot asked her to count backwards. Her mind wandered to Vatican City and she found herself climbing up the steps to the Basilica; 10, 9, 8, 7 …

*****

Jenna pulled on to the driveway and noticed Pete's van was gone. She felt a tinge of sadness that he wouldn't be there waiting for her when she got in, but equally was relieved to have some more time to herself. It was odd, she didn't quite know how they'd ended up living together on a permanent basis.

When he first moved in it was purely as a stop gap whilst he worked things out with Sarah. Yes, he had been at his Mums and therefore wasn't in dire need, but it was clear being back at home with Elsie wasn't necessarily doing him much good either. She hadn't meant to suggest it, but by the time he had settled himself in she was already more than used to having him around.

Knowing that someone else was in the house with her was a huge comfort, although it was odd actually having someone to talk to after so many years of relative solitude. Jenna was amazed how much she'd enjoyed his company, and how naturally their relationship had developed.

Losing Grayson together had made them even closer, but she realised it was at the expense of his marriage. In her mind there was no way he and Sarah could work things out, not after she'd put so much energy in to pushing him away, and not after he had leant so heavily on Jenna instead. Of course, Sarah still didn't know the extent of their relationship; in fact, she knew nothing. The opportunity to tell her just hadn't presented itself, and now she was refusing to take Jenna's calls anyway.

She completely sympathised with Pete, she knew only too well what his thoughts and feelings on the entire situation were; however, she felt her heart breaking for Sarah too. Although she had a funny way of actually showing it, there was no doubt Sarah was besotted with Pete.

Jenna could see she was too emotionally immature to really demonstrate that love, and put someone else first, but that didn't mean she didn't feel it. She'd feel completely betrayed by Pete's behaviour. Their behaviour. No sane person wouldn't be able to understand that.

For the longest of times Will had been unfaithful, but every occasion had been nothing more than sex. Jenna fully understood and accepted what people meant when they said 'it was just sex'. Sex was nothing but a physical urge and need, it didn't have to mean anything, and was therefore easy to forgive if you chose to.

Emotions, well that was something else entirely. When you turned to someone other than the person you'd promised to cherish above all else, that was a vow broken and trust destroyed in a way that 'just' sex couldn't do. It was ultimately why she knew her and Will were over when she'd realised he was involved with Adrienne.

Will had never been entirely hers, not really, and she'd accepted that for long enough. Now she was glad she'd finally set him free, and was amused it had occurred at a time when he no longer wanted liberty. She firmly believed that, in the long run, this was the best thing that could ever happen to him. After all these years she had come to the conclusion that until Will found himself, he would ruin every woman he came in to contact with.

Walking in to the house she shut the front door behind her, placing her handbag on the hall table and picking up the mail Pete had left to one side for her. She made her way to the fridge to grab a bottle of water and caught sight of the post-it waiting for her.

Once she read it her immediate reaction was to head straight over to be by Pete's side, but without knowing what the situation was, she wasn't sure if that might make matters worse for him or Sarah.

The part of her that knew her baby was being brought in to the world desperately wanted to know what was going on. She wanted to know that Sarah, and the child, were both safe. The other part of her, the one that had already delivered a baby that wasn't her own, knew that it would make no difference to Sarah.

Whatever was happening was happening to that woman, and she alone was going through it. The last thing she needed was Jenna pushing her nose in and making her feel overwhelmed. It was a sacred space, and Sarah had every right to enter in to that alone, free from the complications of what the future would bring.

While she wanted to be supportive, she accepted the best way she could do that might be by doing nothing. In the end, she sent a text asking him to call when he could, and saying she was thinking of him.

CHAPTER 38

Pete had spent the last 35 minutes pacing up and down the corridor, desperately trying to keep himself busy to avoid having to think about anything too much. He was a simple man who, when presented with a problem wanted nothing more than to find a solution. The reality of the current situation however was that no single solution seemed to solve all the issues they were facing, which meant he couldn't move forward. Thinking about it wasn't doing him, or anyone else for that matter, any good. Instead he was just gradually going crazy.

The weeks following Grayson's death had been difficult, on so many levels. Simply coming to terms with the loss of his son had been hard enough, but he was thankful to be able to share it with Jenna. He found it ironic that she seemed to understand how he felt better than Sarah could. In fact, Sarah wouldn't even talk about Grayson or how she felt, instead focussing all her energy on despising Jenna.

He'd intended to tell Sarah everything about his relationship with Jenna as soon as possible; the thought of still keeping it a secret from her seemed wrong, and he wanted to open up, to let her in, so she had someone to lean on. There was never the right moment though, her vindictiveness seemed to know no bounds, and there was no way he could add more fuel to the fire.

He was utterly terrified that Sarah would be tempted to keep the baby she was carrying. The entire time the two women had been talking, they'd always agreed they would simply just 'swap' babies as soon as they had been born. Of course, nothing was written down, and even if it had, he wasn't sure there would have been anything legally binding about it. The problem was, given their current situation, did things change?

Morally, he knew they didn't. Sarah wasn't pregnant with her child, and she had no right to keep it. However, Jenna wasn't in a position to hand a child over to Sarah any longer, so Sarah argued there was no reason why she should hand one over to Jenna.

The way Sarah talked it was as though she firmly believed Jenna 'owed her one. An eye for an eye, almost. It made him feel sick to his stomach that, out of grief and jealousy she would deliberately deprive another woman of the child that was rightfully theirs.

The largest part of him wanted to believe there was no way she would be capable of behaving like that, but as the days passed he'd come to accept that she could. He knew that if she found out that he and Jenna had become close, Hell, if she found out anything about them at all, she would be propelled to a new level of revenge seeking.

As things stood, whilst they weren't getting on terribly well, Pete felt he had some degree of involvement with Sarah's decisions and plans for the future. Legally, if not biologically, this baby would be brought in to the world as his child, and that meant he had some say in what happened. If Sarah convinced herself he had been unfaithful, though he hadn't, he would lose the tenuous grip he had on the situation.

Now though he found himself hoping that this change of events, and the speed with which things were happening, would catch Sarah off-guard. The last time they'd spoken she still hadn't firmly made up her mind about what to do. She'd still been avoiding Jenna's phone calls, and Pete had offered to act as a go-between, letting Jenna know how the pregnancy was progressing without Sarah having to have anything to do with her.

Of course, that's precisely what he was doing unofficially anyway. He just hoped it would have given him a good opportunity to avoid explaining how he knew Jenna. Again, there was a surge of guilt. He'd given Sarah such a hard time about keeping her relationship with Jenna a secret, he knew he was no better. However, this turn of events meant he genuinely daren't risk anything that would jeopardise Jenna's chance of becoming a mother to her own child.

It was all just so complicated. He knew Sarah understood that at the heart of all their pain, his, hers and Jenna's, there was a baby. A baby that needed someone to love it and look after it for the rest of its life. Up until now though it had seemed like this was just an abstract concept to Sarah. It was just this baby they talked about, that kicked her throughout the night and that she had no real tie to. This dramatic change in her health meant that in the next few minutes it would become a tangible reality for her and he desperately prayed it might make all the difference to her outlook on things.

Suddenly he heard his name being called, and he turned to see a midwife walking towards him, holding a blanket in her arms. He was immediately reminded of Grayson, and how another midwife, not that long ago, in a ward a few floors away, had handed a similar bundle to Jenna. His heart skipped a beat, realising in that instant the pregnancy was over, and here now, was a new life. Here was Jenna's baby; she was a mother, at last, and he hadn't even managed to speak to her yet to tell her what was happening.

"Mr. Jenkins, congratulations, you have a daughter". The midwife handed him the tiny baby girl and gave him a smile as she guided him towards one of the plastic chairs lining the corridor. "Your wife is doing well, and is currently in recovery. You'll be able to see her shortly, we just need to give her time to come around. The baby is completely fine, and a healthy 6lbs 3ozs; which is good for her age. She didn't need any assistance after she was delivered. She's going to be absolutely fine."

Pete couldn't believe what he was hearing, and was only partially listening. All of his attention was focused on the little girl he now held in his arms. He was busy taking in her tiny fingers, the pout of her lips, which reminded him of Jenna, and the long eyelashes covering her sleeping eyes. He was blown away by how perfect she was and, in that instant, could completely understand why Sarah would struggle to hand this baby over to Jenna.

He knew he had to call her, to let her know what had happened and he reached for his phone, but stopped himself. What on earth could he say to her, and how would they move forward? The reality of the situation was Sarah was still unconscious, he had no idea what her thoughts and feelings were at that moment.

He couldn't very well tell Jenna to come down to the hospital to see her daughter, only for Sarah to refuse her admittance when she got there. Legally speaking, Sarah was this girl's mother; biology had nothing to do with it. At the end of the day she had the final say on what did, or didn't happen to this child. Or did she? He reminded himself that if Sarah was the legal mother, as her husband, he was the legal father.

Regardless of what was and wasn't the case, he knew he had to do something. He couldn't leave Jenna in the dark, not aware that this amazing thing had happened. Somehow, he juggled the baby in his arms, fumbling in his back pocket till he was able to reach his phone, he took a photo and then clicked on Jenna's name.

*****

He sat next to her bed, his head bowed, completely oblivious to the fact she was already awake and had been watching him for the last five minutes. She'd been fascinated by the way he looked at the tiny baby in his arms, even though she was doing nothing more interesting than breathing. It failed to occur to her that the last time he'd held a new born like this there were no rhythmic movements of the chest.

Finally, she coughed to get his attention and he looked up, a huge smile plastered on his face. "How are you?" he asked, before returning his gaze to the baby girl. Sarah tried to sit up, but immediately regretted it, wincing as pain seared through her stomach.

"Not good, it would appear", she said between sharp intakes of air. Automatically, he reached out to pour her a glass of water, and she took a sip, realising it was room temperature. She wondered how long she'd been asleep, and how long he had been sitting by her side.

"The baby is doing well," Pete said, providing her with a complete update on what had happened since she got taken down to surgery. In that moment she found herself not caring about the child she'd been carrying for so long. Catching sight of the profile of the tiny face she realised nothing would ever replace Grayson. This baby girl, gorgeous as she no doubt was, would not change the fact that her own son had died.

For weeks, she thought it would. That having a baby, any baby, in her arms would replace the son she had never got the chance to know. Now, as pain coursed through her body, and she relived the trauma of the last few hours, she knew nothing was going to make it all OK. She could keep this baby, but in the process, she'd be causing someone else so much pain; she wasn't sure if she could actually live with that.

She put her hand out and touched the baby's cheek. "Don't get attached Pete. She's not our princess. We need to let Jenna know she's a Mumma, and she can take her daughter home." Pete immediately felt a sense of relief, knowing how happy Jenna would be.

He'd already sent her photos of her baby, keeping her updated constantly as to how she was doing, but he hadn't been able to let her know what was going to happen long term. Now, he could. Now he could tell her the most amazing news that Sarah had finally seen the light and had made the right choice.

The temptation to simply pick up his phone and call her now was almost overwhelming, but he knew that would spell disaster for everyone. Sarah smiled, misunderstanding the look on his face.

"I know it's hard, but it's the right thing. Please, take her before I change my mind. Jenna's details are in my hospital notes. Get in touch with her, tell her, get the baby to her tonight. I don't want her to be my responsibility any longer. We can sign all the paperwork tomorrow."

He couldn't believe his luck, or how quickly things had changed. Clearly everything she had now been through, the reality of giving birth, even if she had been unconscious throughout it, was enough to make her realise just what was at stake if she kept digging her heels in. Standing, he leant over her bed and gave her a kiss on the forehead then left the room, taking Jenna's daughter with him.

*****

Within minutes of receiving his phone call Jenna had strapped the car seat in to the front of her Mercedes, and was on her way to the hospital. She honestly couldn't believe Sarah had changed her mind, certainly not so quickly, and part of her was waiting for him to phone back and say it had all been a cruel joke on his wife's part.

The more time that passed, and the closer she got to the finish line, the safer she began to feel. After all that had happened she found it hard to believe that anyone was going to end up with the semblance of a happy ending. She knew nothing would change what had already been and gone, she would always be deeply affected by the loss of Grayson, but now, she would have a child of her own.

After all the years of treatment, and the mental and physical pain that had caused, she was finally going to be a mother. Her thoughts again turned to Sarah, and she marvelled at the change of heart. Knowing how attached she felt to Grayson when he was born, she imagined Sarah must have felt the same, and therefore understood the huge sacrifice she was making for her.

Jenna hadn't been given a choice as to whether to keep Grayson. There was no option for her, under the circumstances. However, if he had been alive, if she had been the first to hold him, if she had felt his breath against her skin, she wasn't sure how easily she'd have handed him over. She would have known, with every ounce of her being, that it was the right thing to do.

Sometimes though, the right thing was the most painful, and hardest to follow through with. Silently she thanked Sarah, and knew she would never be able to express her gratitude. She laughed at herself, gratitude seemed such a pathetic word given everything they had gone through to get here.

It didn't take her long to find a space out the front of the maternity hospital, and she pulled in to the pick-up zone, along with a multitude of new Dads. Struggling at first, she finally managed to yank the car seat out of its place, and practically sprinted in to the building. As she made her way to the delivery ward, where Pete would be waiting for her, she found it hard to catch her breath. She knew it was only in part as a result of the physical exertion she had put herself through; in reality it was more to do with the excitement that was almost overwhelming her.

Due to a busy shift it seemed to take forever for someone to buzz her through on to the delivery suite. Panicking, she stood at the reception desk, unsure who to ask for. She didn't want to be sent to Sarah's room, and come face to face with the woman who, at last check despised her, despite what she had now done. Unaware how much the staff on duty knew, she wasn't sure how to explain what it was she wanted.

Just as she was about to ask if anyone knew where Pete Jenkins might be, he came around the corner. Running towards him she came to a stop just before him and peered over the blankets cradled in his arms. The most beautiful little girl she had ever seen opened her eyes and gazed up at her, and in that moment, Jenna believed in love at first sight.

CHAPTER 39

It was 2am and they lay on the sofa together, his arm wrapped around her as she nestled her head on his chest. Her baby daughter lay on her lap, sleeping soundly after a good feed. Jenna smiled, never before had she felt so contented and complete. Finally, she was a mother, and after all that had happened in the last few months, it was still taking some getting used to. In fact, she wasn't entirely convinced she'd ever really get used to it.

Although she had the baby, the nursery, had done some feeds, changed nappies, been thrown up on three times already, and had mastered the art of coaxing a reluctant burp, she still felt she was living a dream. She'd tried to explain it to Pete, and the closest she had come was as though she was an imposter in her own life, and none of this really belonged to her. It was a dream that had finally come true, but it still all seemed like such a fantasy.

The whole way home she had been in fear that Sarah would change her mind, that she'd get home and there would be a phone call from her demanding the baby back. That perhaps this was all part of some game Sarah wanted to play with her, an elaborate revenge she'd planned ever since the moment Grayson died. However, she'd made it home with no contact, and had settled down to an evening of simply staring at her child.

Pete had remained at the hospital for a few hours with Sarah. Jenna knew he wanted to come back home to her, he'd have wanted to spend time with the baby as much as she did, he'd clearly already started bonding with her in the hours after she'd been born and Sarah was in recovery. However, he'd felt it was his duty to stay and support Sarah. Jenna was glad, in part. Though she was amazed how much she actually missed him, and how part of her felt quite guilty for begrudging him the time he was spending away from her, she was actually relieved.

Him staying with Sarah had given her a better insight in to what was going on in this other woman's head. After weeks of veiled threats that Jenna would never see her baby, Sarah had suddenly changed her mind, when it mattered the most. There hadn't been any conversation or discussion with Pete; she'd just done it. Whilst he was there, holding her hand and comforting her, Sarah had explained her change of heart. It genuinely seemed it was based on nothing more than the fact it was the right thing, and she'd at last come to realise that.

Jenna had her own suspicions that it was slightly more complicated than that. Or at the very least, there was a degree more manipulation in Sarah's thought processes than she was currently prepared to admit to.

Pete had made it clear he would never forgive Sarah if she refused to allow Jenna to take custody of her daughter. There was no way he could stand by her side whilst she behaved in such a manner, and destroyed another family, no matter what her motivations for it were. Sarah therefore had to make a choice: the baby, or Pete.

Admittedly, things weren't guaranteed to work out between her and Pete, but it was a gamble to walk away from the man that might be able to give her a shot at a biological child of her own. He'd never agree to it if she'd gone through with her initial plan. Jenna was convinced the only thing keeping Sarah going at the moment was the thought that, somewhere down the line, once the dust had settled, and their grief had turned to something slightly less painful, they'd be able to try again. They would one day have their perfect little family.

As delighted as she was now, lying here in Pete's arms with her daughter, a pain stabbed at her heart when she thought of him returning to a life with Sarah. They'd never talked about how they felt about each other, or what the future held for them regardless of the decision Sarah made, but the truth was they had become a lot closer since Grayson's death.

Almost unbidden thoughts had entered her mind of them raising this child together. Of him being in the garden, kicking a ball around, whilst she prepared dinner. Colourful stick figure drawings depicting their unconventional family plastered over the front of the fridge. Parents evenings, sleepless nights, trips to A&E when she fell off her bike. All the painfully boring and occasionally disruptive events that made up everything about being a parent. That's all she had ever wanted, and it was hard not to imagine sharing that with the man who had come to mean so much to her.

Suddenly Pete kissed her on the head, then touched the baby's face gently with the back of his hand. Without opening her eyes, she moved her tiny hand up and grabbed his little finger. Both he and Jenna smiled at this perfect little moment, another memory to be added to the ones they all still had ahead of them.

"She needs a name," Pete reminded her, "have you given it any thought?".

Jenna frowned. She'd deliberately chosen not to find out whether Sarah was carrying her son or daughter, which meant that up until a few hours ago, she'd had a long list of potential names for either a boy or girl. She still hadn't really come around to the idea that this child was hers to name. She also knew that in reality, Will should be included in the discussions. However, she still hadn't managed to get round to telling him that his daughter had been born. She reasoned his lack of interest to date afforded her a little bit of a reprieve before making the call.

Jenna was about to reply to Pete when they were disturbed by the sound of his phone ringing on the coffee table. Glancing down at the screen he was surprised to see it was an unknown number, and warily he answered it, anticipating an emergency given the time of night.

“Mr. Jenkins?”, a male voice queried on the other end of the line. Pete asked who was calling. “It’s Dr. Williams from St Mary’s. I’m sorry to say that your wife has experienced a complication as a result of her delivery. You might want to come down as quickly as possible. I suggest you bring the baby, she may want to see her once she has returned from recovery.”

*****

Pete found himself frantically pacing the corridors in the hospital for the second time in 24 hours, wondering what on earth was happening and waiting for someone to have a break in their busy shift to update him. Eventually a tall man walked confidentially towards him, held out his hand and introduced himself as Dr. Williams.

“Come with me, Mr. Jenkins, we have a consulting room free where we can talk privately.” With that, he turned back the way he’d come and set off towards the entrance of the ward, taking a left and opening the door to a room that looked to be no more than a broom cupboard. Pete walked past him and took a seat on one of the three dishevelled armchairs placed around the centre of the room.

Once they were both seated Dr. Williams explained how Sarah had experienced a complication as a result of her caesarean. Whilst things had initially looked to have gone well, her uterus had failed to contract, which caused her to start bleeding profusely. Although Dr.

Williams provided him with all the information he had to hand, Pete didn't take any of it in. He was straining to hear the subtleties in the doctor's language – was he referring to Sarah in the past, or the present? Precisely how bad was the news he was about to deliver?

Finally, the doctor got to the point, and advised that the only way to stop the bleeding was to perform an emergency hysterectomy. At first Pete breathed a sigh of relief; she was alive. Initially it was the only thing that mattered, then it dawned on him that as far as Sarah was concerned that might not be the best outcome for her.

He collapsed, burying his face in his hands and wondering what shit storm was about to descend on Jenna and the baby.

*****

The surgery lasted for more than six hours, and it took a further 24 before Sarah regained consciousness. When she was finally wheeled in to her own private room, Pete was waiting for her, though he didn't have the baby with him. The nurse on duty and in charge of Sarah's care had warned him that his wife was confused and disoriented and no doubt in a lot of pain, despite the medication coursing through her body.

As a result, no one had yet told her what had happened, concerned it would scare and upset her too much at this stage in her recovery. It had been agreed it would be left to him to break the news, at a time he felt suitable. He couldn't help but feel it was a cruel act of fate that he would have so much to tell Sarah when she was well enough to hear it.

On the fourth attempt at waking up Sarah managed to stay conscious long enough to hold a conversation. Initially she asked where she was, and then her memory seemed to come back to her all at once. She recalled feeling unwell, and the nurses rushing around her, but after that it had all gone blank. Pete was there to fill in the gaps.

When she heard the news that she could no longer have children, no matter how they were conceived, she broke down. The fact her life had been saved seemed to be off little comfort to her in that moment. For a while she alternated between sitting in silence, staring in to space, and crying so hard he worried her stitches would burst.

After she fell in to another deep sleep Pete took the chance to walk down to the cafeteria to grab a coffee and something to eat. He realised he hadn't eaten for hours, and had barely slept. Though he felt huge concern for Sarah and how she was faring, his biggest priority was Jenna, and the baby.

He was missing them terribly and wanted nothing more than to be at home with them. His feelings for this woman who had started as an unlikely friend were growing by the day, and he was dismayed at how complicated everything would remain for months to come.

He sat down, cradling the paper cup between his hands and enjoying its warmth. Presented with an opportunity to sit and think for the first time in hours he started to play recent events over in his mind. Thinking about Jenna, he realised how much he missed her voice, and decided to give her a call. It had been hours since he'd last updated her on Sarah, and he hated the thought of her being out of the loop.

"How is she?", Jenna asked, genuine concern reaching him through the phone. He sighed, "I honestly don't know. She's in too much shock at the moment to really be able to process everything. It's impossible to say what the future's going to hold for her. For us all, I suppose."

They chatted for a few more minutes, but were both too exhausted to really make much in the way of meaningful small talk. Eventually they said goodnight, Jenna promising to give the baby a kiss for him, and Pete assuring her he would let her know if anything changed with Sarah.

Having finished his luke warm sausage roll he wearily made his way back up to the ward, and returned to Sarah's room. He was surprised to see her propped up on her pillows, trying to pick at a slice of toast the nurse had brought in for her.

"We need to talk", she said as he entered the room and shut the door behind him.

*****

It wasn't so much a conversation as an argument, through hissed whispers, as they desperately tried not to draw attention to themselves. Things had started calmly enough, with Sarah merely explaining how she felt, and what she wanted. The problem was, as far as Pete was concerned, what she wanted was so unreasonable he couldn't help but lose his temper with her.

CHAPTER 40

Jenna sat on the floor in the nursery, her back against the wall with the baby cradled in her arms. The floor was littered with dirty nappies, clumps of cotton wool and a variety of milk-stained baby grows. Her house had never been so untidy, and she had never been so happy.

Pete crept in to the room, avoiding the one squeaky floorboard he had never got around to fixing, and slid down next to her. She rested her head on his shoulder and they sat together in silence for a few minutes.

Finally, he said, "We need to talk", and she nodded, handing the baby over to him so she could stand up, and then transfer her in to her new cot. Satisfied she was perfectly settled, they went down stairs, placing the monitor on the kitchen counter whilst he made a cup of coffee.

On the drive home Pete had desperately been trying to find the best way to explain the situation to Jenna. He'd fumbled over his words, practicing his speech, but now he was facing her he had no idea how to start. There weren't any words that were going to make this less of a shock, or easier for her to handle.

In the end, "She wants her back," was all Pete could manage. There was so much more he could say, but in that moment, those were the only four words that mattered. Jenna's mouth dropped open and she was unable to speak. She wanted to scream no, and offer a hundred reasons why that was impossible, but nothing would come out.

Pushing a mug of coffee towards her Pete nodded, “I know,” he offered at last. “I know.”

While she drank Pete brought her up to speed with what had happened at the hospital. He explained how, after Sarah realised she could no longer have any children following the complications of the birth, she had wanted the baby back. She now saw this baby as her only chance at having the family she’d always desperately wanted, especially because it gave her the little daughter she’d always fantasised about.

He’d tried to talk her down, to sympathise with her and say he understood why that might be her initial reaction, but that things weren’t that simple. He practically pleaded with her, trying to get her to understand the devastation her actions would cause to Jenna, and how none of it was going to help reduce the grief she felt over Grayson.

For the first time Sarah had demonstrated just how savvy she actually was. She’d reminded him that legally speaking she was this baby’s mother, and the only way Jenna would ever be able to make a claim for the child was if both her and Pete gave up their parental rights. Although she had intended to do that this very morning, the need for emergency surgery had got in the way, and the papers had never been signed. Legally, Jenna didn’t have a leg to stand on.

Of course, they'd all discussed it over the last few months, the legal implications and everything, but Pete had never been convinced Sarah had paid that much attention. The agreement had been that the babies would be returned to where they belonged, it didn't matter what the law said.

Whilst she was talking it have been clear that Sarah was utterly convinced that simply saying she wanted the baby would make it so. She didn't seem able to contemplate any form of fight from Jenna, not when she knew Will wasn't going to be by her side to support her. Her exact words were, "What the fuck can she do about it?".

Pete had been furious. No matter how much he understood, and could sympathise with the way Sarah felt, morally he knew everything she was saying was so heartless and calculated. He looked at the woman he'd been married to for so many years and genuinely didn't recognise her. Her quest to become a mother had taken her so far from the person she had once been, that he didn't see how there was any way she could redeem herself.

He'd known for months that their marriage was over, but for some reason had failed to acknowledge it either to himself, or to her. A small part of him had hoped that maybe things would be OK in the end. They would find a way to be again, once the dust had settled. Now he knew it was all too far gone for there to be any hope at all.

Everything they had once been had been completely destroyed during this journey. There was no trust, and now Sarah had removed any semblance of compassion from her soul, he knew he was fighting a lost cause.

That's when he decided he might as well burn the whole house down and be done with it.

"I'm not going to support you in this," he'd said, at last.

Sarah had looked at him, her mouth slightly open, trying to compute what he'd said and what it actually meant.

"You are the baby's legal mother, and I'm her legal father. I have as much right to a say over what happens to her as you do. The only difference is that the second she was born, I didn't discard her and demand that someone else raise her. You did. You abandoned your legal daughter, and I will use that fact to fight you for custody."

The argument had raged, her anger filling the room and spurring him on to retaliate. Before he knew what was happening he'd told her everything about his relationship with Jenna. How they'd met, how they'd talked, how he'd been there when Grayson was born, how he was living at her house and had no intention of moving out.

For one brief moment he reveled in the look on her face, the utter crushing of her soul as the feeling of betrayal swept through her. He knew in that instant he was no longer a good person, and he didn't care. He wanted her to feel something at his hands for once, rather than constantly the other way around.

He tried to make it clear that he'd done nothing with Jenna, that there had been no betrayal of their marriage vows, but Sarah was too far gone to listen. Not for the first time she realised she was no longer sure what he was, or wasn't capable of. He'd been capable of lying to her, of keeping these massive secrets from her, which meant that ultimately he was capable of having an affair. It didn't matter that it made no sense to her, none of this made any sense.

She struggled to lift the empty water jug from the table at the side of her bed and threw it at his head. He ducked, and with that, he'd walked out of the room, knowing that there genuinely was nothing more they had to say to each other.

The only thing that mattered to him at that point was getting home to Jenna, and letting her know he was prepared to fight for her, and her daughter, with everything he had.

*****

After he left, Sarah remained seated in her hospital bed, amazed by everything Pete had said. In all the years they'd been together he'd never stood up to her. She had always been able to get precisely what she wanted from him, often without much in the way of coercion or persuasion. It amazed her, as she had often been under the impression he was weak, totally unable to defend himself or draw a line in the sand.

Today that line had been drawn, and of course it had to be against the one thing she wanted more than anything else in this world. Not only had he stood up to her, but he was now saying he would stand against her. That terrified her more than anything. Having him as an opponent, when she had relied on him silently supporting her from the background, was more than she could begin to compute. How on earth was she going to win this fight on her own? She had no money, no experience, no one by her side.

As she closed her eyes she suddenly remembered that they'd all forgotten one other person who should be having a say in the life of this tiny baby girl. She immediately reached for her phone, pushing through the pain ripping through her stomach as she did so, and started a search for his office number.

If she could handle this correctly, there was no way on earth she was going to be going through on her own from now on. With him by her side, she had as much behind her as Pete did, but she was confident she'd win. There was no way he was going to get away with this, she wanted to destroy him for what he'd done to her. Pete Jenkins would regret the day he chose Jenna and her baby over his wife.

Minutes later the phone was ringing, and had been answered by an Australian accent that caught her off guard.

“Hi, yes, I need to speak to William Cooper, please. No, he’s not expecting me, but I promise you, he’s going to want to take this call.”

*****

“I’ve decided on a name,” Jenna said as she handed him another cup of coffee. Pete raised his eyebrow, encouraging her to carry on.

“Hope,” she said at last. “When everything else is done and gone, all you have left is hope.”

Pete nodded. It was true. Jenna had her, and he had to hope with every essence of his being that between the two of them they could do enough to keep her.

He raised his cup in a toast, “To Hope. If you have it, you have everything. Let the fight begin.”

Thanks goes to …

I've never really understood why every author has pages and pages of thank you's and acknowledgements to write. Surely only one person actually writes a book? Apparently though, writing is a bit like raising children; it takes a village.

So, here goes.

Firstly, thank you to my parents. I once heard that to be a good writer you need to be an avid reader. Now, I'm not saying I've hit the dizzy heights of the first accolade yet, but thanks to my Mum I've certainly managed the latter. I remember as a young child fighting for space on your lap, alongside a book and usually a cat. Thank you for all the nights you read out loud to me, even when you were exhausted.

Then there's Dad. The first person that ever told me I could write, and for years, the only person who constantly told me I had to. You might have thought I didn't listen, but here's proof that I did. I'm just so intensely sorry it took so long, and you missed it.

Next up, Adam, my long-suffering husband. You don't get to run a business, raise five children and write a book without an insane amount of help, and you are that help. You are my biggest fan, and without your support, enthusiasm, and the occasional nag, this book would never have existed. It's as much yours as it is mine. Though, if it's a runaway success I'm totally claiming that credit for myself. You know that, right? I will forever be grateful for the times you discussed the figments of my imagination as though they were old friends, and the other times you merely supplied me with wine.

Also, a massive thanks to the friends I bailed on because I had to spend time with my imaginary ones instead. Thanks especially to those who offered to be my first readers, and who at no point suggested I'd be better off getting a job in a supermarket. My soul thanks you, though my sanity is still looking at job adverts. Bryony, you deserve a special mention for all your help with my dodgy typo's and brain farts. It's mainly down to you that this (hopefully, at least) makes some sense!

I also need to say a massive thanks to my children: Georgia, Charlotte, Henry, Alfred and Quinn. For the days I went a little mad, and stopped being the mother you deserved; thank you. I know you didn't understand, but you accepted. Sometimes, that's worth more. I will never think I am good enough for you, but that's just the curse of parenthood. I love all of you more than chocolate, sleeping, shoes and writing.

Finally, I need to say a massive thank you to everyone who's taken the time to read this book (and spent the money to buy it). I genuinely hope you enjoyed it, and perhaps felt something along the way. Writers don't say this often, but this was my first attempt – I hope it wasn't too terrible.

If you did enjoy it, don't forget, Fighting For Hope, will be out in 2019!

Very Little About The Author Page

I'm reliably informed that "proper writers" have an About The Author Page, where you can find out all about their work, where they grew up and who they live with.

BORING!

Instead, I'm going to tell you my favourite joke.

A duck walks into a bar and asks, "Got any bread?"

The bartender, confused, tells the duck no. The duck thanks him and leaves.

The next day, the duck returns and asks, "Got any bread?"

Again, the bartender tells him, "No -- the bar does not serve bread, has never served bread and, furthermore, will never serve bread." The duck thanks him and leaves.

The next day, the duck returns, but before he can say anything, the bartender yells, "Listen, duck! This is a bar! We do not serve bread! If you ask for bread again, I will nail your stupid duck beak to the bar!"

The duck is silent for a moment, and then asks, "Got any nails?"

Confused, the bartender says no.

"Good!" says the duck. "Got any bread?"

You can genuinely find out more about the author at any of the following:

www.luetchells.com.

facebook.com/PointsOfLu

Instagram: PointsOfLu

Printed in Great Britain
by Amazon

54027907R00227